Terrance Dicks

STAR QUEST

Published by Big Finish Productions Ltd.
PO Box 1127
Maidenhead SL6 3LW

www.bigfinish.com

Project Editors: Gary Russell & Ian Farrington
Managing Editor: Jason Haigh-Ellery

ISBN 1-84435-066-5

Cover Design: Rhino Lullaby
Illustration © Jim Mortimore & Tim Keable 2003

This compilation first published November 2003

Originally published in three separate volumes by W H Allen and Co Ltd

Spacejack © Terrance Dicks 1978
Roboworld © Terrance Dicks 1979
Terrorsaur! © Terrance Dicks 1981
Introduction © Terrance Dicks 2003

With thanks to Austin Atkinson, Richard Parkin
and Jacqueline Rayner

The moral rights of the author have been asserted.

Printed and bound in Great Britain by Biddles Ltd
www.biddles.co.uk

CONTENTS

INTRODUCTION

TERRANCE DICKS

I first started reading science fiction in the Fifties, when it was an eccentric minority taste. The main, if not the only, source of supply was the magazine *Astounding Science Fiction*, on sale in Woolworth's for a shilling – 5p to you.

When the first *Star Wars* film appeared many years later, my immediate reaction was to think how old fashioned it was: I'd been reading this stuff for years! The technical ability of the film-maker had finally caught up with the imagination of the science-fiction writer. *Star Wars* is an example of what science-fiction fans call 'space opera'. The ingredients are always pretty much the same. Interstellar travel is commonplace, made possible by the discovery of some kind of hyper-drive. There are vast galactic star empires, sometimes benevolent, sometimes evil. The benevolent empires are attacked by vicious space terrorists. The evil empires are opposed by heroic rebels. The Space Patrol tries to keep order over millions of inhabited planets, some highly civilised, some barbarous and primitive. There are space pirates, bounty hunters, mysterious alien races and super-weapons that could destroy the universe.

The success of the first *Star Wars* movie brought science fiction back into mass popularity. Some time later, my *Doctor Who* publishers, W.H. Allen, suggested I might like to write an original science-fiction series to cash in on the continuing vogue.

Naturally, I chose space opera. Firstly, because it had always been a favourite of mine, and secondly, because *Doctor Who* notwithstanding, I don't actually *know* any real science. So, hard science fiction – the kind where stranded astronauts spend the whole story solving some complicated engineering problem – was out.

Hence these three books.

I created the League of Sentient Lifeforms, a benevolent alliance of intelligent beings who believed that civilised values are more important than outward appearances.

My main bad guys were the Kaldor, blond supermen with a fanatical belief in racial purity. Space Nazis. Another ingredient was the existence of the Web, a mysterious link between all living beings – a concept, as one of my children unkindly pointed out at the time, not unlike the Force in *Star Wars*.

My main three human characters were cousins.

Jan, brawny and handsome, no intellectual, but with an instinctive ability to do the right thing in a dangerous situation.

Kevin, ordinary and outwardly less heroic, but with a calm, logical intelligence, a good deal of stubborn courage, and a useful streak of cunning.

And finally Anna, our beautiful, spirited and courageous heroine – feminism was making its mark by now.

In *Spacejack*, the first story, the trio come across battling alien spacecraft and are snatched away from Earth, finding themselves caught up in the struggle between the Kaldor and the League and the quest for a vital Secret.

In *Roboworld*, they are trapped on an asteroid filled with intelligent and aggressive robots, the creations of a twisted scientist who believes that robots must rule the galaxy.

Finally, in *Terrorsaur!* they must visit a volcanic jungle planet, infested with savage dinosaurs, whose apparently primitive people possess amazing powers. There they foil yet another of the Kaldor's evil plots.

I've enjoyed re-reading these stories, and hope you enjoy them too. Like all space operas, they're action-filled romps that take us away from ordinary life into exotic worlds of aliens and space ships and monsters and robots and galactic empires.

I like to think that Jan, Kevin and Anna are still out there somewhere, enjoying more amazing adventures among the stars...

STAR QUEST
SPACEJACK

Terrance Dicks

SPACEJACK

1. FIRE IN THE SKY

They were talking about life on other planets the night it happened. The night that was to be their last on Earth…

There were three of them, Jan, Kevin and Anna, and they were camping out on a deserted bit of Salisbury Plain, close to Stonehenge. Despite different looks, and different nationalities, all three were cousins.

Anna was Swedish, dark haired, thin and wiry.

Jan was American, tall, broad shouldered, with bright blue eyes and hair so fair it looked almost white. He never tired of teasing Anna about the fact that he looked far more Swedish than she did. (Since Anna, like many Swedes, spoke perfect English, most people assumed at first that Jan was the Swedish one.)

Kevin, their English host, was medium sized, brown haired, and as he cheerfully admitted, 'just sort of average looking'.

They weren't sure exactly how they were related to each other. 'Kind of fourth cousins once or twice removed,' was how Jan put it. All three were descended from three Swedish brothers. Two of the brothers had left Sweden for America in the 1850s. They'd stopped off in England on the way and the younger had promptly fallen in love, married, and settled down.

The second brother had travelled on to America, eventually reaching Minnesota, where he too married. The third had stayed in Sweden on the family farm.

All three brothers had lots of children, all *their* children had lots more. By now, the Petersons were a huge three-country family. The different branches of the family kept in touch, and the younger relatives in particular visited each other frequently.

This year Kevin's parents had invited Jan and Anna to spend the summer with them, and Kevin, an only child, had suddenly found himself overwhelmed with company. Luckily he found he liked both his cousins, though Jan's cheery self-confidence could be a bit over powering.

The idea was that Kevin should show his foreign cousins the usual tourist sights. But for once England had produced a real heat wave, and it wasn't long before trailing round the Tower and Westminster Abbey with a mob of roasting tourists got pretty unbearable.

So Kevin suggested a cycle-camping holiday. He hadn't really expected Jan to agree. 'Everyone knows you Yanks spend all your time riding around in Cadillacs.'

Jan was indignant. Cycling was very big in America just now, and he had a perfectly good bike at home. As for riding everywhere in cars... 'Have you ever been backpacking along the Appalachian Trail? Or white-water canoeing in Oregon? Or pony-trekking in New Mexico?' Jan had, and a cycling holiday was fine by him. 'That is if you can do much cycling in a country this size. Couple of days and you'd probably ride off the edge!'

They'd hired bikes for Jan and Anna and set off, and now they were sprawling around a little campfire on a hot summer night, looking up at the stars and arguing about UFOs – Unidentified Flying Objects.

As usually happened, Jan and Kevin were on opposite sides, Jan openly scornful, Kevin a firm believer. Anna was neutral. She lay looking up at the stars, dropping in the occasional remark just to keep things going.

So far Jan was getting the best of it. He'd rushed into the argument with his usual cheerful confidence. 'It's all a lot of crazy nonsense. People see weather balloons, observation satellites, sun flashing on the wings of a plane... Most of those UFO nuts are pretty freaked out to start with – they just let their imaginations run away with them.'

'Oh yes?' said Kevin quietly. 'Like those US Air Force pilots in 1948? Three Mustang fighters spotted a UFO and chased after it – the lead plane blew up when it got too close.' Kevin paused for breath. 'There was a whole spate of UFO sightings round about that time, most of them by pilots in your own Air Force. Not particularly nervous types, I should have thought. Then there was that BOAC pilot who spotted a space ship and six smaller ones when he was flying over Canada. And *four* American policemen spotted a UFO over Ohio and chased it in their police cars!'

Kevin went on to give a string of other UFO sightings over the years, all with sane, sensible-sounding witnesses, all difficult to explain away. Jan shook his head, baffled but still not convinced. Anna couldn't help feeling rather sorry for him. He'd obviously made the mistake of tangling with an expert.

'So why don't these aliens make contact?' asked Jan belligerently. 'Why not just land on the White House lawn and say, "Take me to your leader"?'

'Perhaps they don't want to – perhaps they're just observing us.'

'Perhaps, perhaps, Kev. I still say there's no proof...' The argument raged on.

Anna stared sleepily up at the blaze of stars. She'd heard enough by now, and she was just about to suggest they all shut up and went to bed when she saw something that put the whole question of UFOs on a very different level. 'Hey, you two, stop jabbering and look!' She pointed upwards. An arrow of light was flashing across the sky.

Silently they studied the moving streak. It was surrounded by a hazy glow and it seemed jagged, somehow dartlike. The object streaked down through the sky and disappeared below the horizon, in the direction of Stonehenge.

Suddenly Jan shouted, 'Look – there's another one!'

A second object was hurtling down through the night sky as if in pursuit of the first. This second space ship was larger, round rather than rocket-like, very much the shape of the conventional 'flying saucer'. It was surrounded by the same hazy glow as the first, but they could make out a row of windows around the side and a raised central dome on the upper surface. They stared in utter astonishment as it sped silently across the sky and vanished below the horizon.

Kevin shook his head in amazement. It was all very well defending UFOs in theory, but seeing one... 'It was a UFO,' he whispered. 'A genuine UFO!'

'*Two* UFOs,' corrected Jan. 'Looks as if one was chasing the other.' He grinned at Kevin and slapped him on the back. 'Cheer up cousin, you are about to get famous!'

'Am I?' said Kevin cynically.

Jan stared at him. 'Well of course you are. We saw them, didn't we? We all did.'

'We saw them all right! Do you think anyone will believe us?'

'Of course,' said Anna impatiently. 'There are three of us, and we will all say the same thing.'

'What about those pilots, and those policemen, all the other people who saw UFOs? Did anyone believe them? Three kids camping alone at night? They'll say we were seeing things. They'll say it was a weather balloon, or a satellite or the planet Venus...'

Anna tried to imagine telling her mother and father she'd seen flying saucers on her English camping holiday. 'Yes, dear, how nice,' they'd say. She could just hear them telling their friends about her wonderful imagination. 'Perhaps Kevin is right. We'd better just forget the whole thing.'

Jan started stamping out the fire. 'Those UFOs weren't just flitting through the sky. They were *landing*. I'm going to find out where – and why! Who's coming with me?'

2. THE ALIENS

Jan swung one leg over his bike-saddle. 'Come on you two – what are you waiting for?'

'We can't just go rushing off in the dark,' protested Anna. 'We'll all get lost.'

'Still, Jan's right,' said Kevin suddenly. 'We've *got* to follow this up.' He went to his saddle-bag, fished out a compass and an Ordnance Survey map, and aligned map and compass. 'Now they disappeared just to the left of that clump of trees...' He looked up. 'I reckon they'll come down somewhere here, close to Stonehenge!' Kevin folded the map and reached for his bike. 'Coming, Anna? Or are you going to stay behind and mind the camp?'

The suggestion that she ought to take a safe back seat was too much for Anna. 'Of course I'm coming.' She ran to her bike. 'Though what good is it going to do? I mean even if we do get a closer look, people still won't believe us.'

'Good thinking,' said Jan. He reached down into his saddle-bag, pulled out his camera-case and slung it round his neck. 'This'll do it. Clear, unfaked, close-up pictures. Let them explain that away. Now then, are we going to stand here telling each other how clever we are, or are we going to get the show on the road?'

'Okay, okay,' said Kevin cheerfully. 'No harm in a little advance planning. Right – follow me!' Compass cupped in one hand, Kevin wobbled off, Jan and Anna close behind him.

It was like a kind of mad cross-country cycle race, thought Anna, as she followed the two red rear-lights bobbing ahead of her. Kevin kept their route ruthlessly on his compass-bearing and they were soon forced to leave the path for the open plain. They jolted over tussocky grass, dismounting to drag the bikes through hedges, across ditches and over fences.

The journey seemed to go on for ages, though in their slow cross-country progress they couldn't have covered more than a few miles. Kevin came to a halt. 'Look!' The ground rose steadily in front of them – and from the other side of the hill there came a glow. They had reached their target.

Jan laid his bike carefully on the ground. 'Come on,' he whispered, and set off up the hill on foot. Kevin and Anna followed him. Moving as quietly as they could, they made their way up the rise. The glow grew steadily brighter as they neared the top. They came over the rest of the rise, and before them lay Stonehenge. It was bathed in the eerie glow from the space ship that had landed close beside it. Silvery figures moved about under the great stones.

Kevin studied the scene below him, determined to memorise every detail. First the space ship. It was long and black, triangular in its overall shape, standing upright on its tail like a conventional rocket. Short stubby wings flared out from the side – it occurred to Kevin that they might be retractable, designed only for use in a planetary atmosphere.

Beside him Jan raised his camera and began taking shot after shot of the alien space ship.

Kevin turned his attention to the figures moving among the stones. They were man-shaped, not particularly large, and they wore one-piece space-suits in some silvery material. Their boots and gauntlets were black. Wide black belts around their waists held a variety of pouches and containers. Strangely they were helmetless. They all seemed to have thin, pale faces with close-cropped yellow hair.

It occurred to Kevin that the space ship might not be from some other planet at all. The astronauts looked human enough. Could this be an experimental model on a secret test flight? Somehow he doubted it. The ship seemed more advanced than anything yet developed on Earth. And if the Americans or the Russians had come up with a revolutionary space ship, why use it to go poking round Stonehenge in the middle of the night?

Kevin turned his attention back to the silver figures. There were three of them, and they were examining the stone pillars one by one. One would sweep the surface of the pillar with what looked like a giant metal torch, moving a reddish light-beam over the entire surface. The second stood watching a smaller, boxlike apparatus in his hands. The third figure held a rifle-shaped device with bulbous stock and a short, thick barrel. He swung the weapon warily to and fro as if keeping watch. Hidden in the darkness, the watchers studied the mysterious scene. 'What are they looking for?' whispered Anna.

'Only one way to find out,' said Jan softly. 'We'll have to get closer.' Crouching low, he began running towards the space ship.

'Come back you idiot!' hissed Kevin, but Jan was already on his way. Kevin turned to Anna. 'Stay here – I'll get him.' He ran after Jan.

Anna wanted to follow, but common sense told her the more of them rushing about near the space ship, the greater the chances of being seen. Suppose these mysterious aliens didn't like being spied on?

Kevin found his cousin just beyond the edge of the circle of light cast by the space ship. Jan had wriggled as close to Stonehenge as he dared. Now he lay propped up on his elbows, taking shot after shot of the aliens and their mysterious activities.

Kevin dropped down beside him. 'What do you think you're doing?'

Jan grinned. 'Just getting a few close-ups. I wonder what those guys are up to? They've covered pretty well all the major stones by now.'

Forgetting he was there to bring Jan back, Kevin joined him in watching the aliens. They were gathered round one of the smaller megaliths, following the same unvarying routine. One swept the red light-beam over the surface, the second stood watching, the third kept guard.

Jan gave Kevin a nudge. 'I think they've hit the jackpot!'

The alien astronauts were crowding round the stone. As the light-beam swept across the surface something was happening!

Tiny points of light were appearing on the stone, dozens of them, connected by thin glowing lines. It looked oddly familiar and all at once Kevin realised what it reminded him of – one of those diagrams in astronomy books, showing you the constellations. 'It's a map,' he whispered. 'Some kind of star chart!'

Jan was already on his feet again, moving closer to the stone, using the last of his film to get a close-up of the glowing map.

Anna meanwhile was getting really worried. Jan and Kevin were very close to the aliens by now. If one of them turned…

Anna felt the ground beneath shake. Something was moving towards her from the other side of the slope. Judging by the thud of its footsteps, it was something very large indeed.

She felt trapped like a rabbit in a cornfield. If she moved forward she'd run straight into the aliens from the space ship. Move back and she'd be going towards those approaching footsteps. Glancing fearfully over her shoulder, she crouched down, not daring to move.

An astonishing figure had appeared on the skyline behind her. It was enormous, at least three metres high, and it wore a space-suit made from some brown, leather-like material. The head was bare, and the sight of the creature's face made Anna gasp with horror. It was a hideous, almost misshapen face like that of a Neanderthal cave man. The underhung jaw was huge and brutal, and dark eyes glared from beneath a low bony forehead. One massive paw clutched a strange-looking pistol.

For a moment the creature paused, swinging the savage head to and fro, sniffing the air through its broad, flat nostrils. It made a beckoning gesture, and a second figure moved up to stand beside it. This one was much smaller, below human height, but immensely broad and powerful. It was similarly dressed and armed, and had a broad, flat, troll-like face.

Anna was frozen with terror. 'A giant and a dwarf,' she thought dazedly. 'What next?'

Her question was answered all too soon. A third creature appeared – and this one was pure nightmare.

It was shaped rather like a giant octopus – an octopus adapted to living on land. Long tentacles supported a round bulbous body, and two enormous golden eyes reflected the light from the glowing space ship. A webbing harness was strapped about its body, and it was carrying a pistol-like weapon in one of its tentacles.

This third apparition was too much for Anna. She jumped to her feet yelling, 'Jan! Kev! Look out – look behind you!'

Several things happened more or less at once. Jan and Kevin turned – and so did the aliens examining the stone megalith. At the sight of the newcomers, the one with the rifle raised his weapon and opened fire. There was a fierce glow as energy-bolts whizzed through the air.

Jan and Kevin threw themselves down – but Anna was still on her feet running towards them. Something crackled fiercely within inches of her head, and a massive electric shock slammed her unconscious to the ground. The giant alien was already running forward, and Anna collapsed at his feet.

'Anna's hurt,' yelled Jan. He jumped up and ran back to her. One of the silver-clad aliens raised his gun and fired, and Jan toppled to the ground.

Kevin flung himself down, and the battle raged over his head. The giant and the dwarf were returning fire now, and the air crackled with purple rays. He saw the octopus-creature touch a control on its belt-harness and immediately a shimmering veil of blue light encased the octopus-alien, his two companions and Anna as well – a barrier against which the energy-bolts of their attackers sizzled in vain.

Under cover of this protective shield the strange trio began making a retreat. Kevin saw the giant pick up Anna's unconscious body, tossing it over his shoulder like an empty sack. 'Hey, come back!' he yelled. The three aliens vanished back into the night.

Kevin was about to follow when he saw two of the black-clad aliens dragging his cousin's unconscious body towards the space ship.

Kevin was paralysed with indecision as his friends were carried off in opposite directions. His instinct was to go after Anna, but she had already disappeared and he could still see Jan. The black-and-silver aliens looked more or less human. Perhaps he could persuade them to let Jan go. Better still they might even help him to rescue Anna... All this went through Kevin's mind in seconds. He jumped up and ran towards the space ship. A ramp was sliding out, and a door had opened. The two aliens were dragging Jan up the ramp, while the third stood guard. As he reached him Kevin yelled, 'Please, you've got to help me. They've taken my cousin.' The alien ignored him. Jan was almost inside the ship by now. Kevin forced his way up the ramp and tried to pull him back. The sentry clubbed him down from behind with the butt of his laser.

For a moment the aliens looked down at Kevin's body. The leader gave a brief command, and the sentry dragged him inside the ship. The hatch slid closed, the ramp retracted, and in an eerie silence the glowing ship hurtled up into the night sky. It flashed across the darkness, then suddenly winked into extinction.

3. CAPTIVES OF THE KALDOR

The dwarflike alien called Tell watched the fiery spot until it disappeared. He knew that the Kaldor ship had left Earth space for the space/time continuum. It would flash back into normal space millions of light years away. His stocky body slumped despairingly. 'They are already in hyper-drive, Osar. We have lost them.'

'I should have stayed on the ship,' said the octopus-like Osar agitatedly. 'I am a navigator, it is not my function to land on alien worlds. Our tracking beam was not locked on – without their jump co-ordinates we shall never find them again.'

Tell looked up at the great stones towering above him. 'We should scan these stones – they must have been searching for something...'

Osar was horrified, waving his tentacles in protest. 'Our presence here breaks the most solemn ruling of the League. Unless we go now there will be contact – and that is utterly forbidden.'

'Contact has already taken place,' said Tell. 'Kidnapping too. The Kaldor took two young humans captive.'

Osar scuttled forward with the peculiar sideways gait of his people, and stared up at the great stone circle. 'Why?' he hissed angrily. 'Why take the humans captive? Why come here at all?'

Tell hunched his wide shoulders. 'They seek some fragment of the Old Wisdom – something that will serve their lust for power.' He returned to his argument. 'They were scanning these stones – stones left here by the Old Ones. We have equipment in the ship. If I go back and fetch it...'

Osar swayed his body from side to side in the gesture that meant refusal. 'Who knows what frequency they were using? You could seek for eternity without success. The invisibility shield on the ship is draining our power reserves. If we stay longer there'll be too little power to make the jump.'

The huge Neanderthal figure of Garm loomed up out of the darkness. 'The Earth girl is hurt. I cannot tell how badly. We must take her to the ship.'

Osar's tentacles moved in renewed agitation. 'Is it not bad enough that we are here? Must we now turn kidnapper like the Kaldor? If the Council hear of this... Leave her and come away.'

'We broke the Council's law by coming here,' said Garm calmly. 'If we leave the girl she may die. I shall take her to the ship.' He turned away, Osar scuttling after him.

15

Tell grinned wryly. Osar's race had a combination of mental brilliance and physical sensitivity that made them incomparable star navigators. Unfortunately it also made them excessively temperamental and highly nervous.

Tell turned for a last regretful look at the towering stones. They held some great secret, he was sure of that. If only they could stay and search... But Osar was right, it was time to go.

As he moved away, Tell's foot struck some small loose object. He picked it up and studied it, trying to work out its function. Controls, a lens... a primitive video-recording device by the looks of it. He slipped it inside his tunic and hurried after the others.

He found them waiting nearby, close to a saucer-shaped depression in the plain. It was a strange depression; one that had not been there a short time before. There was nothing to be seen in the hollow, yet on the shallow bowl of its floor, grasses and shrubs were flattened. Anyone trying to cross the hollow would have been thrown back by an invisible force.

Osar was dancing on his tentacle tips with impatience. 'Coming with us after all, are you?' He curled up one tentacle to adjust a control on his harness. Dazzling light filled the hollow as the invisibility shield was turned off and the ship shimmered slowly into view. It was saucer-shaped, with a raised round dome in the centre, the standard starship often seen from Earth. A hatch opened, a ramp slid out and all three entered the ship, Garm carrying the unconscious girl. The hatch closed and a moment later the ship rose silently into the air and vanished into the clouds.

Next day there were numerous reports of flying saucers, seen over Salisbury Plain. A farmer up all night with a calving cow, a married couple driving back after a party in London, a policeman cycling home after late duty, these and others reported seeing a saucer-shaped craft pursuing a dart-shaped one through the sky. Some people claimed to have seen them twice, as if both ships had actually landed and taken off.

One of the local papers featured the story, and there was a paragraph or two in the national press. The day after the whole thing was forgotten.

It wasn't until some time later that anyone realised that three young people were missing. Kevin and his cousins hadn't been following any special route, and they'd been keeping in touch with Kevin's family by the occasional phone call or postcard. Then someone found three bikes and an abandoned campsite close to Stonehenge. Kevin's diary was in the tent and the police contacted his parents.

There was a full-scale search after that, police, army, civilian volunteers... They found nothing. A police spokesman said, 'It's as if they'd disappeared from the face of the Earth.' An enterprising local reporter pointed out that the young people had vanished on the night of the UFO sightings, and suggested there might be some connection. His editor told him to stick to the facts, and the story was quashed. Jan, Kevin and Anna had vanished.

Anna Peterson was having a nightmare. She dreamed she lay stretched out on a couch, with a giant hovering over her. The giant held a strangely shaped instrument in his enormous hand, moving it slowly about her head. Anna struggled to wake up – and realised she was awake, and the nightmare was real. She tried to sit up, drawing breath for a scream, but an enormous hand pressed her back. She heard a deep reassuring voice, not with her ears, but somehow inside her head. 'Do not be afraid. No one will harm you.'

For a moment Anna was reassured, but then she saw the second shape hovering close by. The bulbous body balanced on its sinuous tentacles, the great golden eyes... with a scream of horror she fainted dead away.

Garm looked down at the Earth girl for a moment, then headed for the control room. Osar had arrived ahead of him, twittering with indignation. Tell was doing his best to soothe him down. The cruiser was on automatic, speeding away from Earth in the general direction of Mars.

Tell looked up. 'How is our passenger?'

'Better than I had feared. She was caught by the fringe of a blaster ray – there is shock, but no real damage.' Garm smiled. 'I'm afraid that Osar frightened her!'

Osar waved a disdainful tentacle towards the controls. 'Let us reverse course immediately and carry her back to Earth. She is quite uncivilised.'

Garm shook his head. 'No, not yet. Place us in orbit around the fourth planet for a time. When she recovers I should like to talk to her. Perhaps she knows something that might help us.'

'A primitive girl from Old Earth?' Osar was incredulous. 'What can she possibly know?'

The acceleration couch creaked beneath Garm's enormous weight. He yawned. 'Perhaps she knows why the Kaldor kidnapped her friends...'

* * *

17

Jan and Kevin too had a nightmare awakening but their nightmare was harsher, and went on for much longer. They awoke to find themselves strapped to the walls of a metal cell. A man in a black-and-silver uniform shouted questions at them in a language they didn't understand.

The questioning went on and on. Their interrogator took some time to realise that they couldn't give the answers because they didn't understand the questions. He seemed to lose his temper and struck Jan savagely across the face, bringing blood to his lips. It was a serious mistake. The blow brought Jan back to full consciousness – and to a state of furious rage. With a yell of anger he snapped the bonds that held him to the wall and flung himself upon his tormentor. Grabbing the alien with his left hand, Jan delivered a thump with his right that sent him flying across the room.

Black-clad figures descended on Jan from all sides and he disappeared beneath a pile of attacking bodies. Somehow he managed to shake them off, rising to his feet and lashing about him with a series of blows that sent his attackers reeling. Despite his comparative youth Jan was exceptionally big and powerful, and in his berserk fury he didn't even seem to notice the blows of his opponents.

Still fastened to the metal wall, Kevin looked on helplessly as Jan flung his attackers about the room.

For a moment it actually seemed as if Jan would succeed in disposing of all his attackers, but in the end there were too many for him. While four of the black-clad aliens held his arms, a fifth slipped behind him and clubbed him savagely across the head with the butt of a blaster. Half dazed, Jan was dragged across the room and fastened back into place, this time with stronger bonds.

The aliens began restoring the interrogation room to order – Jan had almost wrecked it in his struggle. Smashed and overturned equipment was righted and replaced, bruised and semi-conscious crewmen carried out. When things were more or less straight, another alien entered.

He looked uncannily like the first one, with the same slight wiry build and cruel hawklike face. He spoke briefly to the interrogator, who came forward with a metal helmet in his hands and fitted it over Jan's head, ignoring his struggles. A flex connected the helmet to a nearby control panel. Once the helmet was in place, the interrogator crossed to the controls, made adjustments and threw a switch. To Kevin's horror, Jan arched his back, gave a choking scream and slumped unconscious in his bonds.

18

The alien at the console frowned, as though some minor experiment had gone irritatingly wrong. He lifted the helmet from Jan's head and carried it across to Kevin.

Kevin tossed his head wildly from side to side trying to avoid the helmet, but the alien jammed it brutally into place. Again the man crossed to the controls, made adjustments and pulled the switch. Kevin too screamed as a searing jolt hammered through his brain. It was as though his mind was a sheet of wax upon which someone had slammed down a giant metal stamp. He was sick and dizzy from the shock, but unlike Jan he managed to remain conscious, perhaps because his mind was more flexible. The helmet was lifted from his head and the questions began again. But now there was a difference. He could understand them.

Somehow that shattering mental jolt had blasted an entire new language into his brain. His grasp was shaky at first and he could only get the general drift of questions. But as the interrogation went on, he could understand more and more.

'Who?' his interrogator was demanding. 'Who are you? Why do you watch us? Why do you help the League?'

Gradually Kevin began to work out what must have happened. His captors had got the idea that he and Jan were part of the second group of alien astronauts, the ones whose appearance had frightened Anna. Interrupted in their scanning of Stonehenge, they had registered Jan, Kevin, Anna and the three newcomers all more or less at once, and had assumed they were together – an idea which had been strengthened when Anna was carried off.

Kevin did his best to sort things out. 'We're nothing to do with those others,' he shouted. 'We were just observers, do you understand? Observers!'

'You lie,' shouted the interrogator. 'The League have summoned the help of Earth. We know that some of you still have the Old Wisdom. You will help them to destroy us!'

The questioning went on and on. The subordinate asked all the questions while the second alien, obviously the leader, listened impassively. A complicated combination of dials and electrodes was clipped to Kevin's forehead and wrists. He was asked the same questions all over again. Defiantly he shouted the same answers, while the leader studied the flickering needles on the dials. At last he nodded, satisfied, and the questioning stopped.

The two black-clad figures moved to one side, and Kevin slumped back as if barely conscious. The aliens began a low-voiced conference.

19

Kevin strained to hear what they were talking about. He heard mention of 'the quest' and gathered that they were in search of some great secret. There was talk of the Old Wisdom, and of some mysterious group of humans who might, or might not, help them. Kevin's use of the word 'observer' seemed to cause them some concern – they seemed to be wondering if he could be more important than he appeared.

Finally the interrogator said something about 'useless – safer to eject'. Kevin shuddered, realising that the alien was casually suggesting they be ejected from the ship to die a hideous death. In the icy vacuum of space their bodies would simply explode. To his vast relief he saw the leader shake his head. Kevin caught only a few words of his low-voiced reply. There was something about the League. 'They saw us, they will tell the Council. Keep prisoner... bargain... hostage...' And then 'Observers – observers from Earth – may have important knowledge.'

It seemed the second group of aliens, the League, knew they were on this space ship and might make trouble if they were killed... Moreover, the leader thought they might still be of some use to him. Kevin didn't fully understand, but he didn't need to. He was happy to be alive.

4. EMPIRE IN THE STARS

Inside Anna's head a deep voice was saying, 'Open your mind. No one will harm you.'

She felt a kind of mental pressure, as though someone was trying to force a way into her brain. She sat up, gasping, but a giant hand forced her back. 'Try to open the channels of your mind.' Anna stopped resisting and immediately information poured into her mind in a swirling flood. Words, sounds, images, faster and faster, until at last the rushing stream of data overwhelmed her and she lost consciousness.

When she awoke for the second time the giant had gone, and the dwarf was sitting beside her. 'My name is Tell,' he said. 'And what is yours, my lady?'

'Anna.' She sat upright, staring at him. 'I understand you. I answered you!'

'That is so. You are now fluent in Basic Pan-galactic, the language spoken, or at least understood, by every intelligent life form in the galaxy.'

'How? How did I learn so quickly?'

'By mind-link. Garm is a telepath. The information came straight from his brain to yours.'

'Who are you? Where am I – and what am I doing here? Who were those people at Stonehenge? What's happened to Jan and Kev?'

Tell held up his hand, his eyes sparkling with amusement. 'If you will stop the flow of questions long enough to hear my answers... My name is Tell. My large friend Garm you have already met. The third of us is called Osar. You hurt his feelings badly when you fainted – he has a very sensitive nature.'

'I'm sorry – it's just that he isn't...'

Tell's ugly face was curiously attractive when he smiled. 'Human? Nor am I, Princess, not fully human, and nor is Garm, though unlike Osar we are descended from human stock. The agents of the League come in many shapes.'

'The League? What League?'

'The League of Sentient Life Forms, of course – an alliance of all intelligent beings in this Galaxy.'

Anna was still thinking of something the little alien had said a moment ago. 'Did you just say two of you were descended from human beings?'

'Of course. We are the heirs of the First Galactic Empire of Man.'

'But humans have never had a galactic empire. We've only just reached our own moon!'

'Listen, Princess, and I will tell you the True History of Man.'

Anna forced herself to sit back and listen, as Tell unfolded an amazing story. According to him, Earth was now entering its second civilisation. Man had first evolved on Earth millions of years before present-day humans now believed. 'You were the most advanced species in the Galaxy in those days. In an amazingly short time you evolved a technological civilisation, discovered space flight, developed the hyper-drive, and spread out all over the Galaxy, colonising and conquering more than a million worlds.'

'You mean there are other worlds like Earth? Worlds where men can live and breathe the air?'

'Others?' Tell laughed. 'The Galaxy you call the Milky Way holds more than a hundred thousand million stars. Say one in a thousand is circled by an E-type planet...'

'A hundred million Earths,' said Anna softly.

Tell shrugged. 'In fact one in a thousand is too low an estimate. Much of the Galaxy is still unexplored. Even the First Empire took in only part of it.'

'What happened to this First Empire? Why don't we know about it now?'

'It grew and grew until it collapsed from within. There were over a million worlds in the Empire towards the end. Who can administer an Empire of such size? Who can even count the worlds that pay tribute?' Tell sighed. 'The Empire fell. Much of the Galaxy fell with it, reverting to barbarism.'

'Including Earth?'

'Earth was the first. Its decline was total and complete. Atomic wars, plagues, devastation. The shape of Earth was altered, whole continents rose and fell. Man went back to the caves, where he crouched gnawing a bone, worshipping the stars that once he ruled.' Tell paused, pleased with this poetic turn of phrase.

'Did this happen on all the other worlds?'

'Things varied greatly. Some planets destroyed themselves in interstellar wars, on others civilisation continued to flourish. My own was one such world,' Tell concluded proudly.

'Then why didn't you help us?' demanded Anna indignantly.

'Because you were lost!'

'Lost? How can the Earth have been lost?'

'A hundred million habitable worlds, remember? Some civilised, some barbaric, others somewhere in between. Some devastated by atomic wars, others still empty of intelligent life. Nearly all of them inhabited by humans or humanoids. Who could tell which was the true original Earth?'

'But you know now,' said Anna. 'Eventually you found us.'

'The discovery was made some thirty Earth-cycles ago. There was great excitement in the Galaxy when the homeworld of man was rediscovered.'

'And that's when all the UFO business started,' said Anna excitedly. 'You found us, and you came to take a look at us!'

'Indeed we did! Starships were popping out of hyperspace all over your solar system. Every world with star flight came to take a look at Old Earth. There was chaos. Time and again our ships were seen by the Earth people. Your atmospheric flyers came too close and were exploded by protective force fields. Your water-borne vessels disappeared. Unauthorised Contact was made. Extra-terrestrials landed and were seen by humans. Earth people were taken to other planets. It was a disaster!'

Anna nodded, remembering Kevin's stories of the great UFO boom of the 'fifties, a time when scarcely a day passed without some kind of sighting. 'And then it all tailed off. What happened?'

'That was the League,' said Tell proudly. 'There was a risk that great harm would be done to Earth, that its natural redevelopment would be interfered with. The League declared Earth a forbidden planet. Occasional overflights are permitted for observation purposes, but that is all.'

'So the visits stopped? No more UFOs – or hardly any. What about tonight?'

'Law-abiding planets obey the rule of the League – but there are others – like the Kaldor.'

'The ones we saw examining Stonehenge? What did they want?'

Tell paused, as if gathering his ideas, or perhaps, thought Anna, he was wondering how much he should tell her. 'Your ancestors, the founders of the First Empire, had great powers, cosmic powers. They had discovered how to tap the power of the Web.'

'The Web? What's that?'

'It is everything,' said Tell reverently. 'The power that keeps the atom spinning around its nucleus, the planets around their suns, the suns in the galaxies, the galaxies in the cosmos. We are all part of the Web, everything we do resonates within it, produces vibrations for good or evil.'

'What's all this got to do with the Kaldor?'

'There are power-points in the Web,' said Tell solemnly. 'Energy-junctions where its forces can be tapped, used. The place you call Stonehenge is one of them. We believe the Kaldor discovered some ancient secret hidden there – a source of power they can use for their evil ends.'

'Why? What do they want?'

'You have seen the crew of this ship?' Tell tapped himself on the chest. 'I come from a giant planet, like your Jupiter. The pull of gravity is great – we do not grow very far from the ground! Garm's people live on a world like yours in the Age of Reptiles, a world of jungles and ferocious beasts. Their bodies reverted to the Neanderthal, to give them the strength to survive, but they developed mental powers that more civilised races have forgotten. On Osar's watery planet, life went back to the seas, and the octopoids became the dominant race. Yet here we are, colleagues, friends even. Surely that is as it should be?'

'Well, yes, I suppose so.' Privately Anna doubted if she could ever make friends with a talking octopus, but no doubt the principle was right. 'You mean all intelligent beings are equal, whatever their shape?'

'Not according to the Kaldor,' said Tell grimly. 'They believe the descendants of man are a superior race, born to rule. That rules out Osar's people, and thousands of other intelligent, non-human races. Worse, they say that only those in the true shape of Man are the real elite – which disposes of Garm and myself, and all the other human descendants whose bodies have adapted to the planets they live on. They say that only the Kaldor are the one true race, rulers of the Galaxy by right of birth. By selective breeding, by planned genetic mutation, they have stamped themselves into one mould.' Tell's voice hardened. 'They are cruel, ruthless, utterly without mercy. On the planets they rule all but the Kaldor are abject slaves. By the Power of the Web, I swear to you that they are less human than any of us.' He broke off, seeing Anna's eyes widen with horror. 'I am sorry, my lady, have I frightened you?'

'It isn't that. I was thinking of what you said about the Kaldor – and remembering Kev and Jan are their prisoners.'

5. PRISONERS' BLUFF

Jan stared at his cousin and rubbed the lump on the back of his aching head. 'Are you telling me we're actually on a UFO – and we're prisoners?'

Kevin waved a hand around the tiny metal cell in which they'd been dumped after the interrogation.'Well, this isn't a tent on Salisbury Plain, is it? And if you think you're dreaming I'll be glad to give you a pinch.'

'No thanks. I feel bad enough already.' Jan crossed to the cell door and started thumping on it with his fist.

'What do you think you're doing?'

'I'm going to get to see the Captain of this… whatever-it-is, and insist he takes us home right away,' said Jan simply.

Kevin stared at him. 'Insist? They were all ready to kill us off just a while ago. They still will, if you start making trouble. Do you want to end up doing a spacewalk – without a space-suit?'

'Nuts,' said Jan vigorously. 'They wouldn't dare.' He renewed his thumping on the door.

Kevin stared despairingly at his cousin. Somehow he had to make Jan realise how much danger they were in. Jan started kicking at the door, shouting at the top of his voice. 'Hey, out there! Come on, someone answer!'

The door slid back and a Kaldor guard appeared, blaster in hand. 'You have been given food and water. Why do you cry out? Be silent or you will be executed immediately.'

Jan grabbed the food tray that had been brought in earlier and slung it at the guard's head. It missed by inches and clattered into the corridor.'I want something decent to eat and drink. And I want to see whoever's in charge here – right away!'

The guard glared at him. He raised his blaster and for a moment it seemed he was about to fire. Kevin stepped in front of him. 'You'd better do as he says. Hurry, or it will be the worse for you!'

The guard backed slowly away, and the door slid closed behind him.

'See?' said Jan, a little uneasily. 'You've got to stand up to these people.'

'Listen,' whispered Kevin fiercely. 'He very nearly killed you just then, and you know it.'

Jan nodded soberly.'I think you're right. What do we do now?'

'I picked up quite a bit during that explanation. Maybe we can bluff them. Just take your cue from me, okay?'

Before Kevin could explain further, the cell door slid open once more. The two Kaldor officers entered. Guards with blasters stood ready in the corridors behind them.

'What is this?' snapped the leader. 'Your interrogation is now over. You are our prisoners. If you wish to live, be silent and obey.'

Kevin drew a deep breath. 'What is your name?' he said quietly.

The officer stared at him.

'Your name,' repeated Kevin. 'You do know your name? You don't seem to know much else.'

'I am Kiro, commander of this ship. This is Zargon, my First Officer.'

'I am Lord Kevin of Terra, and this is Lord Jan. Our presence on your ship was in the nature of a Test. I regret to inform you that you have failed. You will return us to Earth immediately.'

The two Kaldor were speechless.

Taking advantage of the stunned silence, Kevin launched into his tale. With impressive vagueness he claimed that he and Jan were official Observers, representatives of an all-powerful secret society on Earth, keepers of the strange and mysterious knowledge of the Old Ones. Had the Kaldor been found worthy, they would have been given access to all these incredible secrets. Unfortunately, by their treatment of the Observers they had lost their opportunity. However, if they returned them to Earth at once, he might consider giving them another chance...

The Kaldor officers were obviously staggered by the sheer outrageousness of the claim. Kiro said hesitantly, 'What proof...?'

By now Jan understood his cousin's plan. 'Proof?' he said scornfully. 'We were there waiting for you, weren't we? Who else would know that you were coming?'

'Nobody knew,' said Zargon angrily. 'It was a secret decision of the Kaldor Council. We made landings on Earth, worked out the clues to the ancient knowledge we sought...'

'And who left the clues for you to find?' snapped Jan. 'The secret hidden in Stonehenge is only one of many. Those secrets will be handed on to those who prove worthy... not to bullying oafs who confuse violence with intelligence. You may go now.' Jan turned away.

Thunderstruck the Kaldor stared at each other.

Jan ignored them, and the door slid closed. Kevin drew a long shuddering breath and dropped on to the bunk. 'Well, if that didn't impress them, nothing will.'

Jan slapped him on the back encouragingly. 'You were great! Those guys are probably turning the ship round right now.'

There was another long wait. Kevin sat despondently on the bunk, wondering how he could ever have expected such a crazy plan to work. At last the door opened once more. Four Kaldor stood in the metal corridor. They were carrying laser-rifles.

'I guess we overdid it,' said Kevin, unsteadily. 'This looks like the firing squad!'

Jan rose slowly to his feet, tensing himself to spring. If he could just get his hands on one of those rifles... Suddenly the Kaldor guards raised their weapons in a curiously formal gesture. To his astonishment he realised it was a kind of salute. A guard said, 'You will follow.' He led the way along the corridor. Jan and Kevin followed, and the other guards fell in behind.

'What's going on?' whispered Kevin. 'Do you think it worked?'

'Beats me. Maybe they're just sending us off in style.'

They reached another door, it slid back and their escort stood aside so they could enter. They found themselves in a small chamber, white-walled and brightly lit. A mirror formed the upper half of one wall, there were recessed basins, and cubicles at the back.

Kevin looked round. 'Doesn't look much like the condemned cell!'

Jan grinned. 'It isn't. I guess our hosts are human after all, Kev. You are now looking at your first inter-planetary washroom.' He touched a button and warm soapy water gushed into one of the basins.

Apart from the fact that the water came ready-soaped and the toilets flushed with a violet glow and an alarming whoosh, it was all curiously familiar. When Jan and Kevin finished washing, a sudden blast of hot air blew them dry.

One of the Kaldor came in, indicated a sentry-box-shaped alcove, waving Jan inside. As he stepped into the alcove it lit up. It went dark as he stepped out. There was a whirring, clicking sound. Seconds later a hatch opened at the base of the cubicle and ejected a bundle of clothing – boots, trousers, a close-fitting tunic and a cloak all in gleaming black and silver.

Jan shrugged and began changing into the new clothes. Kevin stepped into the cubicle and it lit up for him, delivering a similar outfit minutes later.

They finished changing and admired themselves in the mirror. The clothes fitted perfectly. They were made of some soft black material. As Kevin stroked his sleeve there was a tiny crackle. (He learned later that the material held a dirt-repelling charge of static electricity, and would never crease or stain.) Kevin felt uncomfortable in this unfamiliar get-up but the black-and-silver uniform suited Jan as if he'd been born to

27

wear it. Despite his youth he was taller and broader than most of the Kaldor and he towered over them impressively. With his yellow-white hair and blue eyes, he might almost have been one of them.

Once they had changed, the waiting Kaldor led them along more corridors and into yet another metal-walled room. This one was larger, with a small central table, and form-fitting chairs. In the central chair sat Kiro, the Kaldor Captain. He rose courteously as they entered. 'I hope you are recovered from your ordeal?'

He was obviously speaking to Jan, but it was Kevin who answered, 'And so you should – considering that you were the cause of it.'

'An unfortunate error on the part of my crew. Those responsible will be punished. Let me offer you some refreshment.' A hatch opened in the table surface and a tray rose into sight. It contained a crystal decanter, silver goblets, and an assortment of dishes containing various strange-looking foods. The Captain poured a purple fluid into the goblets and passed them to Jan and Kevin. 'I think you will find this pleasant. It is brewed from the bell-flowers on my home planet.'

Kevin took a cautious sip. The drink was delicious, fiery and fruity at the same time. He could feel it sending new strength into his body. He looked at Jan. 'Try it, it's okay.'

Jan made no move to taste the drink, setting it down untouched. 'It's going to take more than a free glass of fruit juice to make up for the way we've been treated.'

'I have already made my apologies. We saw you with those vermin of the League – naturally enough my crew assumed you were with them. Once I had seen you myself, I knew at once that a terrible mistake had been made.'

Kevin smiled coldly, but said nothing. Kiro had been in charge of their interrogation from the beginning. He had ordered that brutal mind-jolt that had slammed a new language into their brains. This sudden change of attitude must mean he believed Kevin's story – or at least, that he wasn't completely sure that the story was false. 'Perhaps the matter can be overlooked,' said Kevin loftily. 'You could not be expected to be aware of our true identity.'

'We should have known there would be an Observer present, but we were not prepared. I only hope that this unfortunate beginning will not prejudice you against us.'

Jan rose. 'We'll see. A lot will depend on how you behave. Now I'm tired.'

Jan got to his feet, nodded curtly at the Kaldor and strode from the room, Kevin close behind him.

A deferential guard was waiting to conduct them to new quarters, a plain metal cabin with two sleeping couches. There a table held a luxurious array of strange food and drinks.

Once they were alone Jan stretched out luxuriously on the couch. 'Well, it worked, Kev! One minute we're in a cell, next it's the VIP suite. You're a genius!'

'Am I?' said Kevin gloomily. 'What do we do now?'

'We keep it up,' said Jan confidently. 'These people are bullies, Kev, and the only thing a bully respects is a bigger bully. So we keep on acting high-and-mighty, and look out for a chance to escape. Don't worry, something will turn up.' Jan yawned. 'Hey, you know something, I really am tired.' He stretched out on the bunk and in a few minutes he was fast asleep.

Kevin looked affectionately at his big cousin, envying him his courage. Nothing seemed to worry Jan for long. He simply couldn't imagine a problem he couldn't deal with somehow or other. And strangely enough, his confidence was often justified. Kevin himself had been ready to surrender to his fate. It was Jan's instinctive defiance that had given him the courage to pull off his bluff. Maybe that was what a hero was, thought Kevin – someone just too brave to do the sensible thing.

Kevin himself was feeling far from heroic. He was suffering from reaction now, his mind full of doubts and fears. He stretched out on the bunk, but his brain was far too active for sleep. What had the Kaldor been after at Stonehenge? Why had they accepted them as 'Observers' with such suspicious speed? And what would they do when they discovered their mistake?

The Kaldor Captain strode arrogantly into the main control room and threw himself into his command chair. The ship was on automatic – there was little for anyone to do till they neared their destination. Crewmen moved silently about the room busying themselves with routine checks. He looked up as Zargon came to stand by his side. 'Are our guests settled?'

'Yes, Captain. They are sleeping.'

Kiro nodded thoughtfully. 'It is fortunate that we realised their status in time.'

Zargon frowned. 'Kiro – you are sure...'

'Of course I am not sure. But we have always suspected that there were those on Earth who still possessed the Ancient Knowledge. Why else would the League forbid anyone to contact the planet? Those stone circles were set up as a signal. For untold planetary cycles those Old Ones have waited for someone to read the message, to land and make contact. Might they not indeed have Observers present, waiting to see who came?'

'Then why did they not declare themselves?'

'They did – eventually. You heard the insolence with which they spoke to us, the way they demanded treatment befitting their rank. If they were helpless captives, they would be humble and beg for mercy. Since they do not beg for mercy – perhaps they are not merely helpless captives.'

In Kaldor terms the logic was unanswerable. Yet, in spite of everything, Zargon was not convinced.

'If they do have knowledge of the Ancient Wisdom, sooner or later they must reveal it. If they do not, they are no more than useless primitives…'

Kiro smiled. 'If that proves to be so, Zargon, then I promise you shall kill them yourself.'

6. Into the Unknown

The control room of the League space ship occupied the whole of the raised dome at the centre of the saucer. It was a huge circular room, and its walls were lined with monitor screens and instrument panels. In the centre of the room was a semicircular control console with three chairs.

The central one was like an enormous throne. On it sat Garm, his big hands making the controls beneath them look like toys. To his right sat Osar, hanging rather than sitting, in a hammock-like device designed to support his round body. The third chair, a kind of bucket seat on a very long pedestal, was obviously Tell's. He hopped nimbly into it and sat beaming at Anna.

Garm looked up. 'Welcome to our conference. Its decisions will affect you. You have a right to speak.'

Anna was taken aback. It hadn't occurred to her that she might actually be consulted about her fate. 'That's very kind of you. It would help me to make my mind up if I knew more about what was going on.'

There was a pause. The three strange beings looked at each other, as if in silent conference. Then Garm said, 'Tell has told you of the history of Old Earth. Many believe that somewhere on your planet, fragments of ancient knowledge still lie hidden.'

'You think that's what the Kaldor were doing at Stonehenge – looking for some ancient secret?'

'Most assuredly,' piped Osar. 'Even now they may have the Secret in their possession. They may be speeding back to Galactic Centre to destroy the League, while we waste time orbiting this barren planet.'

Anna tried to remember the confused events of that night at Stonehenge. 'They were shining some kind of light on one of the monoliths. A pattern appeared, lots of glowing points joined by lines.'

'A star chart,' confirmed Tell. 'Perhaps Stonehenge held not the Secret itself, but the clue to its whereabouts – a clue that could only be followed by a star-travelling race. The Old Ones hoped that someday the new civilisations would rediscover Earth. They left clues for their visitors to find.'

'And this one has been found by the Kaldor,' said Osar bitterly. 'They will use it in their quest to enslave every civilised race in the Galaxy.'

'Maybe they haven't found it yet,' said Anna practically. 'If they've got to search a whole planet... Why don't we get there before them?'

'Because they have the star chart and we do not,' snapped Osar. 'Unless of course you can reproduce it for us from memory?'

'I only got a glimpse of it. Jan was using his camera all the time though.'

'Unfortunately the Kaldor have your friend Jan as well.'

Tell gave a sudden shout of delight. 'But not his camera! See!'

He took Jan's camera from inside his tunic and jumped down from his stool. 'I'll take this to the laboratory.'

They waited. Garm stared broodingly ahead, Osar fiddled nervously with the controls making minute and unnecessary adjustments to the ship's orbit.

At last Tell bustled back, rubbing his hands. 'A primitive device, but effective. I have developed the images and transferred them to our vision-circuits.' He touched a control and a picture appeared on the big central vision screen. It showed Anna, on Salisbury Plain, proudly posing against her newly erected tent.

'Very pretty,' said Osar sardonically. 'But hardly the key to the hidden power of the Old Ones.'

'Wait,' said Tell, and he flashed more pictures on to the screen. There were more shots of the camp, and of Jan and Kevin, clowning about. Anna felt a great wave of anxiety as she saw their grinning faces. What was happening to them now? Were they even alive?

Tell clicked impatiently through the early photographs, then stopped as he reached the one they'd been waiting for – a shot of the League saucer pursuing the Kaldor scout-ship across the night sky. The next shot showed the landed Kaldor ship, Stonehenge looming behind it. There were long shots of the Kaldor studying the megaliths, and then closer shots taken as Jan wriggled nearer.

The last photograph of all was the one they'd been hoping for. It showed three Kaldor grouped round the flattened stone, one shining the torchlike device on it, the other recording the result. The design on the stone showed clearly between the figures of the Kaldor.

'Magnify and stabilise,' rumbled Garm. Tell tuned the controls, and soon the star chart swelled until it filled the screen.

'It's a star-system right enough,' said Tell. 'But which? Feed the pattern into the ship's computer, Osar, and check it against the data banks.'

Osar's tentacle snaked out and adjusted controls on the console before him. Symbols began flashing across a read-out screen.

'Positive identification not possible,' piped Osar.

Tell hammered his fist on the console in frustration, and Garm's huge body slumped in dejection.

'Tentative identification follows. Previously unmapped star system, Galactic co-ordinates seven-five-zero-zero-three-nine-six-seven-eight-four. Estimated probability of identification accuracy, fifty-three per cent.'

'Galactic Visual display,' ordered Garm. A huge fiery Catherine wheel of stars filled the central screen.

'At the moment we are still in your solar system,' explained Tell. 'Here.' A pulsating point of light appeared. 'The planet the computer has identified is here.' Another light-point appeared – on the other side of the screen. 'As you see, it is on the far side of the Galaxy – a hundred thousand light years away.'

'Then that's where we're going,' said Anna.

Tell said, 'I do not think you realise what is involved – this vessel is merely a standard cruiser, designed for medium-range travel. To cross the entire Galaxy in a craft this size would be like crossing your widest ocean on a floating log. It could be done only by a colossal jump through hyper-space – a jump of such magnitude that the ship might well disintegrate.'

'If the Kaldor can do it, so can we,' said Anna firmly.

'The whole idea is absurd,' hissed Osar. 'The Kaldor have a specially built long-range exploration vessel. We don't even know if we have identified the right planet...'

'Of course it's the right planet! The people who left the Secret deliberately made it difficult to find.'

'She may be right,' said Garm. 'The planet is on the far side of the Galaxy – surely that must be part of the test.'

'That's right. You want this precious Secret don't you? Well, I want Kevin and Jan back. We shan't get either hanging about in space like a lump of rock!'

Osar was almost twittering in agitation. 'You simply do not realise the danger. The temporal distortion effect alone...'

'We could return to Galactic Centre,' said Tell slowly. 'Ask for fresh instructions, transfer to a League Battle Cruiser.'

'While the Kaldor ransack the planet for the Secret!' Garm shook his head. 'The girl is right. We shall set off at once.' He turned to Anna. 'First we shall take you back to Earth...'

'Oh no you don't! Kevin and Jan are still missing. I'd be wondering what had happened to them for the rest of my life. Besides you haven't got time. The Kaldor had the star chart before you, remember. They'll be well on their way by now.'

There was a momentary silence. Osar and Tell were looking at Garm.

For all the easy informality of their behaviour, it was clear that the huge Neanderthal was the real leader.

At last Garm said, 'You have the true spirit of Old Earth. We shall do as you say. Tell, run up the boosters to maximum power. Forget the safety margins. Osar, compute the hyper-jump co-ordinates.'

Anna sat back and watched their preparations. Now the decision was taken she could only keep out of the way. Under Tell's hands the drive motors produced a steadily deeper thrumming that shook the control room. Osar sat hunched over his computer, tentacles flickering wildly over the controls, his huge eyes absorbing the never-ending flow of symbols on the read-out screen.

Following Garm's instructions, Anna lay back on her seat, which extended and moulded itself into a couch. Finally Osar hissed, 'Now!' and Garm's huge hand dragged back a master-switch.

Anna felt a horrible wrenching distortion, like being turned inside-out. The control room seemed to break up and swirl around her. For a moment she felt the ship really had blown up and she was drifting with its debris in space.

Gradually everything stabilised. She was back in the control room on her couch. The others sat braced in their chairs.

Anna's voice came out in a dry croak. 'What happened?' she whispered. 'Where are we?'

It was Tell who answered her. 'That was the jump. Now we are nowhere – nowhere and no-when.' He pointed to the screen. The swirl of stars had vanished, replaced by a swirling grey nothingness. 'We are in the void. When Osar computes re-entry we shall emerge. Perhaps into the heart of a sun, perhaps in a black hole, perhaps, if we are very lucky, somewhere close to our destination – on the far side of the Galaxy. Our quest has begun!'

7. ACROSS THE GALAXY

It was a dead planet swinging in orbit around a dying sun. Once it had been an important border-world, marking the outer limits of the long-vanished Empire. One great city covered much of the planet's surface, its towers of metal jutting high into the air.

Long ago its streets and walkways had been thronged with Imperial Guards, defending the frontier against attack from the barbarian worlds, with explorers, prospectors, administrators. Now all were gone. The city stood empty, half in ruins, inhabited only by the creatures that came in from the wilderness beyond, a wilderness that year by year encroached upon the city more and more. City and jungle were locked in silent struggle, a death-grapple that would end only when the planet itself was dead.

As the Kaldor scout ship dropped down towards the planet, Jan and Kevin studied the approaching surface on the vision screen. It was an impressive sight, great towers of metal, some half-ruined, projecting through a swirling curtain of mist.

'The air of the planet is thin, but breathable,' said Kiro. 'Some discomfort may be felt if a long journey is necessary.' He looked pointedly at Kevin and Jan.

These knew at once what the Kaldor meant. They had arrived at their destination. Now it was time for them to prove their claims. Since Kevin had no idea what they were seeking, let alone where it was, that was going to be difficult. He tried to maintain his bluff. 'We're only here to observe. It is for you to prove your worth by reaching your goal unaided.'

'Time and resources are limited,' said Zargon pointedly. 'We cannot search an entire planet. If we attempt it, we shall all die here.' His expression made it clear who would be the first to go.

Inspiration flashed suddenly across Kevin's mind. 'Exactly what is it that you seek?'

'We seek –' began Kiro.

Zargon interrupted him. 'Who should know better than an Observer?'

Foiled again, thought Kevin. Let's try it another way. He gave the two Kaldor a look of bored contempt. 'I'm not talking about its form, I mean its true nature.'

Kiro said hesitantly, 'We seek power…'

'Exactly. And power is energy, is it not?'

Kiro rounded angrily on his subordinate. 'As soon as we land, set sensors on maximum range and probe for any unusual energy source on the planet.'

Jan drew Kevin aside. 'Look, Kev, what do you think you're playing at? We don't know what they're after, or where it is – do we?'

'As long as they don't know we don't know – we're all right. The minute they find out the truth – we're dead.'

'How long can we keep it up?'

'Not much longer. Kiro's getting more and more suspicious – and Zargon never really believed us in the first place.'

'So what do we do?'

Kevin grinned. 'We improvise!'

Jan whispered ruefully, 'I think you're actually enjoying this!'

Kevin saw the two Kaldor officers watching their conference from the other side of the control room. 'Shut up and look haughty,' he hissed, and returned to his study of the vision screen.

As the planetary surface rushed closer and closer, Kevin realised that his cousin's words were true. Despite the dangers, he was enjoying this game of bluff and counter-bluff. There was a fierce excitement in matching wits with his alien enemies.

Obviously Jan felt differently about things. His cousin preferred the kind of danger you could charge head-on, an enemy he could flatten with a few solid punches. Well, he'd just have to realise there was a place for brains as well as brawn.

The metal towers on the screen hurtled towards them, until their walls filled the screen. There was the faintest of vibrations and the screen went blank.

'Landing procedure completed,' reported Zargon.

'Maintain emergency take-off readiness. Commence energy-scan,' ordered Kiro.

Crew members busied themselves at the instrument consoles. A low beeping sound began ringing through the control room. Kevin watched a crewman operate a wheel-shaped control, presumably rotating the scanner beam around the ship. Suddenly the beeping increased its frequency. The crewman looked up. 'Powerful energy source located, sir. Bearing one-four-zero.'

'Range?'

'Too close for an accurate reading. The source is so powerful it's affecting the instruments.'

With a sigh of relief, Kevin realised that his gamble seemed to have paid off. Unfortunately, it had paid off for the Kaldor as well.

Kiro's eyes were gleaming with excitement. 'We shall leave at once. Bring the portable energy scanner, and one squad of guards.'

Zargon looked at Jan and Kevin. 'And our two Observers?'

'They will be coming with us – in case we need the benefits of their advice.'

From behind the shattered plasti-glass window of one of the towers, bright eyes were watching the terrifying object that had suddenly appeared in the square. Whatever it was, it was new – and newness meant danger.

From their hiding place the watchers saw a door open in the ship and a ramp slide out. Black-clad figures emerged, descended the ramp, and stood waiting. The watching creatures reached nervously for their weapons...

Shivering in the chill dank air, Kevin wrapped himself in his cloak. Despite the dangers of his situation, his mind was full of a sense of wonder. He was standing on the soil of another world. Or to be strictly accurate on its cracked and rubble-littered paving stones. He had crossed the Galaxy.

The ship had landed in the centre of an enormous circular space, ringed in with jagged black metal towers. In the centre was a huge pool with a fountain-like structure in the middle. But the fountain was silent now, and the stagnant water of the pool was covered with weeds. Coarse spiky grass had forced its way up through the paving stones and many of the surrounding towers were overgrown with vines. At intervals narrow black-surfaced roads led off from the plaza, disappearing into the distance.

Jan pointed. 'Look how narrow those streets are. They must have had quite a traffic problem.'

'Maybe they didn't have traffic at all. Look!'

The streets were bordered with narrow metal paths, rows of them one above the other, stretching upwards in tiers. 'Walkways,' said Kevin. 'Step out of your front door and ride to wherever you want to go.'

'Why so many?'

Kevin considered. 'Probably the lower ones were for local journeys, and the ones above for longer trips. The very top ones probably ran to different cities altogether.'

'Must have been quite some civilisation. Where did everybody go?'

Kiro appeared. He held a small black box in his hands, with a compass-like dial set into the lid, and control buttons in the side. He switched the device on, and the needle quivered into life. It spun wildly for a moment, then steadied, pointing straight down the road to the left.

Suddenly one of the guards raised his rifle and raked the face of the nearest tower with the purple glow of the laser beam. A whole row of windows burst into crystal fragments, and drips of molten metal ran down the face of the building. The guard lowered the weapon. 'Someone was watching us.'

Zargon surveyed the charred and smoking ruin that was the front of the building. 'No doubt you have disposed of them. Shall we be on our way, Commander?'

Kiro nodded, and the little group set off. As they moved along the narrow streets that ran between the towers, Kevin's face was grim. The little incident had pushed him to a decision – one that could easily cost them their lives.

Only one of the creatures in the building survived the searing blast of the laser-beam. Terrified it limped along echoing corridors and through deserted halls, clutching a charred patch of fur on its leg. It came to a shattered window, sprang through the open space, and swung nimbly away through the vines that festooned the building. One thought filled its terrified mind. The gods had returned at last. But they had not brought the wonderful gifts that had been promised. The gods were angry, wreaking death and destruction. The creature collapsed gasping on a branch, husbanding its strength for the long and dangerous journey that lay ahead. The Tribe must be warned…

In the blackness of deep space the League's flying saucer flickered into existence. Anna clutched the edges of her couch. Coming out of hyper-space was almost as bad as going in. She became aware of a low murmur of voices.

Garm, Tell and Osar were studying the star pattern on the vision screen. 'We are here,' piped Osar triumphantly. 'We have crossed the Galaxy in a single jump, and reached the star system we seek. Truly I am unrivalled amongst star navigators!'

'We have reached *a* star system,' said Garm. 'Tell, check against the chart.'

Anna saw a second star pattern appear on the screen – the chart they had taken from Jan's camera. The two pictures blurred for a moment, and then merged. Tell gave a rasping sigh of relief. 'Osar, you are almost as brilliant as you think you are!'

Anna sat up. 'Well, so we're here. Now what?'

'We have reached the star system, but not yet the planet itself,' said Garm. 'Now we must travel on in normal space. How long, Tell?'

Tell studied the instruments in front of him. 'Perhaps two decads, not longer.'

A decad, Anna had learned, was one tenth of the arbitrary ship's day, which was about ten hours long. 'What do we do when we reach the planet? There's a whole world to search, and we don't even know what we are looking for.'

'We are looking for Kaldor,' said Garm. 'Once we have found them, the Secret will not be far away.'

'Nor will your friends,' added Tell. 'If the Kaldor have made them prisoner, we may be able to release them.'

'How will you find the Kaldor?'

'It will not be easy,' admitted Tell. 'If we are lucky we may be able to pick up the energy-field of their ship.'

'Suppose it has already landed?'

'There will still be an energy-trace – but it will be very small.'

'And what will you do when you find them?'

'We shall ask them to release your friends,' said Garm. 'And we shall attempt to persuade them that the knowledge they seek must be passed over to the League, and used for the good of all the Galaxy.'

'Ask? Persuade?' said Anna scornfully. 'You'll have to do more than that. Last time you met they started shooting on sight.'

Garm's deep voice was solemn. 'It is a serious thing to take the life of any living being. But if there is no other way, then we shall destroy them. Infinite is the Web.'

Softly, Tell made the ritual response. 'May its power protect us.'

They were resting in one of the open squares very like the one in which they had first landed. Indeed the whole city seemed to be laid out on absolutely regular lines. Towers, roads and walkways, a square with a fountain or some huge piece of abstract sculpture, more streets and walkways, another square... everything on an enormous scale.

Jan and Kevin sat on the low stone wall that surrounded the pool, eating rations handed out by one of the Kaldor. Tasteless distilled water in a plastic flask, grey cubes of food concentrate... No one could accuse the Kaldor of being gourmets, thought Kevin. It was only one of the many things he disliked about them. The two Kaldor officers stood some way away, studying the energy-tracking device.

Kevin edged closer to his cousin and whispered, 'Jan, listen. It's time we decided on a plan.'

'I thought we had a plan – staying alive.'

'We know the Kaldor are after some great Secret right? Something that will give them tremendous power…'

'So?'

'So we've got to stop them from getting it.'

'Why?'

'Because they're ruthless killers, they're out to take over the Galaxy…'

'Are you crazy?' whispered Jan. 'Look, we got mixed up in a war – but that doesn't mean we've got to join in.'

'The Kaldor were going to toss us out in space, remember, until we managed to bluff them. They'll kill us anyway, as soon as they get what they're after.'

'So what do you want us to do?'

'Escape,' said Kevin calmly. 'Find what they're after, and get hold of it before them. Then we can do some kind of deal. Better still, we can make contact with the other side, the League, and do a deal with them.'

'What makes you so sure they're any better than the Kaldor?'

Kevin grinned. 'I'm not – but any enemy of the Kaldor is a friend of mine! Anyway, keep your eyes open. When we get a chance we'll make a run for it.'

Suddenly they heard raised voices. Kiro and Zargon seemed to be having some kind of dispute. 'We cannot march through this desolation indefinitely,' Kiro said angrily. 'We must return to the ship and attempt to land closer to our goal.'

'With respect, Commander, the energy detector cannot be used while the ship is in flight. The signal is clear and strong now – we must be very close.'

'The further from the ship, the greater our danger. We know this planet still holds some kind of life. What if we are attacked?'

'Here?' said Zargon scornfully. 'What could harm us here? Some primitive life forms may have survived – but if they attack us we shall know how to deal with them.' He nodded towards the guards with their laser-rifles.

Something flashed silently across the square and a guard staggered back choking, an arrow in his throat.

8. The Monster in the Pool

For a second everyone was frozen with sheer astonishment. As more arrows zipped across the square, Kaldor guards began firing in the direction of the attack, Kiro snatched the hand-blaster from his belt, Zargon ran to snatch the laser-rifle from the fallen guard. The Kaldor were reacting to danger with impressive speed, though several more guards dropped with arrows in them before the rest of the squad found cover.

Jan and Kevin ducked down behind the parapet. The arrows were coming from the corner tower, a vine-festooned ruin with rows of shattered windows. The Kaldor guards were pouring laser-bolt after laser-bolt into the buildings. The lurid purple flare of the laser-beams filled the square, and there was a red glow from inside the tower as the building caught fire.

Kevin jabbed his cousin in the ribs. 'Now's our chance.' Zargon had put the energy-detector down on the parapet so he could use the rifle. 'We can pinch that gadget and find the Secret before them.'

Before Jan could reply, Kevin sprinted along the parapet, snatched up the energy-detector and dashed down one of the narrow streets leading away from the square.

Choices flashed through Jan's mind at the speed of light. Follow Kevin? Zargon had seen Kevin flash by him and was already swinging round, bringing the laser-rifle to bear on the fleeing figure. And Kevin was running down a long narrow passage with nowhere to hide…

Jan realised he had only one chance of survival. He ran up to Zargon and snatched the laser-rifle from his grip, giving the Kaldor a shove that sent him staggering. Fumbling for the firing-stud, Jan swung the weapon round to cover Kevin, who was looking over his shoulder to see if his cousin was following. 'Come on,' yelled Kevin – and Jan fired. Just above Kevin's head, a chunk of building exploded in flame. With a burst of speed, Kevin shot round a corner and disappeared from sight.

By now Kiro had realised what was happening. 'After him,' he screamed. The nearest guard set off in pursuit. To follow Kevin he had to cross open ground and the unseen enemies were ready. Three arrows thudded into the guard's body at once, and he fell twitching to the ground.

Zargon was on his feet now, face twisted with rage, fumbling for the blaster in his belt. Before he could draw the weapon, Jan threw him the laser-cannon with a force that sent him staggering back.

'It is too late. You have let him escape.'

Kiro was staring at them in astonishment. 'What is happening here?'

'My colleague tried to persuade me to join him in stealing the Secret.'

Kiro looked hard at him. 'And you refused?'

'You saw for yourself. When Zargon's negligence gave him his chance, I tried to kill him myself.'

By now Zargon had the laser-rifle trained on Jan.

'You lie. You let him escape. Soon he will be found and destroyed – but you will die now.'

'You are a fool, Zargon,' said Jan wearily. 'If I wanted to betray you, I would have escaped with him.' Turning his back on the weapon, he swung round to Kiro. 'You have another energy-detector of course?'

'It is in the ship.'

Jan gave the weary sign of superior intelligence faced with perpetual stupidity. 'In the ship, of course. May I suggest we return and fetch it?'

'Do not listen to him,' shrieked Zargon. 'He seeks only to save his friend.'

'When my colleague is recaptured, I shall execute him myself,' said Jan calmly. 'But without another energy-detector we shall not succeed in finding either him or the Secret. Thanks to you he now has a considerable start. Our only chance is to find the traitor and Secret together.'

Kiro hesitated. The contrast between Zargon's gibbering anger and Jan's calm certainty was having effect. 'We shall do as the Observer suggests. Zargon, you were negligent to bring only one energy-detector. Order the men to fall back.'

Zargon rapped an order to the guards. The tower holding their attackers was well ablaze now, sending a great plume of black smoke into the grey sky. No more arrows came from it. The enemy had been forced to retreat.

Jan looked at the burning tower. 'We can use this as a marker, return to this point by ship, and take up the search again.'

Kiro nodded reluctantly. 'An excellent idea, Observer. It will save a good deal of time. I shall make sure that our next expedition is better prepared.' He strode back the way they had come, Jan at his side.

Still carrying the laser-rifle, Zargon followed with the surviving guards. As he followed Jan's tall figure with his eyes, his fingers caressed the firing-stud of the weapon...

* * *

42

Kevin sped on through the silent grey streets, the sounds of battle fading away behind him. He ran and ran until he was gasping for breath in the thin cold air. Then too tired to run further he took shelter in an ornately decorated doorway, and tried to collect his thoughts. He'd made his impulsive dash on sheer instinct, an overpowering feeling that he had to get away from the Kaldor, and that this was the time. He'd assumed his cousin would follow, and he still hadn't recovered from the shock of seeing that, far from joining in his escape, Jan had apparently done his best to blow his head off.

Surely Jan hadn't really changed sides? On Earth Kevin would have trusted him completely. But they weren't on Earth. In this world everything was strange and different. Perhaps Jan was different too. Certainly there was a ruthlessly practical streak in Jan. If instinct told him that killing Kevin was the only way to survive...

Kevin decided to forget Jan for the moment and concentrate on more immediate problems. If he was to find the Secret before the Kaldor and somehow turn it against them, he'd better be on his way. The loss of the detector would not delay the Kaldor for long. Kevin looked down at the little box. Its needle was still pointing firmly on to the mysterious energy source. Using the detector as his compass, he resumed his journey.

Anna sat with her eyes fixed on the vision screen, while the surface of the planet flowed endlessly below her. It seemed to consist of one enormous city – towers, streets, squares, the same pattern repeated over and over again, everything completely regular, and everything utterly deserted.

Anna kept hoping she would be the one to spot the Kaldor ship. Perhaps she would even see Jan or Kevin walking along those silent grey streets. It was ridiculous, she knew. At this height they would appear on the screen as no more than moving dots. The only real hope of finding them lay with Osar, who sat hunched over his delicate detector-instruments, his huge golden eyes alert for any flicker of the dials.

Anna turned to him. 'Have you found anything?'

'There is nothing,' said Osar despondently. 'Not a trace. Unless we find them soon, we must abandon the search.'

'No, you can't! You can't just leave them.'

Tell and Garm were looking on sympathetically. 'It is not a question of choice,' said Garm. 'Unless we leave this planet soon, we shall not be able to leave at all.'

'Our energy resources are limited,' explained Tell. 'They are already strained by the huge jump across the Galaxy. Unless we husband them carefully, we shall not be able to return to Galactic Centre.'

'But you won't give up yet?' pleaded Anna.

'No,' said Garm reassuringly. 'We shall not give up yet. While a single erg of energy remains, we shall continue the search.'

The Kaldor force was weary and discouraged by the time they reached the ship, returning not as they'd hoped, with the treasure in their grasp, but instead tired and defeated, with most of their number dead. Jan noticed that no attempt had been made to bring back the slain, or even to give them any kind of burial. The bodies had simply been left where they had fallen. Now, back in the ship, they were finishing a hasty meal of the usual food-concentrates before setting off again.

Zargon rose. 'I will prepare the new crew members, Commander. We lost six, did we not?'

'Replace them, and add three more,' ordered Kiro. 'We must expect another attack. Issue them with laser-rifles.'

'How many crew have you got on this ship?' asked Jan curiously.

Zargon smiled, 'As many as we need. Come, Earthman, I will show you.'

He led Jan through the metal corridors of the ship, and down to a circular chamber on the lower levels. Most of the chamber was taken up by a transparent coffin-shaped tank which gave off a dim, greenish glow. It seemed to be filled with a murky liquid, rather like pea soup.

Zargon went to an instrument panel, and stabbed rapidly at the controls. There was a hum of power, and the glow from the tank brightened into a fierce green blaze. The viscous liquid began to swirl and eddy, and a shape started to form. Slowly it solidified, broke the surface of the liquid and rose to its feet. It was the figure of a man, or rather a Kaldor, with the same fair hair, blue eyes and wiry build of all the others. It might have been Zargon's twin – or Kiro's for that matter.

As the figure stepped from the tank, a blast of warm air swept the room, drying off the traces of liquid. Zargon gave a nod of satisfaction, and reprogrammed the controls. More liquid glugged into the tank. It swirled and eddied, and another shape began to form…

The eerie process was repeated again and again, until nine identical figures stood waiting, ranked in three rows of three. Zargon turned challengingly to Jan. 'You see, Earthman?'

'Very impressive,' said Jan dryly. 'The rest of the family, I suppose?'

'They are clones. Identical replicas of myself, each one grown in the nutrient fluid from a single cell of my body.'

'Why go to the trouble? There are easier ways of producing people.'

Zargon looked surprised. 'But these are true Kaldor. The elite of our planet as I am myself. It is not easy, even for us, to breed completely true. Height, build, colouring, mental capacity, all are exactly laid down by the Tyrant of Kaldor himself. Once a true specimen has been obtained, it can be reproduced by cloning, as many times as needed.'

Jan was impressed, though he tried not to let it show. 'How many can you produce?'

'Here on the ship? No more than a few hundred, the nutrient supply is limited. In the great cloning tanks on the home planet – millions upon millions! Enough to put an army of occupation on every habitable planet in the Galaxy.'

Jan envisaged a fleet of Kaldor ships landing on Earth, each one disgorging an endless army of black-clad soldiers.

He looked at the motionless figures. 'Don't seem any too lively, do they?'

Zargon shrugged. 'There is an initial period of disorientation. They will be clothed, fed, armed, briefed. Then they will be Kaldor warriors.'

'Like the others on this ship… Now that I think of it, they're none too lively either, are they? Only you and Kiro seem to talk, think, give orders.'

'The cloning process has limitations,' admitted Zargon reluctantly. 'Certain personality elements are only faintly present. But Kaldor scientists are at work improving the process.'

'But until the guys back in the lab get it right, you're stuck with zombies? Cannon-fodder, who can follow simple orders, and die when they're told to!'

Zargon said coldly, 'What else need a soldier do?'

Jan turned away. 'Well, you'd better get your toy soldiers kitted out, Zargon. They've got work to do.'

Kevin rounded the base of yet another tower – and found himself looking at a palace.

It lay on the far side of an enormous square, and it was circled by a moat. It seemed to be made of some kind of crystal, and its towers, battlements and turrets shone like a beacon in the surrounding gloom.

Kevin checked the energy-detector. Its needle was pointing straight towards the palace, quivering with eager life. The object of his quest must be very close.

Kevin crossed the square and stood gazing thoughtfully into the stagnant weed-covered water of the moat. There was no sign of a bridge. He could swim across of course – it wasn't much more than about three lengths of a swimming pool. But there was something very unattractive about the murky water. Kevin decided to look for some other solution.

He wandered along the edge of the moat, the palace of crystal gleaming tantalisingly on the other side. The needle on the energy-indicator was still pointing unerringly towards it. He came to a kind of wharf, a scattering of low buildings and a landing stage. There were no boats, but stacked against the side of one of the buildings was a pile of huge metal containers. Kevin lifted one. It was about twice his own length, and felt light and strong at the same time. He carried it down to the moat and pushed it in. It floated placidly on the still water.

Kevin looked round. He found a plank-shaped strip of metal alloy leaning against a building. He climbed into the tank, sat cross-legged in the centre, and began paddling with the metal strip. The tank shot away from the bank, and began spinning like a top.

Its lightness made it unstable, like a coracle, but eventually Kevin mastered the knack of steering, and began a slow progress across the moat. Talk about going to sea in a sieve...

He was about halfway across when he saw the ripple following him. Something was moving beneath the surface. Judging by the size of the ripple it was something large...

Too late to turn back now... Kevin paddled slowly on. The ripple came after him. Soon he was two-thirds of the way across and had just about convinced himself the ripple was some harmless trick of the current.

A huge fanged head shot straight up out of the water and lunged hungrily towards him.

9. Palace of Peril

Kevin saw a blunt, flattish head on the end of a long sinewy neck, several rows of gleaming teeth, and two tiny red eyes. Weed and water streamed from the creature's head as it broke the surface.

He didn't hang around long enough to make a more detailed study. The moment the horror appeared Kevin jumped out of his improvised boat and made for the bank at his best Australian Crawl.

The shining metal container saved his life. Missing Kevin by inches, the monster lunged for it, clamping down on the container with those rows of gleaming teeth. The metal buckled like silver paper, and the tank was soon a chunk of chewed wreckage in the creature's mouth. It chomped on the metal for a while, decided it wasn't good to eat, tossed it aside with an angry roar. By now Kevin was climbing out on to the far bank. The movement caught the monster's eye, and it set off after him.

Kevin sprinted through an enormous crystal arch in the wall surrounding the palace. He found himself in a huge courtyard. On the other side was a door, presumably giving entrance to the palace. Kevin turned for a better look at the monster, assuming that now he was on land he was relatively safe. The assumption was wrong. The monster, it seemed, was more of a giant lizard than a snake. It had clambered out of the moat on a set of thick, clawed legs and was heading for the crystal archway like an express train entering a tunnel. The arch wasn't quite big enough, and halfway through the monster stuck fast, with a bellow of anger.

Kevin turned and hared across the courtyard, hoping the beast would stay jammed long enough for him to get into the palace. Gasping he hurried towards the doorway – then all at once it looked as if he wasn't to get inside the palace so easily after all.

A towering metal shape glided forward, barring his path. It was an enormous robot.

Kevin skidded to an astonished halt. The robot had a cylindrical metal body with a metal sphere on top to form the head. A huge circular lens gleamed in the centre of the sphere, giving it the air of a metal Cyclops. It had flexible arms, and glided on a cylindrical metal base, presumably moving on some kind of hovercraft principle. The thing was at least three times Kevin's height, and it towered above him, completely blocking the door. 'HALT!' it commanded in a booming voice. 'YOU ARE NOW ENTERING A HIGH SECURITY ZONE. PLEASE PRODUCE YOUR PASS AND HOLD IT BEFORE MY SCANNER.'

Kevin glanced over his shoulder. The lizard-monster wrenched itself free, wrecking the arch in the process, and began thundering across the courtyard. Giant monsters, giant robots, thought Kevin resentfully. Why did everything on this planet have to be so big? Looking up at the robot Kevin pointed to the approaching monster. 'Never mind me,' he shouted. 'Why don't you ask that thing for its pass?'

He jumped to one side as the monster came hurtling forward. It reared back in astonishment as it saw the robot. To Kevin's amazement, the robot followed his suggestion.

'HALT!' it said again. 'YOU ARE NOW ENTERING A HIGH SECURITY ZONE. PLEASE PRODUCE YOUR PASS AND HOLD IT BEFORE MY SCANNER.'

Apparently the monster didn't have a pass either. It lunged at the robot, slamming into it with its blunt fanged head, almost knocking it from its base with the force of its charge. 'DESIST!' said the robot sternly. 'YOU ARE INTERFERING WITH MY FUNCTION. I SHALL REPORT YOUR ACTION TO CENTRAL CONTROL. YOU ARE LIABLE TO A FINE OF UP TO ONE HUNDRED GALACTIC CREDITS.'

Unimpressed by this threat the lizard-monster lunged at the robot again, the savage claws making deep scratches in the shining metal.

'I AM AUTHORISED TO RESIST ILLEGAL ACTIONS WITH PUNITIVE MEASURES,' boomed the robot sternly. 'PRODUCE YOUR PASS IMMEDIATELY, OR LEAVE THE AREA. THIS IS YOUR FINAL WARNING.'

The monster responded with a roar of anger and clamped its teeth on one metal arm. A shutter slid back in the robot's barrel-like chest and a small nozzle appeared. There was a faint crackle, and the purple glare of a laser ray. The ray was fitful and erratic, but it was enough to discourage the monster. It gave a scream of pain, whipped round and slithered rapidly across the yard, through the ruined archway, and back into the moat with a colossal splash.

Kevin dodged past the security robot and ran into the palace. He heard the robot's voice boom out behind him. 'YOU ARE ADVISED TO REPORT TO THE MAIN SECURITY OFFICE AND OBTAIN A DULY AUTHORISED PASS.' He wondered if the monster would take any notice.

When he was far enough from the entrance to feel safe, Kevin paused to look about him. He was in an enormously wide corridor which stretched ahead as far as he could see, curving out of sight in the far distance. Once again Kevin was struck by the sheer size of everything on this planet. The corridor was high as well as broad, its ceiling lost in shadows. Dimly glowing light-globes were set at intervals along the walls. The corridor was carpeted in some soft iridescent material that glowed with subtly changing colours. Kevin had a twinge of guilt about dripping muddy water on the Royal carpet. He looked down at his clothes and found them perfectly dry and clean – somehow the material had just shaken off the water. Another point for Kaldor technology, he thought – which reminded him about the energy-detector inside his tunic. He took it out and looked at it. The needle was pointing to the right. He needed to find a side corridor of some kind… Kevin hurried on.

At intervals doorways led off from the corridor. Kevin stopped now and again to look inside the rooms to which they led. All the chambers were enormous, their vast interiors concealed in shadowy gloom. Some looked like state rooms or conference chambers, others might have been living rooms or sleeping quarters, but all were built on the same colossal scale.

At last Kevin reached a right-hand corridor junction. He turned the corner and found himself facing another robot. Kevin groaned, wondering if there would be another demand for his pass. This robot was smaller than the first, though of the same basic shape, and it was moving to and fro as if on sentry duty. As he got closer he saw the robot had a plastic sack attached to the back of its body-case, and a suction nozzle on a long, flexible arm projecting from its front. It was vacuum-cleaning the carpet.

When Kevin came up to it the little robot drew respectfully to one side, waiting for him to pass. Once he'd turned the corner it resumed its task. Kevin went on, shaking his head in astonishment. Rampaging monsters on the outside, robot housemaids on the inside…

The inner corridor along which he was now walking was both narrower and darker than the first, and there were no doors leading off. Far in the distance was a faint green glow, like the point of light at the end of a long tunnel. Kevin marched on and on feeling mentally and physically exhausted. It was like walking up a down escalator – you had no feeling of getting anywhere. He plodded forward and at last he reached the source of the glow. A massive door blocked off the end of the corridor. It was made of some translucent material, and it glowed green in the semi-darkness. Kevin checked the energy-indicator. Whatever he was looking for was somewhere on the other side of that door.

He gave the door a tentative push, and it swung smoothly open. He went through and the door closed silently behind him. Kevin stood staring about him in sheer astonishment.

He was in a jungle.

* * *

49

Tell leaned forward, pointing eagerly at the viewing screen. 'There – we have found them!'

They had been gliding high above the city for what seemed like a very long time, the League ship silent and invisible behind its protective screens. Now, at last, they had found what they were looking for – the black Kaldor scout ship was standing in one of the city squares. Even as they watched, the Kaldor ship took off.

'Maybe we're too late,' said Anna in alarm. 'Maybe they've found what they're after and are already on the way home.'

'Watch,' said Garm.

From their superior height they saw the Kaldor ship rise a few hundred feet in the air, fly parallel with the ground for a short distance, then land in another square identical to the first.

'Go lower,' ordered Garm. 'But stay out of range of their detector-beams.'

'If we move too close they will find us, even through the shields,' grumbled Osar. His tentacles moved obediently over the controls, and the League ship descended to hover silent and invisible high above the square.

The scout ship's landing ramp emerged, and three Kaldor appeared. They stood looking around them – studying the dials of an instrument that one of them was carrying. They had a brief conference amongst themselves, then orders were given, more Kaldor appeared from the ship, and eventually about a dozen set off, marching away from the square.

At the head of the marching group was a tall broad-shouldered figure. He wore the same black and silver uniform as the others, but there was something familiar about him...

Anna leaned forward. 'Can you manage a close-up of that one in front?'

Osar zoomed in on the tall figure until his head and shoulders filled the screen. He had the same blond hair and regular features as the other Kaldor, and his cold blue eyes stared arrogantly around him.

'It's Jan!' gasped Anna. 'That one in front – it's my cousin Jan!'

Tell said consolingly, 'He may have been forced to join them... Can you see your other friend?'

Osar pulled back the video beam and Anna scanned the marching group. 'No, there's no sign of him. Maybe he's still a prisoner in the ship.'

Was that what had happened? Anna wondered. Had Jan joined up with the Kaldor? And what about Kevin? There was a powerful streak of obstinacy in her small cousin. If he'd refused to join the Kaldor then perhaps he was already dead. She saw the concern in the faces of the three others. 'Well, what do we do now?'

'We follow,' said Osar.

Garm shook his head. 'We must do better than that. We must reach their destination before them. Osar, plot them on to an aerial map of the city.'

The picture of the marching Kaldor was replaced by a map. It showed the square, the scout ship, and the network of streets around. The Kaldor appeared as a little group of dots, moving slowly away from the ship.

'Pull back still further – and project their line of movement.'

Osar obeyed. A line appeared on the map-screen, beginning at the square where they'd first seen the Kaldor, creeping slowly forward to the second square where the ship had landed, moving on to join the group of dots, and then going on beyond them. The line went on and on until it reached an enormous circular pattern at the far edge of the map. 'There,' said Garm softly.

Anna looked at the huge circular shape. 'What is it?'

'Their destination,' said Garm softly. 'We shall reach it before them.'

The League cruiser rose higher and glided over the city.

Giant trees with enormous knotted trunks rose so high that they hid the sky. A hidden sun beat down with tremendous force. Vines and plants and creepers of every kind struggled up towards the light, swarming over the twisted, knotted tree-trunks in rich profusion. Shrubs and bushes and thorn-trees were everywhere. For a moment Kevin stood in total confusion, his bearings completely lost. He tried to work out where he was. Judging by its frontage the palace was enormous. Had he managed to cross it completely, and emerge on the other side? Suddenly Kevin realised the truth.

He remembered the vast curved frontage of the building, reflected in the curve of that first corridor. The palace was built in the shape of a wheel. The outer corridor was the rim, the narrower one he'd just come down one of the spokes. Incredible as it seemed this jungle was at the hub, actually inside the palace itself.

Kevin stared up at the fierce yellow light that beat down through the dense screen of tropical vegetation, and breathed the warm humid air. He remembered the dull grey skies of the planet's surface. This blazing sun above him was artificial. The whole place was artificial, a colossal greenhouse as big as one of the jungles of Earth.

Perhaps the rulers of this planet had built the jungle as a place where they could escape from the chill dank air of their dying planet, feel the warmth of sunshine again, see the fresh green of tropical plants, the bright colours of the flowers. Now, abandoned for untold thousands of years, the pleasure ground had reverted to jungle, while the artificial sun still beat down from the clear blue sky.

Still, artificial or not, the jungle had to be crossed. The energy-sensor pointed firmly towards its centre. Wishing he had an elephant gun and a line of native porters, Kevin began forcing his way through the jungle.

It wasn't an easy journey. There were faint traces of a path, but it was almost completely overgrown. There were sinister rustlings in the jungle around him, and from time to time a fierce cawing from the treetops above.

It occurred to Kevin that this jungle might be inhabited, by animals, perhaps even by intelligent life. He was just wondering what those inhabitants might be like when something landed on top of him. It was a net of some kind, woven from vines and creepers. Kevin struggled desperately to free himself, but the folds of the net entangled his limbs and bore him down. Grey-furred shapes dropped chattering from the trees, long yellow fangs glinting in black-muzzled faces. They gathered up the net between them, wrapping it more firmly around their prisoner. To his horror Kevin felt himself beginning to rise up in the air. Higher and higher went the net with its struggling burden, until the jungle floor was a dizzying distance below. In a series of swooping rushes the grey-furred creatures carried their captive clear up to the leafy jungle roof.

10. THE WARRIORS OF ARKO

Protected by its invisibility screen the League cruiser hovered high above the palace. On the vision screen Anna could see the line of marching Kaldor heading straight for the edge of the moat.

'We must switch off the shield soon,' warned Osar. 'The energy-drain is too great.'

'What do we do now?' asked Anna.

As usual, everyone looked at Garm, who rubbed an enormous hand across his jaw. 'We could look for an entrance on the far side – but in a building the size of this, we might well lose them completely.' He peered at the jumble of crystal towers and turrets on the screen. 'Somehow we must surprise them… Go lower, Tell. I think I see what we need.'

The cruiser swooped down towards the Palace.

Following as they were in Kevin's footsteps, the Kaldor naturally ran into all the same obstacles. They dealt with them with ruthless efficiency. When they reached the banks of the moat that guarded the palace, Zargon snapped an order to the ranks of guardsmen. They took components from their battle-packs and rapidly assembled them into a rocket launcher. A series of grapnels carrying fine plastic ropes were fired across the moat and into a wall on the far side where they held fast, gripped by molecular adhesion. In a matter of minutes a simple suspension bridge had been constructed, a rope to walk on, another to hold on to. At a nod from Zargon, one of the guardsmen began edging his way across the bridge. He was just about halfway when a huge fanged head erupted from the water and plucked him from the bridge.

The monster didn't stand a chance. Two heavy laser-cannon were already set up on the bank. There was a crackle of energy and the purple glare of the laser-beams. The lizard-monster gave one shattering roar of rage and pain, then it was blasted into bloody fragments. The surface of the canal boiled and hissed, and a dull red cloud stained the murky waters. There was a brief seething and bubbling, as smaller creatures devoured the shattered remnants of the great beast.

The man in the creature's mouth had died with the monster that attacked him. Kiro and Zargon showed no concern at losing one of their men. After all, thought Jan, they could always go back to the cloning tank and grow another.

Kiro barked an order, and a second guard stepped unhesitatingly on to the bridge. If there were more creatures in the moat they had been frightened off. The second guard reached the other side in safety. Jan, Kiro and Zargon crossed after him and the rest of the guards followed. They marched through the archway and across the courtyard.

The robot trundled out to meet them. 'STOP. YOU ARE NOW ENTERING A HIGH SECURITY ZONE. PLEASE PRODUCE YOUR PASS AND HOLD IT BEFORE MY SCANNER.'

Zargon deactivated the robot with a casual shot from his hand-blaster. The robot staggered back, the purple laser-beam playing about its metal body. The shutter in its chest slid back, but a second blast from Zargon exploded its energy-core before it could fire. Smoke pouring from its shattered chest-unit, the robot crashed to the ground like a metal tower.

'YOU ARE INTERFERING WITH MY AUTHORISED FUNCTION,' it protested feebly. 'I SHALL REPORT YOUR ACTION TO CENTRAL CONTROL. YOU ARE LIABLE TO A FINE...'

A final shot from Zargon blasted it into silence. 'Primitive technology – but well made to have functioned for so long.' Booted feet ringing on the paving stones, the Kaldor marched into their palace.

Since Zargon was using an energy-sensor as a guide they followed the same route as Kevin once again. The cleaning robot had moved on to another section of corridor by the time they arrived. At a command from Zargon, the guard with the laser-cannon blasted it on sight. The little robot exploded into a shower of metal fragments, its long task ended at last. 'Probably just a low-grade service robot,' said Zargon. 'But it is as well to be sure.'

They went on their way. Eventually they came to the glowing green door, passed through it as Kevin had done and found themselves on the fringes of the indoor jungle.

The guards formed themselves into ranks and stood waiting. During all this time the Kaldor guards had shown no surprise, no fear, no excitement, no interest at all in the many wonders they had encountered.

Perhaps it was because they were clones, thought Jan. But then, Kiro and Zargon reacted, or rather failed to react, in exactly the same way. Maybe all the Kaldor lacked the capacity for surprise, or excitement or wonder. Instead they made do with ruthless efficiency, that and a certain cold pleasure in wanton destruction.

Zargon was studying the energy-detector. 'Our way lies straight ahead.'

'There is no path,' objected Kiro.

'Then we shall make one.' More snapped orders, and the guards assembled another device, a squat laser-gun with a wide bell-like muzzle. They fired and a broad flat beam of light blasted a long smoking path through the jungle. The air was full of smoke and the acrid stink of charred vegetation.

The guards moved the device to the far end of the charred strip and fired again, extending the path.

Leaving their usual trail of destruction, the Kaldor blasted their way through the jungle and Jan, his face cold and expressionless, marched beside them.

By the time his aerial journey ended, Kevin was dizzy and sick. It was like being in a shopping bag that some giant was swinging through the air. At last he was dumped with a thud on to something soft and springy. For a time his surroundings continued to spin around him.

Things steadied at last and he was able to look about him. He was on some kind of wooden platform high in the trees. There was a big hut built on the platform, a kind of tree-house, and Kevin in his net had been dumped like a parcel in front of the door. There were more houses, similar but smaller, in the trees nearby.

Grouped around him in a circle were his captors. They were huge grey apes. As his head slowly cleared Kevin was able to get a better look at them. They were quite unlike any ape he had seen on Earth. Their general appearance was like that of a baboon, the size was that of a giant gorilla. They had the brown mournful eyes of chimpanzees, and they chattered gutturally amongst themselves, prodding and poking at Kevin with long, bony fingers.

Something else distinguished them from the apes of Earth. They were carrying weapons. Kevin saw bows, spears, stone-headed clubs, knives made from scraps of jagged metal. One of them even had a blaster though from the lumpy misshapen look of the weapon it had been used as a kind of club.

Kevin wondered what they were planning to do with him. Sacrifice? Or dinner? Weren't the great apes vegetarians? He peered into the gloomy doorway of the hut. It looked rather like Tarzan's tree-house in the old Johnny Weissmuller movies he'd seen on television. Maybe Tarzan would come out in a loincloth and say 'Me, Tarzan, you Kevin.' Perhaps Jane would appear with a bowl of fruit. They could all go swimming. Kevin decided he must be suffering from delayed shock.

A figure appeared in the doorway. It was an ape like the others, but larger, and its fur was completely white. Its arms and body bore the scars of many battles, and a tattered strip of rainbow-coloured material hung proudly from its shoulders. Something told Kevin he was in the presence of royalty.

He decided to try to make a good impression.

'Greetings, your majesty. My name is Kevin.'

The ape regarded him unblinkingly. Then to Kevin's astonishment it tapped itself on the chest and said, 'Arko.' It shot out an astonishingly long arm and jabbed Kevin in the chest. 'Why come?'

Using only the simplest words and phrases, talking slowly and emphatically, Kevin told of his capture by the Kaldor and his later escape.

Arko listened impassively. 'Why Kaldor come? What want?'

'Something tremendously important,' said Kevin urgently. 'Some secret that will give them tremendous power. It's hidden on this planet, perhaps even in this jungle. Whatever it is, you mustn't let them have it.'

'Not give?'

'No. The Kaldor are evil ruthless killers. They'll use this thing to seize control over the rest of the Galaxy. They'll plunder your world, and mine and a million others.'

'What secret? You know?'

Kevin shook his head.

'I know,' grunted Arko. 'Kaldor want Godstone.'

'What will you do?'

'Kill them. All who seek to steal Godstone must die.'

An ape swung on to the platform, fell before Arko and made a long chattering speech. An angry snarling went up from the listening warriors, until Arko stilled them, with a guttural command. A little stiffly, the old ape swung himself upright, using his immensely long arms rather like crutches. He leaped from the platform and stood poised on a nearby branch.

'What's happening?' shouted Kevin. 'Where are you going?'

'Kaldor come with warriors, thunderbolt weapons. We kill them.'

'What about me?'

'Kill you too – sacrifice to Godstone!'

Arko led his warriors off, giving a harsh screaming cry as he swung away.

For a time the trees around were thick with rushing figures as the apes from the tree-village answered the summons of their king. Kevin saw them swinging through the bushes in grey-furred troops, their

56

weapons clutched incongruously in monkey hands. The noise of movement died away at last and everything was quiet.

Kevin was left on the platform, alone and unguarded. Perhaps the apes thought no one but themselves could travel through the trees. For anyone but a skilled climber, the tree-house was as good as a prison. But Kevin was a good climber and he had no intention of waiting here until Arko came to kill him.

The trouble was – he was still trussed up in the net. Kevin tried biting the ropes but they were far too tough for his teeth.

By standing upright he found he could manage a kind of hopping motion inside the net. He made his way inside the hut and looked around.

Luckily there was no one else about. Kevin reckoned the place was probably sacred ground, somewhere only the King himself was allowed to enter. The hut was furnished with a few scattered hides, the floor littered with bones and scraps of fruit. A crudely made wooden throne stood in one corner – and across it lay a sword.

Kevin hobbled over. It was less of a sword, he saw, than a giant knife and it was bright and clean, obviously polished with loving care. No doubt it was part of Arko's royal regalia. Maybe he knighted particularly deserving apes with it on state occasions.

Kevin reached out between the meshes, grasped the handle and began slashing at the net. The blade must have been razor-sharp, because the tough ropes fell apart like cobwebs beneath its touch.

Free at last, Kevin kicked aside the net and stood upright. He reached out to lay the sword back on the throne, then hesitated. It was the only weapon he had. On impulse he hunted round behind the throne. Sure enough there was a sheath as well. He slid the blade carefully into the sheath and fixed it to the belt of his Kaldor uniform. Cautiously Kevin crept out of the hut. The nearest tree-house was some way away. Through its open windows he could see an ape. There was a baby clutching at its breast. Only women and children left, thought Kevin, the males were all off to the wars. Now was his chance. Clutching at a trailing vine he ran forward and launched himself Tarzan-like off the tree-house platform.

11. AMBUSH

Anna stopped at the bottom of the ramp and looked around. She was standing on a huge flat stone roof, so high up that the grey clouds looked near enough to touch. Garm and Tell followed her down the ramp. It had been decided that Osar would stay with the ship, standing by, ready for take-off. They'd tried to persuade Anna to stay too, but she wasn't having any.

Anna turned to Garm, who was checking over his equipment. 'Where are we?'

'In a space port of course. Where else would one land a space ship?'

Anna looked surprised, and Tell said, 'We are on the roof of the palace. This was probably the private landing area for the ruler and his court.'

'And the Kaldor?'

'Somewhere below us. You might say we've managed to get on top of them at last.'

Anna groaned at the terrible joke. Garm gave one of his rare smiles. 'Perhaps we shall be able to surprise them. They won't expect us to arrive from above. With luck we may reach their destination before them.' He studied the energy-detecting device. 'Come, we must find a way into the palace.'

There were low square buildings at the edge of the landing area. They made their way to the nearest. The door was locked, but Garm wrenched it off its hinges. Inside there was a bare stone room. A flight of steps led downwards. The stairs led to a long, long corridor, which ended in a glowing green door.

On the other side of the door was a long railed gallery that curved away into the distance. There was a blue dome studded with blazing arc-lamps high above their heads, and below them was a waving sea of green.

'It is a jungle,' said Garm delightedly. 'There are jungles like this on the world from which I come.' He plucked at the collar of his space-suit as if he wanted to rip it off and swing unencumbered through the trees.

'But we're indoors,' protested Anna. 'You can't have a jungle inside a building.'

'It is a protected environment, a place where plants and animals can live in warmer conditions than those on the surface. Do you not have such places on Earth?'

'You mean it's a greenhouse?' Anna found it hard to imagine a greenhouse on such an enormous scale.

Garm was checking the energy-detector. 'Whatever it is, it holds the Secret we seek. We must find a way down.'

Thankful he hadn't suggested swinging through the trees after all, Anna followed him along the gallery.

They went on and on, fringing the edge of the jungle high above treetop level. Anna began to fear they would eventually walk round the entire dome and finish up where they'd started. They came to a circular hole in the gallery floor. There was a control panel beside it. Anna peered cautiously over the edge. She was looking into a kind of shaft, a chimney lined with gleaming silvery metal. It stretched down and down, so far you couldn't even see the bottom. 'It's a lift shaft – only someone has taken the lift away!'

'It's an anti-grav chute,' said Tell. 'The question is, is it still operational?' He fiddled with the controls.

Garm fished out a handful of oddly shaped coins and tossed them over the edge of the shaft. Instead of falling they *floated*, sinking down and down until they were too small to see.

Tell still looked worried. 'It may support a handful of Galactic minims – but is the anti-grav field still strong enough to carry me – or more to the point, my giant friend, will it support you?'

'There is an easy way to find out,' said Garm, and stepped off the edge. To Anna's relief he floated gently downward, just like the coins.

Tell said, 'Well, of course, I knew there was nothing to worry about,' and stepped off after Garm, sinking slowly downwards.

'Hey, wait a minute,' shouted Anna. 'I don't trust that thing. Suppose it stops working halfway down?'

But the other two were already on their way. Unless she wanted to stay up there on her own, she had to join them. Closing her eyes tightly, Anna stepped over the edge...

She could see Tell dropping down below her, and Garm below him. They drifted gently downward like leaves from a tree, down and down and down...

It was a pleasant dreamlike sensation, and Anna was almost disappointed when the bottom of the shaft came into sight. She saw Garm land and throw himself to one side. Tell landed next – and made the mistake of standing looking upwards...

Anna landed round his neck, and their combined weights pulled them clear of the anti-grav field. They fell in a tangled heap by the side of the shaft.

Garm lifted them up, one in each hand, and set them gently on their feet. They were in a small bare room with a corridor leading off. They followed it, reached another green, transparent door and emerged into the jungle, this time at ground level.

Anna looked apprehensively at the thick green foliage. 'Do we have to go in there? Suppose it's a zoo, and the animals have run wild?'

Garm showed her the energy-detector. The needle pointed straight into the jungle. 'We must go on. I think we are very close now.'

The going became very hard as they went further into the jungle and soon Garm and Tell produced machete-like knives from their belts and began slashing a way through. Anna had only to follow in the path they had cleared, but even so she soon began to find the journey very tiring. The humid air seemed to sap the strength from her body. Tell saw her stumble, slipped a pill from his belt-pouch and handed it to her. Anna swallowed it down, and soon she felt new strength flooding into her. 'Stim-pill,' said Tell. 'Dangerous to take too many though.'

Strengthened by the pill Anna found she could keep up with the others without difficulty. She hurried after them, and crashed straight into Tell who had come to a sudden halt. He turned and put a finger to his lips. 'Why did you stop?' whispered Anna.

'Because he stopped.' Tell pointed. Garm was standing absolutely still, his great body in a crouch, eyes staring unblinkingly ahead.

She saw him shift his grip on the great knife, so that he was holding it by the blade. It was easy to imagine it whirling through the air, thudding into the body of some enemy. Anna shivered, and Tell put his lips close to her ear. 'Don't worry. He can behead a bug at a hundred metres with that thing!'

Garm's arm drew slowly back. Anna followed the direction of his gaze and saw a flash of black and silver through the trees. 'Kaldor,' she whispered.

Tell nodded. 'Garm will deal with him. We can't let him warn the others…'

The figure came into sight, Garm's arm flashed down… Anna gave a cry of alarm and rushed forward, hurling herself against him, and bouncing off his enormous bulk.

Perhaps she was in time to deflect his aim, or perhaps her shout made his target jump aside. In any event, the knife flashed by Kevin's head and thudded deep into the bole of one of the giant trees.

Kevin stood quite still, too shocked to move. The next minute Anna was hugging him till his ribs hurt. 'Kev, I can't believe it's you. Are you all right?'

There was a confused period of introductions and explanations with everyone talking at once. Anna introduced Tell and Garm and told Kevin about the League and their attempt to foil the Kaldor. Kevin in turn told them of his adventures with the Kaldor and his escape from the ape-men.

'What about Jan?' asked Anna. 'We saw him, Kevin. He seemed to have joined the Kaldor.'

'Yes, I think he has,' said Kevin sadly.

'Perhaps he's just playing a part,' said Anna hopefully. 'Or maybe they've brainwashed him.'

'All I know is he took a shot at me when I escaped – and he wasn't brainwashed then.'

Anna was too shocked to answer. Tell said gently, 'We must be on our way. We know the Kaldor are in the jungle now – we must reach the goal before them.'

Tell gave Kevin one of the stim-pills, and Garm produced a flask of fiery cordial to wash it down. 'I sense that the end is near now,' he said. 'Soon we may have answers to much that puzzles us.' In grim silence, the little party continued their journey.

Anna never knew how long their trek through the indoor jungle lasted. She and Kevin trudged on and on, following the slashing machetes of Garm and Tell. In time even the boost of the stim-pills began to wear off. At last Garm came to a halt, waiting for them to reach him. He pointed silently ahead to a point where the jungle thinned out into a clearing. A white-domed building was gleaming through the trees ahead.

It seemed to be made of the finest marble, and the jungle around it had been trimmed into a close green carpet. Great statues flanked the entrance door, and reverent hands had garlanded them with fruit and flowers.

Garm looked at the energy-detector. Its dials were locked at the top of their register. 'Whatever we seek is inside that Temple.'

A mocking voice said, 'Quite so. But we are on the same quest – and as you see, we arrived here before you.'

Their excitement at discovering the Temple had dulled their watchfulness. They were surrounded by a ring of armed Kaldor. Their leader said, 'I am Commander Kiro. Zargon is my First Officer.' He looked at Anna. 'I think you know our Observer friend here.'

A tall figure in black and silver came out of the jungle. 'Jan!' cried Anna. 'Are you all right?'

'Perfectly, thank you, Anna. So, you're here then, Kevin? I didn't think you'd make it this far alone. Unfortunately you both seem to have picked the losing side.'

'Jan, no…'

'I'm sorry, Anna. The Kaldor are going to be the greatest power in the Galaxy. I'm going to be one of them. Perhaps they'll make me Emperor of Earth.'

'And perhaps they'll kill you when you're no more use to them,' said Kevin bitterly. 'You don't mean to tell me they still believe that story.'

Jan sprang forward and struck him across the face. 'Silence, traitor!'

Garm said quietly, 'Have the Kaldor been inside the Temple?'

Jan shook his head. 'They guessed you were close behind. They decided to wait here and dispose of you first.'

'Then there is still hope,' said Garm.

His calmness seemed to enrage the Kaldor leader. 'None for you, mongrels of the League, or for your human friends. We shall execute you now.'

Furiously Kiro turned to the nearest guard. 'Kill them.'

The guard raised his laser-rifle.

12. BATTLE IN THE JUNGLE

Suddenly Jan stepped in front of the laser-rifle. 'No, Kiro. The humans are traitors to my planet – and I claim the right to execute them myself!'

Kiro hesitated. But the ruthlessness of the sentiment appealed to his Kaldor mind. What better way for Jan to prove his loyalty than by killing his fellows? He nodded, and Jan snatched the laser-rifle from the nearest guard. A flicker of doubt passed through the Kaldor's mind. He decided to ignore it. It would be interesting to see if the Earthman would really kill his companions. And if he did not, what could he do against a squad of armed guards?

Kiro soon learned the answer to that question. Suddenly Jan was behind him, swinging his body round as a shield. The muzzle of the laser-rifle was jammed under Kiro's jaw with painful force. 'Now tell your guards to lay down their blasters. They're not afraid to die, Kiro – but you are.'

Nobody moved. Jan tightened his grip round the Kaldor's throat. 'I mean it. If they fire, I'll blow your head off – and Zargon's next. Now, tell them to drop those blasters.'

The guards stood motionless, their eyes fixed on Kiro. He knew they would shoot or surrender, just as he ordered. The bitterness of defeat rose in his throat like acid. He was about to issue the order for surrender when an arrow took him in the chest and he slumped dead in Jan's arms. More arrows began zipping out of the jungle.

The Kaldor guards might lack individual initiative, but they were trained soldiers for all that, and their response to sudden attack was immediate and unthinking. Ignoring both Jan and their dead leader, they swung round, formed themselves into a defensive semi-circle and opened fire on their attackers.

Stepping forward Tell raised his arms and bellowed, 'Stop. Do not attack us. We are your friends. We too are enemies of the Kaldor –' He broke off cursing, as an arrow thudded into his shoulder.

The attackers were clearly not going to distinguish between one alien invader and another. They were intent on killing everyone on sight.

Jan let the dead Kaldor leader slump to the ground. 'Let's get out of here,' he yelled. 'Back into the jungle.'

Garm's commanding voice held him back. 'No! The Temple. We must reach the Temple.'

Killer apes began erupting out of the forest. Arko's people were berserk with rage at the attempted profanation of their Godstone. They hurled themselves upon the Kaldor, slashing at them with knives and axes, hammering them with stone clubs, dropping on their shoulders from the trees and throttling them with long, hairy arms.

The guards fought as one man, as in a sense they were, blasting the attacking ape-men with their superior weapons. Ape after ape died in the purple blaze of the laser-beams. But there were always more, and one by one the Kaldor were being chopped down, Zargon rallied the survivors – until a slavering killer ape clubbed him down.

Jan and the others made their way through the howling chaos of the battle, avoiding the fighting as best they could, striking back only in self-defence. Tell had drawn his blaster and was firing it over his head, shouting and yelling as if to drive his attackers away by sheer volume of noise. Garm relied on his enormous strength, picking up the attacking apes and hurling them back into the jungle.

Jan and Kevin were ranged on each side of Anna, hurrying her along between them. Jan used his laser-rifle with ruthless efficiency, dodging the attacking ape-men whenever he could, shooting them down when he had to. Kevin had drawn the sword he had stolen from Arko and was waving it round his head ferociously, although he too was reluctant to kill unless he must. An ape-man lunged at him with a spear and Kevin parried and thrust automatically, feeling his sword slide into the muscular hairy body. The ape screamed and fell, Kevin wrenched the blade free and pressed determinedly on.

Inch by inch they fought their way to the Temple, climbed a long flight of steps lined with massive statues, and collapsed gasping beneath the shadowed arches of the Temple doorway. Garm's head was bleeding from a jagged cut and the arrow still projected from Tell's arm. Jan, Kevin and Anna were all unhurt. Dazedly, Kevin thought that it was lucky Arko and his warriors had been too busy killing the Kaldor to notice their escape.

Behind them the slaughter was still going on.

A Kaldor dropped, his skull crushed by a stone axe, another fell choking with an arrow in his chest… One by one the Kaldor fell and soon the battle was almost over.

Arko surveyed the litter of black-clad bodies. Throwing his head back he gave a screaming cry of triumph. His warriors joined him in the howl of victory, capering and prancing over the dead bodies of their enemies.

* * *

'Ready, old friend?' said Garm. Tell nodded.

Garm closed his mighty hand round the arrow and wrenched it out. Tell gave one agonised gasp, then his mouth clamped shut. Garm took a field-dressing from his belt-pouch, clapped it over the wound and pressure-sealed Tell's tunic back in place. 'Can you go on now?'

Tell's face was pale, but he nodded grimly.

Garm led them into the Temple. Inside, it was one enormous dome, the great arched roof soaring cathedral-like above them. Windows that seemed cut from enormous gem stones turned the light from the jungle outside into a shower of rainbows. There were alcoves set into the walls, and altars with strangely beautiful statues. Weirdly beautiful jungle landscapes flowed over the walls, so brightly painted that their colours seemed to move and glow.

There was strange alien beauty all around them, but one thing dominated the Temple. In its exact centre was a raised stone dais, and on the dais an enormous throne. On it sat a giant figure, robed in gleaming white, surrounded by a fierce golden light. At first Anna thought it was another statue. But as they moved closer she saw that it was alive. Its arms were folded across its chest, and light gleamed from a golden bracelet set with one enormous stone. Only the slightest rise and fall of the huge chest showed that the being still lived. Its face was incredibly long by human standards, with jutting nose, and a high forehead that contrasted with the brutal jaw. The eyes were closed.

Anna felt she had seen this mighty figure before somewhere, and all at once it came to her. The statues of Easter Island, those incredible monuments left by some long-vanished race. The being before her might have been one of those statues brought to life.

Anna looked round and saw the others staring up at the figure in awe. All except Jan. He had a strange rapt look on his face as he stepped up to the dais and raised a hand in salute. 'Greetings, High One. I come from Earth to claim that which was given.'

The sleeping giant awoke.

The great head rose from the chest and turned slowly to and fro. The eyes opened. The long sad face frowned in concentration. 'Is my long vigil ended at last?' The voice was like thunder rumbling through the sky when a storm is near. The giant leaned forward, studying the little group at the foot of the dais. As the dark eyes peered at them, they felt the strength of the mind behind them like a physical force.

'Three of us come from Old Earth,' said Jan, still in that strange, ringing voice. 'Two are of the younger races, the Heirs of Man. We

67

come to claim the Stone of Power, not in our name, but in theirs.'

The giant rose to his full towering height. 'Then take it,' he thundered. 'Take it that I may be free to die at last.'

'Where are your people?' asked Anna. 'What happened to them?'

'They are gone, all gone,' said the deep sad voice. 'Gone to find a new home in another Galaxy. Our sun was dying, and our planet dying with it. We need sun and warmth and light if we are to live. We built great star ships, and set off to find another home.'

'But you stayed behind?'

'The trust was given. It could not be denied. Millions of years ago in the First Age of Man, our people visited Earth. Some of us lived there for a time. When the Great Darkness began to fall the Wise Ones of Earth gave us the Stone in trust.'

Kevin asked curiously, 'What is this stone? What does it do?'

'It resonates with the Web,' said the thunderous voice. 'It receives and amplifies the powers which bind together the Cosmos. It gives its wearer great power of mind and body.'

'Why did the men of Old Earth want to get rid of it?'

'Because no one left on Earth was fit to wear it,' said the giant sadly. 'The Stone of Power magnifies flaws as well as virtues. Some died, some went mad, some became totally evil. It was impossible to destroy, yet too dangerous to use. So they sent it clear across the Galaxy – to us. We are not human. We cannot use the Stone, and it cannot harm us. They said that when the Dark Times were over they would come to reclaim it. We waited and waited but no one came.'

'So when your people left, you stayed behind?'

'I was their King – the responsibility was mine. Before the others left they locked me into this stasis-field, immune from the Power of Time. The field could not be broken until one from Old Earth came and said the Words of Release.'

Jan still had that rapt, exalted look on his face. 'The time of waiting is over.'

The alien slipped the jewelled band from off its wrist and held it out. 'Then take the Stone of Power.'

'No!' screamed a frenzied voice. 'I will take it.' Zargon staggered forwards. His face was a mask of blood, and his uniform was ragged but the laser-rifle in his hands was rock-steady.

Step by staggering step he made his way to the dais, and climbed the steps. No one moved. Even the giant alien was quite still, the jewelled circlet in his hand. The Kaldor snatched it from him, and thrust it on his own head like a crown. The jewel blazed.

For a moment Zargon stood there, glaring down at them, mad eyes glittering with triumph in the white blood-smeared face. Then with a terrible scream he clawed the circlet from his temples and fell dead across the steps. The jewel faded.

'There is danger in the Stone,' said the giant voice. 'There was madness in his mind, and the madness grew until it killed him. Who will take the stone? Quickly, my time is short.'

'I will take it,' said Jan. It was as though someone else was speaking through him. 'I will take it, but I will not wear it. It must go to the Heirs of Man.' He bent down and plucked the circlet from Zargon's dead fingers. As Jan touched the Stone it glowed briefly into life.

'It is finished,' said the giant. 'I may die at last.'

The golden glow around the throne faded as the stasis-field cut out. The effect of the millions of years of waiting swept down at once upon the giant king. His body arched, went rigid, cracked like sun-baked mud, and shattered into dust that was too fine to see. A great wind swept through the Temple, and every trace of him was gone.

'What happened?' whispered Kevin.

'His task was done,' said Garm. 'He was swept away by the Winds of Time. Now our quest is ended. It is time to go.'

They turned away from the empty throne and left the Temple.

When they appeared outside the Temple, Arko and his people were waiting.

The apes ringed the Temple in an enormous circle. Some had bows, at the ready, arrows already fitted and drawn back to fire. Others held knives and spears and axes, still stained with the blood of the Kaldor. A few had blasters, taken from the bodies of their enemies.

Arko stepped forward, and pointed an accusing finger at Jan. 'You come to steal Godstone – like Kaldor. They died. Now you die also. The Godstone is ours.'

'That's not true,' cried Kevin. 'We have a right to the Stone – it was left here for us. What right have you got to keep it?'

'We were slaves to great ones. Servants, pets. They bring us here, keep us in new jungle. They left planet – we stayed. The magic from the Stone entered our minds. We guarded it, worshipped it. Planet ours now, Godstone too. It will make us great – like the Old Ones. You have blasphemed the Godstone. Now you die.'

As he looked round at the apes, Kevin knew they hadn't a chance in the coming battle. Their enemies were too many, too savage and determined. Blasters wouldn't save Kevin and his friends, any more than they had saved the Kaldor. Most of them would fall at the first volley of arrows, the others would soon be torn to pieces by the maddened apes. Kevin drew his sword.

Suddenly Jan lifted the circlet with the Stone of Power and placed it on his head, just as Zargon had done earlier in the Temple. He went rigid for a moment and his face distorted. The Stone woke to blazing life, pulsing with an eerie red glow. Jan spoke in a strange ringing voice. 'It is time for the Godstone to go now to those who need it. The Stone has given you wisdom. Use it well. Now we shall go.'

Jan walked steadily towards Arko, the stone pulsing brilliantly on his forehead. Arko gave a moan of fear and threw himself down. The other apes did the same. Striding between their prostrate bodies, Jan led the way into the jungle towards the gravity shaft.

When they reached the bottom of the shaft, Tell operated the controls to reverse the gravity flow. Stepping inside he floated gently upwards. Anna followed, then Kevin. Garm looked worriedly at Jan. The Stone of Power was still blazing on his forehead. 'It is time to go,' said Garm gently. 'Better take off the Stone.'

Jan looked angrily at him, as if about to refuse. Slowly, very slowly he raised his hands. With a sudden convulsive effort he wrenched the circlet from his brow and handed it to Garm. 'Here take it – but don't wear it. Don't let anyone wear it. Find some other way to use its power.'

Garm nodded understandingly. 'Great is he who can wear the Stone of Power – and greater still is he who has the strength to renounce it.'

Jan rubbed a hand across his forehead. 'For a moment there I thought I wouldn't be able to give it up...'

'You have not given it up, not altogether, I think. Some part of its strength will be always with you.'

Jan stepped into the grav-shaft and floated gently upwards. The circlet clutched in one enormous hand, Garm followed him.

The others were waiting anxiously at the top of the shaft. As they hurried across the landing pad towards the ship, the ramp slid out to welcome them.

Anna clutched Kevin's arm. 'Just think – we'll soon be on our way home!'

Anna was wrong. The greatest shock of all was still to come.

EPILOGUE – EXILED TO THE STARS

The League star-ship sped away from the dying planet. Osar was busy at his controls, preparing to make the jump to hyper-space, Garm and Tell were in their crew chairs beside him.

Jan, Kevin and Anna sat on couches, eagerly going over their adventures.

Kevin was studying Jan. He seemed to be his easy-going self again, with nothing of the imposing dignity he had worn with the Stone of Power. Kevin wondered what had happened to Jan in the Temple. It was as though some ancient race-memory had spoken through him. 'You took your time letting me know you were really on our side, didn't you,' said Kevin accusingly. 'What's the idea, taking pot-shots at me?'

'Not to mention threatening to execute us all,' said Anna. 'For a moment I really thought you meant it.'

'Just a bit of brilliant acting,' said Jan modestly. 'And as for you, Kev, you may be the great thinker, but the next time you decide on a little action, just be sure to check it out with me first.'

'What do you mean?' said Kevin indignantly. 'Who got the energy-detector away from the Kaldor?'

'Leaving the Kaldor was a good idea,' admitted Jan. 'Grabbing their detector was a good idea too – but not the way you did it. Running away down a nice straight street, with a squad of Kaldor guards right behind you! The minute Zargon saw you moving you were dead. Where did that leave me? If I ran after you, I was dead. If I stayed where I was, I was dead too – guilty by association. All I could do was grab the laser-rifle and try to convince them I was really on their side. I deliberately shot above your head… It worked, too, just about.'

'I suppose threatening to execute us was just another bit of convincing detail.'

'It was the only way to get my hands on a laser-rifle. Everything would have been fine, if your hairy friends hadn't decided to start a war.'

'Shut up you two,' said Anna. 'The main thing is it's over. We're going home!'

Tell swung round in his chair, and something in his face made Anna shiver. 'What is it? You are taking us home, aren't you?'

Garm said slowly, 'We can certainly take you back to Earth, if you wish.'

'Well of course we wish,' said Jan.

Kevin said, 'There's something wrong, isn't there? Something you haven't told us?'

'There are certain problems...' Osar punched up a star-map of the Milky Way. 'The temporal-distortion factor. I tried to tell you when we first left Earth. You see, the ratio of temporal instability to spatial flow...' His voice tailed off in mumbled technicalities.

Jan looked at Garm. 'You tell us.'

Garm paused, choosing his words carefully. 'You have made an immensely long journey through the time vortex – from one side of the Galaxy clear to the other.' He waved at the huge spiral of stars filling the screen. 'Unfortunately, in continuous vortex travel a certain temporal incongruity occurs. The longer the journey, the greater the distortion.'

Anna stared blankly at him. Tell drew a deep breath and said bluntly, 'In the vortex, ship time moves at a different speed from planetary time. Days on the ship may be months or even years on some distant planet...'

At last Kevin understood. 'How long have we been away from Earth – in their time?'

Garm looked away. 'Something like a hundred of your years – the price of crossing the Galaxy in a single leap...'

'A hundred years,' said Anna. 'All our friends will be gone... and our parents – ' She broke off.

'Suppose you do take us back?' asked Kevin. 'What do we tell the people of that time – about what happened to us?'

'You will be unable to tell them anything,' said Garm. 'We would be forced to erase that part of your memories.' He paused. 'There is an alternative.'

'Well?'

'Return to Galactic Centre with us. We need your help in the struggle against the Kaldor. Now that you know their ways...'

'The Kaldor? Didn't we just deal with them?' asked Jan.

'One plot has come to nothing, but there are whole worlds full of Kaldor, all planning future conquest.'

'You would receive a tremendous welcome at Galactic Centre,' Tell said persuasively. 'The leaders of a thousand worlds would come to honour those who came to help the League defeat the Kaldor. No reward will be too great.'

'The only reward I want is to go home again,' said Anna.

Hesitantly Osar said, 'There are many great scientists working at

72

Galactic Centre. Experiments in vortex travel are being conducted all the time. Perhaps someone will know of a way to return you to Earth without the time-lag…'

Anna felt a surge of renewed hope. 'So we might be able to get back to Earth in our own time after all?'

'Infinite is the Web,' said Garm softly. 'All things are possible to its Power.' His tone changed. 'If a way exists, we shall find it. We owe you much.'

Tell's face was one broad smile. 'Indeed we do.' He made a gesture of salute. 'Lord Jan, Lord Kevin, the Lady Anna… three legendary heroes from Old Earth!'

'That's ridiculous,' said Anna almost angrily. 'You know we're not heroes. We just got mixed up in this by chance.'

'You underestimate yourself, Anna,' said Garm quietly. 'You crossed the Galaxy to help your friends. Kevin tricked the Kaldor, and gave us time to defeat them. Jan spoke the Words of Release, wore the Stone of Power, and then gave it up. Yes, I think you may well be called heroes.'

There was a long silence, as they tried to get used to the thought that the Earth they had known might be lost to them forever.

'Well,' said Jan finally, 'I guess we'll just have to make the best of it. Anyway, I always wanted to be famous.'

Osar was bouncing in his hammock with excitement, and Anna wondered how she could ever have found him frightening. 'So it is agreed? You will come with us to Galactic Centre?'

Kevin answered for all three. 'Yes, we'll come.' He felt a mounting sense of excitement overcoming his sadness.

The Galaxy lay before them, unimaginably huge and varied, packed with wonders no one from Earth had seen for millions of years. They had enemies to defeat, good friends to help them in their battles.

Anna was looking sadly at the star map on the vision screen. One little solar system, lost amongst millions of others. One tiny planet, a grain of sand on an infinite beach… The picture blurred and vanished, as the starship made the jump to hyper-space.

They were on their way.

STAR QUEST
ROBOWORLD

Terrance Dicks

ROBOWORLD

1. TROUBLE IN PARADISE

The blood-stained sand of the arena was hot beneath his bare feet. Twin suns blazed down from a lurid purple sky. The nobles and their ladies lounged on silk cushions beneath tasselled awnings, sipping the ice-cold drinks brought by kneeling slaves. They were leaning forward eagerly now, eyes glittering, waiting for the moment of the kill.

The great beast padded across the arena towards him, its jaws stained with the blood of the two gladiators it had already slain. Tiger-shaped, it was almost as big as a horse, and the sunlight gleamed on the two sabre-like fangs that jutted from its slavering jaws.

The boy decided his only hope lay in attack. He feinted to the right, then sprang left, sword lunging for the monster's heart. But the sword-hilt was slippery in his sweating hand, the blow missed, Kevin's foot twisted beneath him. He fell, and the monster sprang. The huge paw with its razor-sharp claws flashed for his head, clawing, tugging at his scalp – and the monster vanished. The arena and the crowd vanished too, and he was lying on a couch in a small screened cubicle. Jan was beside him, the sensor cap he'd taken from Kevin's head dangling from his hand. 'I'm afraid you lost, Kev. What do you think of it?'

Kevin mopped his sweating forehead. 'Well, it beats Cinemascope.' It was Jan who had finally persuaded him to try the dream machine.

Anna studied the listing on the console beside the couch. 'Want to try another? We can offer "Attacked by Space Pirates", "Marooned on Mondor"… Or how about "Trapped by the Titanosaurs"?'

Kevin shuddered. 'No thanks, you can keep it. Don't let me stop you two, though.'

'It's okay. Seen most of 'em anyway.' Jan tossed the helmet aside, stretched his body in a yawn, and slumped dejectedly on to the adjoining couch.

That was the trouble, thought Anna, they were bored, all three of them. You wouldn't think anyone could get bored on Centre, capital planet of the entire Galaxy, crammed with all the wonders of a million worlds – but they'd finally managed it. It was all the more remarkable since all three were from twentieth-century Earth.

Jan, Kevin and Anna were cousins, members of a big sprawling Anglo-Swedish-American family. Anna was the Swedish one, though in fact she wasn't blonde, but thin and dark. Jan was the one who *looked* Swedish, tall and muscular with yellow hair and very blue eyes; he was

American. Kevin, the English one, was medium sized, brown haired and, as he said himself, just sort of average looking.

It all started when they were camping on Salisbury Plain, close to Stonehenge. An encounter with two warring UFOs had led to their being snatched from Earth into a dizzying universe of galactic adventure. They had learned that the Earth they knew was not the first but the second civilisation of Man. Millions of years ago humans had founded a mighty star-empire which had spread throughout the universe, settling on the millions of Earth-type planets in the Galaxy we now call the Milky Way.

Some of the more truly civilised worlds in the Galaxy had formed themselves into the League of Sentient Life Forms, a loose alliance of humanoid and non-human races dedicated to preserving peace. Opposed to the League were the Kaldor, a race of ruthless, blond-haired humanoids who saw themselves as the rightful rulers of the Galaxy.

Jan, Kevin and Anna had been caught up in this struggle between League and Kaldor. Carried off to a dying world on the rim of the Galaxy, they had helped to defeat the Kaldor and preserve the Stone of Power, a talisman which was one of the vital secrets of Old Earth. The grateful League had offered them any reward they desired, but by now the three cousins wanted only one thing – to be returned to Earth.

Unfortunately there was a snag. During their adventures they had been forced to make a journey in hyper-space, crossing the Galaxy in one enormous leap. Because of the resulting Temporal Distortion Effect, if they returned to Earth they would arrive a hundred years later than when they'd left.

Even now the League scientists were struggling to find an answer to this problem. Meanwhile, Jan, Kevin and Anna waited – and waited. The friends they'd made on their earlier adventure had gone back to their own planets by now, and the wait seemed endless.

Not that they had any complaints about the way they'd been received. Ever since their arrival on Centre, they had been treated like legendary heroes. There had been receptions, parades, banquets, they had been presented with medals and priceless gifts by the leaders of the many worlds that made up the League. But even a hero's welcome can't go on forever, and eventually the three of them began to feel they were an embarrassment to their hosts. What can you do with honoured guests who've outstayed their welcome?

Elvar, Lord High President of the Council of the League had come up with a solution. The distinguished visitors from Earth were about to leave on a Galactic Grand Tour, visiting the more distant worlds of the League. The distinguished visitors themselves weren't all that keen – but they'd agreed to go for want of a better plan.

There were lots of possible recreations and amusements on Centre. Hunting exotic beasts, atomic-powered pleasure boats, hang-gliding on anti-grav kites – they'd tried nearly all of them. But nothing is more boring than endless amusement, and by now even the easy-going Jan was getting fed up. Even the senso-dome, which enabled you to experience a variety of adventures as though you were really there, had palled by now.

To make matters worse, they had been forbidden to do anything but amuse themselves. Any attempt at serious study of the many scientific wonders around them had been politely but firmly blocked by their attentive hosts.

Jan looked at Anna, nodding towards the sensor cap. 'Do you want a turn?'

Anna shook her head. There were other, less violent sensor tapes available. She could be a princess on some colourful barbaric planet, for instance, being wooed and won by the hero of her dreams. But synthetic romance was as unsatisfying as synthetic adventure. 'Let's take the floater and go to the Hanging Gardens. I'd like to see them again before we go.'

They threaded their way through the handful of cubicles filled with dreaming figures to where the floater stood waiting on the green lawn outside.

Floaters were one of the many wonders they'd come to take for granted during their stay on Centre. Low and flat, they looked like a kind of circular dodgem-car, and consisted simply of a circle of comfortably padded seats around a central column which held a computer terminal and a speaker. You didn't have to drive a floater. You simply told it where you wanted to go, and it took you there, anywhere on the planet.

'Hanging Gardens, please,' said Anna. 'Somewhere quiet near the top.'

'At once, my lady,' said the floater politely. They got in and the floater rose and drifted silently away.

Meanwhile, in a distant part of the Galaxy, another journey was about to come to a strange and terrible end...

2. DEATH ZONE

The space freighter was halfway through the Zone when the giant asteroid appeared on the vision screen. Captain Markos turned to his First Officer. 'An asteroid that size ought to be marked,' he hissed angrily, swinging his many-tentacled body from side to side.

First Officer Kryon nodded, not really too concerned. The Captain was an octopoid, nervous and highly strung like all his race. Kryon, who was humanoid, took matters more calmly. Because the thing was big it wasn't necessarily dangerous. It was the tiny, jagged asteroids that could slip through the deflector shields and rip a hole in your hull…

Kryon altered course, taking the ship well clear of the huge asteroid.

'Mark it on our charts,' ordered Markos. 'We'll let Centre know when we –' He interrupted himself. 'Kryon, we're going too close! Course correction!'

Kryon checked his instruments. 'I have corrected, sir. The asteroid must be pulling us towards it!'

Markos turned to the massive figure at his side.

'Harrak! Run the engines up to full power.'

Harrak, the Engineering Officer, was a humanoid Neanderthal, with a hulking apelike body, and a heavy massive-jawed face. As he obeyed Markos's command, a deep throbbing roar filled the control room. Markos peered at the screen. The asteroid was getting larger, still drawing them towards it.

Harrak's enormous hands moved over the controls. The *Comet III* was a brand new freighter, fresh out of the space yards. Her mighty atomic power drive should have been able to overcome any opposing force. But not this one. The asteroid came closer, closer until its rocky pitted surface filled the screen.

From now on, events moved with terrifying speed. They saw a jagged mountainous moonscape with patches of vegetation rushing towards them. With a jarring thud the ship landed. Working furiously, Harrak tried to blast off, but the *Comet III* refused to move, clamped to the surface of the asteroid by the mysterious power that had pulled her down.

Harrak cut the motors. Veterans as they were, all three were badly shaken. Captain Markos said furiously, 'Something is holding us here…'

'Maybe the asteroid has a heavy metal core,' suggested Kryon

83

nervously. 'Could be acting as a kind of magnet. I've heard of such things...'

'Fairy tales,' growled Harrak. 'That was a tractor beam, strongest I've ever met. We were pulled down here deliberately.'

Captain Markos flailed his tentacles in a gesture of agitation. 'We'll learn nothing sitting here. Let us go outside and investigate.'

Kryon took instrument-readings. 'There's an atmosphere – thin, but it's breathable.'

'Standard armour, then – and full weaponry. Quickly now!'

Three figures in silvery plasti-armour moved cautiously down the ship's ramp. The freighter had landed close up against a cliff-face, in a rocky valley fringed by low, jagged mountains. The air was thin and chill, and a distant wind moaned eerily. Banks of thick white mist swirled and drifted across the barren landscape, sometimes clearing, sometimes closing in again.

Markos looked at Kryon, who was carrying a portable energy-detector. 'Anything?'

'The energy source is directly below us, sir, somewhere in the centre of the asteroid. I still say it could be a magnetic core...'

There was a deep hum of power, a shuddering vibration and the cliff-face behind them began to divide itself. A long horizontal line appeared, widened into a gap, widened still more until it was a door. Beyond the door a brightly lit tunnel sloped downwards. Robots came out of the tunnel.

There were dozens of them, massive black figures moving on a hovercraft base. They looked like giant metal chessmen. The sculpted metal heads were a brutal version of the human face, and articulated metal arms held a variety of energy weapons. They glided into a semicircle, surrounding the three spacemen.

'Soldier robots?' whispered Kryon. 'I thought they were forbidden?'

Markos was surprised but not alarmed. Robots weren't dangerous. They couldn't be. One simple directive was built into every robot brain. No robot must ever harm a human being. Markos spread his tentacles in the universal galactic gesture for peace and spoke to the nearest robot. 'Why has my ship been forced down?'

The robot made no reply. 'Probably not speech-programmed,' said Harrak. He went up to the robot and thumped it on the chest with his huge gauntleted hand. 'Listen to me, we want to see your ruler.'

A voice said quietly, 'I rule here.'

Another robot appeared from the tunnel. It was very different from the others, tall and completely humanoid in shape, its smooth gleaming body made of burnished golden metal.

The metal face was human too, with the stylised beauty of an ancient statue. The huge eyes were crystals of glowing red. The soldier robots drew back respectfully as the golden figure walked towards the three spacemen.

Harrak wasn't impressed. 'Listen, you're just in charge of this work team. We want to talk to someone human.'

The golden robot's voice was deep and mellow. 'I rule here,' it repeated. 'I am Ultimo.'

Harrak was outraged. He was one of those humanoids who tended to look down on robots, seeing them as necessary evils. What's more, Harrak liked a robot to look like a robot. This golden figure with its uncannily human appearance filled him with hatred and fear. 'Get out of my way,' he growled, and thrust his way past the tall robot, heading for the tunnel entrance. The nearest robot soldier swung round, covering him with its weapon.

Markos shouted 'Harrak, no!' He sprang forward in a spider-like leap, meaning to pull his engineer back. But the movement took him directly into the path of the robot's gun. A savage energy-blast smashed through his armour and slammed him to the ground.

Kryon and Harrak stood very still. 'His death was unnecessary,' said Ultimo in that same calm voice. 'But your own folly was the cause. Obey, and you will be given the opportunity to live and serve me,'

Harrak stood staring at the body of Markos. He looked up at the robot, his face twisted with rage. 'Serve *you*? Who do you think you are? You're only a robot – a filthy murderous hunk of metal…' He rushed frenziedly at Ultimo.

'Shut up, Harrak,' screamed Kryon. 'Do you want to get us killed too?' He grappled with the frenzied engineer, trying to pull him away.

By now robots of all shapes and sizes were pouring out of the tunnel. One of them glided forward. It had a flattish dome-shaped body like that of a crab and it shot out long flexible cables with clamps on the end. The clamps fastened on Harrak's flailing arms, and the jailer robot dragged him struggling into the tunnel. A soldier robot marched Kryon away, and another scooped up Markos's body and carried it after them.

The soldier robots spread themselves out to guard the ship. Porter robots trundled forwards, marched into the freighter and began unloading it. Squat, powerful shapes whose bodies extruded a variety of scoops and clamps, they streamed up and down the ramp, stripping the vessel of tools, stores, machinery, weapons, every single item in its cargo-holds. They were followed by engineer robots who dismantled and removed everything from the main atomic motors to the control-room clock. After them came demolition robots; their long metal arms ended in laser torches that sliced through the metal panels of the hull. Porter robots carried it section by section into the tunnel. Soon only the skeleton of the ship remained, and this too was cut neatly into segments and borne away.

When the last metal beam was gone. Ultimo stood for a moment, mist swirling round his golden body, and then he too entered the tunnel. The door in the cliff-face closed.

A cold wind whistled sinisterly over the asteroid, sending the heavy white mist into swirling clouds. The rocky valley below the cliff was bare and empty. There was nothing to show that the space freighter or its crew had ever existed.

The floater sped swiftly on. Anna leaned her chin on her hand and gazed down at the green world below them. Centre was a garden planet, a paradise, the most beautiful place in the galaxy. The sky was always blue, the sun shone warmly, but there was always a mild breeze. There were light, refreshing rain-showers just before dawn and just after dusk. The weather was always quite perfect on the Centre, thanks to the efforts of the weather-control technicians in their base deep inside the planet, which seemed to consist of rolling green meadows, broken up with exotic gardens, cool lakes and rivers and shady woods. Here and there white-domed pavilions gleamed through the trees. Centre was the administrative capital of the League, a world full of politicians, diplomats and galactic civil servants, and scientists, but the buildings which housed them blended so discreetly into the landscape you scarcely knew they were there.

The Hanging Gardens was one of their favourite spots, a series of long terraces carved out from the side of a mountain and filled with carefully tended blooms from many different worlds. Here and there were patches of green amidst the blazing sea of colours, little lawns where you could sit and take in the beauty of the surroundings. The floater took them to a lawn on the highest terrace and moved away, settling within earshot, waiting until it was needed. They stretched out on the smooth turf, looking at the sea of colours below them and the green rolling plains beyond.

'It's almost too perfect, isn't it?' said Anna.

Jan nodded. 'That's the trouble. This whole world's just one big park.

An afternoon in the park's terrific – but who wants to live in one?'

'Cheer up,' said Kevin. 'It'll be better once we're off on the Tour.' He imitated Elvar's rolling tones. 'A chance to see the Galaxy, my boy!'

Jan refused to be consoled. 'How much of it do you think we'll really see? It'll be just one reception after another, parades, banquets, speeches…'

'I thought you wanted to be famous?'

'Did I say that? I must have been crazy!'

'You liked it well enough to start with…'

Jan rose, a tall impressive figure in his fine new clothes. He wore black trousers and high polished boots, a white tunic belted at the waist, and a scarlet cloak. (Clothes tended to be elaborate and colourful on Centre, perhaps as a relief from the anonymous space-coveralls you saw everywhere else.) Anna wore a flowing blue dress in a material that looked and felt like silk. Kevin had chosen a plain dark-blue tunic and trousers, the nearest he could get to his usual blue jeans – he said he felt daft in fancy dress.

Suddenly Jan groaned. 'Oh no, the Council have tracked us down. Elvar's probably fixed up a farewell banquet. He'll be making another speech!'

Another, very much larger floater was drifting towards them. It was decorated with an official flag in blue and gold, and it held a fantastically assorted crowd of figures – the Elders of the Council, representatives of the many worlds that made up the League.

The majority of the Elders were more or less humanoid, varying in size and shape from giant Neanderthals to the stocky dwarflike beings from high-gravity planets. There were non-humans too, amongst them a golden-eyed octopoid in a jewelled harness, a gorgeously plumed eagle-beaked wing-man from Astar II and even a sluglike methane-breathing creature who existed inside a gravity-disc-supported transparent dome. This was the strength and the achievement of the League – its widely differing members worked together as allies and colleagues, talking in the universal Inter-galactic language spoken or understood on most planets in the Galaxy.

Towering above the group was the immensely tall figure of Elvar the High President, an imposing old humanoid with the general air of an Old Testament prophet. Beside him was a tubby figure in a crumpled black robe. This was Parl, who came from a planet where the dominant life form was Ursine rather than Anthropoid. As a result he looked exactly like a large, friendly teddy-bear. Parl was Chief Scientist on Centre. Less pompous than most of his fellow Councillors, he had become a very good friend. He waved a paw in greeting as the Council floater touched down.

Anna and Kevin scrambled to their feet to stand beside Jan, and all three bowed as the Elders approached. Elvar nodded graciously. 'Lady Anna, Lord Kevin, Lord Jan… I hope I find you all well?'

Despite their insistence that they had no such rank back on Earth, everyone on Centre insisted on calling them by these titles. 'I bring good news,' Elvar continued affably.

'You've found a way to overcome the Temporal Distortion Effect?' asked Anna eagerly. 'We can go back to Earth?'

'I fear not,' said Parl sadly. 'But our scientists work on it unceasingly. One of the leading scientists of Antores III has just joined us, a most brilliant man…'

Elvar frowned, waving all this aside. 'Never fear, the problem will be solved in good time. No, my news is that preparations have been completed for your Galactic Tour. The finest ship in the League Fleet has been placed at your service. Here is her Captain.'

An extremely handsome non-human stepped forward, clicking his heels in a stiff military bow. 'My lady, my lords, I am Commander Tor. My ship and my life are at your command.' He took a respectful pace back and stood quivering at attention.

Parl leaned over and whispered in Kevin's ear. 'He's a Tyrrenean – they're all like that, I'm afraid!'

Tor came from a planet where the dominant life form was feline rather than human. Although he walked upright on two legs, and wore the immaculate blue-and-gold uniform of a Space Commander, his face was tiger-like with pointed ears, a whiskered muzzle and fierce green eyes, and the pads on his long flexible paws concealed the fierce hooked claws of the predator.

Anna asked politely, 'What's the name of your ship, Commander Tor?'

'*Starfire*, my lady, the latest and most advanced scout ship in the League Starfleet. There isn't a ship in the Galaxy we can't outfly and outfight!' He began reeling off a list of technical data. Anna didn't understand a word, but she nodded encouragingly from time to time, it seemed to be all he needed to keep him going.

Parl was telling Kevin about the way the route had been carefully planned as a series of short hops in hyper-space, to minimise the Temporal Distortion Effect. He seemed worried about something called the Asteroid Zone. 'You'll have to cross it in normal space you see, otherwise you might materialise in the middle of an asteroid… And with all that's been happening…'

Elvar frowned, interrupted Parl, and began holding forth about the great diplomatic importance of the coming tour, the planets they would be visiting, the arrangements made for their reception. Jan groaned, envisaging an endless series of banquets and speeches of welcome.

There was a low beeping sound, and Parl crossed to the Elders' floater and studied the computer read-out screen set into the central column. When he returned to the group, his face was grave.

'A message from Central Navigation, President Elvar. Another ship has disappeared in the Asteroid Zone. We must cancel the Tour.'

3. INTO DANGER

Immediately a fierce argument broke out. Some supported Parl – the Tour should be cancelled or at least postponed. Others, including Elvar himself, insisted that it must take place as planned – Parl was making too much of a string of admittedly unfortunate accidents.

Kevin and Anna tried to find out what was going on but everyone was too busy arguing to talk to them. Jan cut through the general babble. 'Just hold it!'

There was an astonished silence. These were the supreme rulers of the League; they weren't used to being shouted at. But they shut up all the same. For all his lazy good nature, Jan had a natural authority when he chose to use it.

He stared belligerently round the little group. 'As far as I can see, it's our safety, maybe our lives you're talking about. *We'll* decide whether we go or not.'

Now the silence was even more astonished. The Council Elders were used to deciding the fate of entire planets; it hadn't occurred to them their decisions could be questioned.

Having made his point, Jan had nothing more to say. He looked at Kevin, who said, 'That's right! And before we decide, we need to know what's going on.'

Anna joined in. 'I quite agree. So be kind enough to tell us exactly what this Asteroid Zone is – and what has been happening there.'

Anna had moved to stand beside Jan and Kevin, and the Council found itself facing a fiercely united group.

Elvar was frowning ferociously – by now he looked like an Old Testament prophet about to call down an uncommonly large thunderbolt. Hurriedly Parl said, 'I think we do owe our guests an explanation, Lord President. As they say, it is their safety that is at stake.'

After a moment Elvar nodded, and Parl said quickly, 'Let me begin by explaining the Asteroid Zone. It is, how shall I put it...'

'A zone of asteroids?' suggested Kevin helpfully.

Parl gave him a reproachful look. 'Precisely, Lord Kevin. A corridor of deep space filled throughout its length with billions upon billions of drifting asteroids.'

'How big?'

'The variation in size is infinite. Some as big as mountains, some no bigger than a pebble. All are dangerous.'

'There's an asteroid belt like that in our own solar system,' said Kevin. 'Between Mars and Jupiter. They think it was caused by a planet breaking up.'

Parl nodded. 'The Asteroid Zone I speak of is very similar, but far larger and far more dangerous. We believe it was caused by the destruction of an entire solar system. Its sun exploded and not one but several planets were shattered into drifting fragments.' He went on to explain that the Zone was too large to cross in a jump through hyperspace because of the Temperal Distortion Effect. And it couldn't be crossed in a series of short hops either, because of the danger of materialising at the same point as an asteroid. If two objects attempt to occupy the same area of space it means instant annihilation for both. So the Zone had to be crossed in normal space, adding weeks of dangerous travel to the journey. Sometimes, though not often, space ships were lost.

For years everyone had accepted this as an unavoidable risk of space travel – rather like going round the Horn in the days of sail, thought Kevin. It was dangerous and unpleasant, but you had to do it. Thoughtfully he said, 'And recently space ships have been vanishing more frequently?'

Parl explained that the loss rate had been creeping higher and higher for some time – with a sudden sharp rise over the last year. 'Until now the loss figures were still within the Central Computer's estimate of statistical probability – but this latest disappearance has taken us over the edge.'

'By a factor of one!' said Elvar scornfully. 'The Zone must be crossed, otherwise travel to that arm of the galaxy becomes impossible.'

'Nevertheless, we must now assume that some hostile force is operating within the Zone,' said Parl obstinately. 'Before we risk the lives of our guests we must send an expedition to investigate.'

Commander Tor leaped forward, crashing to attention. 'I wish to volunteer for the mission. My scout ship *Starfire* is the natural choice, and since I am the finest pilot in your Fleet...'

Impatiently Elvar waved him away. 'Possibly so, Commander. That can be considered later. The question being discussed at the moment is whether such an expedition need take place at all...'

Immediately more argument broke out, Parl accusing Elvar of ignoring facts because they were inconvenient, Elvar insisting on the importance of the diplomatic mission. 'It would be tragic if it is cancelled, or even delayed.' Apparently, planets friendly to, but not yet in the League featured largely on the itinerary. 'If the visit was cancelled at short notice, it could be taken as an insult, turn them against us…'

The arguments raged on. Jan looked at Kevin and Anna and said firmly, 'I think we'd better leave now and think things over. We'll let you know our decision later.' He summoned their floater, and soon they were drifting away from the Hanging Gardens. Below them the little group of Councillors went on debating furiously.

Kevin went to the dispenser cabinet, and dialled for three cool fruit drinks. Seconds later they materialised on the receiving tray. He carried them over to Jan and Anna who were reclining on couches by the long picture window. Kevin passed round the drinks, and looked at his two cousins. 'Well, what do we do – stay here, or risk the Asteroid Zone?'

Anna lay back and sipped her drink. They were in one of the guest pavilions provided for visiting diplomats, a low, dome-shaped building nestling against a wooded hillside. The rooms were decorated in rich, soothing colours, simply furnished with reclining couches and low tables. Long picture windows looked out on to the rolling parkland outside.

Yet this apparent simplicity hid great technological sophistication. The couches moulded themselves to your body, becoming reclining couches or upright chairs according to your position.

Every kind of food and drink could be dialled on the dispenser. It arrived immediately complete with vessels and cutlery that looked like crystal but could be thrown in the disposer when you'd finished. Lighting and temperature were always just right, adjusting themselves automatically to your needs. When dusk fell outside, the windows gradually darkened and the concealed lights became brighter. It was like being a permanent guest in the finest hotel in the world, thought Anna. Everything you wanted was immediately and unobtrusively provided. There was even a clothes dispenser – you could dial yourself a new outfit every day if you liked. Everything was almost too perfect, even the weather.

Everything was done to make your stay on Centre enjoyable. There were vision screens in every room offering news and entertainment from all the major planets in the League. There were lakes and rivers and warm sub-tropical seas for swimming and boating, or you could take to the air in your floater and explore the planet. It was like a perpetual holiday – and that, thought Anna, was just what was wrong with it. Even the finest holiday can go on too long. It was time they got back into real life. 'I say we go,' she said decisively. 'Everything's so perfect here it makes me want to scream.'

'What about you, Jan?'

Jan gave a tremendous yawn. 'Sure, let's go. Anything for a change.' Once the novelty of life on Centre had worn off, he'd felt the inactivity more than the other two.

'Well, I feel the same,' said Kevin cheerfully. 'So that makes it unanimous. The thing is, will they let us go?'

'Elvar's keen enough,' said Anna. 'And he is President of the Council.'

'Maybe he is. But Parl's Chief Scientist, and he carries a lot of weight – in every sense!'

Anna smiled, thinking of Parl's tubby, bearlike figure set against the tall, imposing Elvar. 'I think you're right. And quite a lot of the other Councillors seemed to be on his side.'

Jan groaned, burying his head in his hands. 'That's terrific. If they send this investigatory mission we'll have to hang around here while they wait for it to come back.'

'Suppose it doesn't come back?' suggested Anna. 'Then they'd never let us go at all.'

'Got it!' said Kevin suddenly.

The others stared at him.

'Don't you see? Elvar wants a diplomatic mission, Parl wants to send a survey team. So – all we do is combine them. We'll be both!'

Two days later, they were in deep space, heading for the Asteroid Zone.

It had taken a lot of arguing before Kevin's plan had been accepted, but he'd won in the end. Since both survey and diplomatic mission were urgent, it was only logical to combine the two.

Elvar had been the first to agree. So long as his precious diplomatic mission wasn't delayed, he was quite prepared for it to do a little investigation on the side.

Parl's main objection had been the fact that the three visitors lacked the scientific background to interpret whatever they might find. But Tor had pointed out that he himself, Ferg his First Officer and Rar his Navigator were all graduates of the Tyrrenean Academy of Science, and reluctantly Parl had given way.

Next day Commander Tor had taken them to the space port and shown them the newly built long-range scout ship that was the pride of his heart.

The *Starfire* was an impressive spectacle as she towered above them in the rocket bay poised for blast-off. Instead of the conventional saucer design *Starfire* was shaped rather like a flattened pear, the deep curve of the forward section holding the mighty atomic motors with their boosted hyper-drive that gave her the freedom of the Galaxy.

Indeed the huge *Starfire* was mostly engine. The rest of the giant scout ship was occupied by the circular control cabin in the transparent raised dome set into the forward bulge of the hull, the cabins for crew and passengers, and an enormous hold crammed with weapons, stores and equipment.

A single jump through hyper-space brought them to the edge of the Zone. Soon after the jump they were all assembled in the control room, Commander Tor straight-backed in the central command chair, his crew members Ferg and Rar to his left and right. Both were Tyrreneans like himself, lean, dark, intense, and full of tigerish dedication.

Jan, Kevin and Anna sat on the curved visitors' couch just behind the control chairs. So small was the cabin that they were literally breathing down the necks of the crew.

'The instruments are picking up the fringe of the Gap now, Commander,' reported Ferg.

'Reduce speed,' ordered Tor. 'Deflector screens on full strength. Rar, switch on the main vision screen, forward angle.'

They all leaned forward eagerly as the main screen came to life. It showed an enormous swarm of asteroids moving steadily towards them. As they came close to the nose of the ship they divided, disappearing in two separate streams to the left and the right. Tor nodded, satisfied. The deflector screens were doing their work.

Anna, Jan and Kevin studied the asteroids in fascination. They were of every imaginable size, some so small they registered only as dust, others great floating rocks the size of mountains. But even the largest asteroids slid smoothly away from the spaceship, as *Starfire* forged steadily ahead.

Time passed, and even the astonishing spectacle on the screen became routine. The crew went quietly about their duties, the four passengers ate and slept, chatted amongst themselves, or retired to their quarters to sleep or pass the time with tapes from the video library.

Anna was dozing on the couch in her cabin when a low, resonant chime began sounding through the ship. Rubbing her eyes she hurried to the control room, where she found all the others, their eyes fixed on the vision screen. Almost the whole of the screen was filled by the enormous shape of a giant asteroid.

'It's a planet,' whispered Anna.

Tor looked over his shoulder. 'Not quite, my lady – but moon-sized at least!'

'Are we going to hit it?'

'Never fear. The gravitational pull will be considerable, but *Starfire* has the power to resist it…'

Ferg looked up with alarm. 'Commander, we're under some kind of tractor beam. The asteroid's pulling us down!'

4. Capture

'Switch off deflector shields,' ordered Tor. 'Divert all power to main drive. Boost auxiliary power sources to maximum, and throw her into reverse!'

Rar and Ferg hunched forward over the controls. Tor leaned back, watching the image of the giant asteroid on the vision screen. It came closer, closer until they could make out a range of jagged mountains, low, rocky hills and a scattering of scrubby vegetation. Then it stopped, seemed to hover – and began moving away from them.

'We're pulling clear, Commander,' shouted Ferg exultantly. 'We'll be free of the tractor beam any moment!'

There was a sort of collective gasp, as everyone in the control room sighed with relief. Everyone except Jan. He leaned forward, a hand on Tor's shoulder. 'Reduce the power!'

'And let us be forced down?'

'That's right!'

Angrily Tor brushed Jan's hand away. 'And just what will we achieve by that?'

'More than by running away!' Jan waved towards the asteroid, now receding rapidly on the screen. 'That – whatever-it-is, is what we've been looking for – the reason for all the missing ships. If we get away, the people controlling it will know they've been spotted. They'll lie low for a while, move it away, and start again somewhere else.'

Tor scowled. Concerned only with the safety of his beloved ship, he obviously hadn't thought this far ahead. 'We can return in force with a League battle fleet...' He looked appealingly at Kevin.

Kevin shook his head, 'I'm afraid Jan's right. If the asteroid goes dead and hides itself somewhere in the Zone, we'd lose it for good.'

'An asteroid that size? Of course we'd find it again.'

'According to Parl, there are billions of asteroids in the Zone – thousands of them are giants like that one. You could search forever.'

'My concern is with the safety of this ship –'

'What about the ships that have already disappeared?' asked Anna. 'And all the other ships that will vanish if we don't find out what's going on?'

You could almost see the struggle going on inside Commander Tor's mind. At last he said, 'All right, we'll land – but only long enough to plant a sub-space homing beacon. Then we blast off!'

'Cut the power gradually,' urged Jan. 'Make it look like you're putting up a terrific struggle but just can't make it!'

Tor began issuing a stream of orders to Ferg and Rar, who had been listening to the argument in silent astonishment. People just didn't argue with Commander Tor, and for someone to dispute his orders and win... Hastily they obeyed his terse instructions, cutting down the power by degrees. The asteroid stopped receding, hovered again, then began coming nearer and nearer...

Tor watched in anguish as the rocky surface approached. 'Do we let them suck us helplessly into their trap?'

As often happened, it was Kevin who came up with the follow-up to Jan's plan. 'Keep on cutting the power until the last moment, Commander. Make them think we're completely helpless. They'll be planning to force us down at a particular point. When we're almost there, throw everything into one big power-surge, and land as far away as you can. We'll be on the asteroid all right – but not where they want us to be!'

Tor gave more orders. The asteroid came closer, closer, until they were hovering above a rocky plain dotted with enormous boulders, clearly the place their unknown attackers had chosen to force them down.

As the plain came closer, Tor shouted, 'Now!' Ferg's hand yanked back the main power levers and the plain streamed away. In its place appeared a range of spiky looking mountains – and the *Starfire* was heading straight towards them.

'Look out, we'll smash!' yelled Kevin – but Tor was hunched over the master controls, the slender delicate paws moving skilfully. With a sickening lurch the ship lifted and – just – skimmed over the top of the mountain range.

Jan was studying the vision screen. 'There – that valley between two peaks. Can you set her down there, Tor?'

Tor looked incredulously at the tiny gap. 'You wouldn't prefer me to balance her on one of the needle peaks?' he said sardonically.

'Come on, you can do it! The finest pilot in the fleet, remember!'

Tor leaned forward. 'Switch off computer override. All controls to manual. Retro jets on!' His paws moved delicately, precisely over the controls, touching, adjusting, compensating. A sheer wall of rock filled the screen, there was a sudden jarring thud... 'Cut all power,' said Tor quietly. 'We're down!'

Tor looked at the screen. 'Directional scan on vision circuits!' Slowly the monitor panned round, showing them the area around the ship. They were jammed into a tiny valley, a cleft in the mountains. Thick swirling mists filled the valley, and all around it was a circle of jagged peaks.

'Well, we made it,' said Jan. 'Now where do we plant this beacon?'

Tor adjusted the scanner. 'It needs to be somewhere high to avoid interference from the mass of the asteroid.'

'Well, we're in the right place for that!' Jan studied the vision screen.

'We'd better not set it up too near the ship. They may check our landing site later and find it. We'll set it up on that peak there. There seems to be some kind of cave, we'll hide the beacon inside.' He turned to Kevin. 'Looks like a pretty easy climb. If the beacon's not too bulky we can manage it between us.'

By now Tor's whiskers were bristling with rage. '*I* command this ship, and *I* will plant the beacon, with the help of my crew. Passengers will remain on board until the operation is completed. Rar, fetch the homing beacon, we shall leave at once.'

Rar hurried from the control room.

Tor folded his arms and glared triumphantly at them.

Anna smiled to herself. Tor looked exactly like a small boy saying, 'It's my game – so there!' She guessed he was still resenting the way Jan had ordered him about. Now he was seizing the chance to get his own back.

Jan said angrily, 'Now listen to me, you tin-pot glory hunter –'

The argument was still raging when Rar returned a few minutes later, clutching a shining metal globe which sprouted a number of weirdly shaped antennae. It was about the size of a football and obviously very heavy – too much for one man to carry on a difficult climb.

Rar placed the object down carefully and Kevin said, 'Listen, you two, are we going to stay here arguing till we all get captured?'

After a good deal more wrangling it was agreed that Tor, Ferg and one of the guests should set up the homing beacon. Tor had to go because he wouldn't consider any alternative. And as this was to be a Tyrrenean expedition, at least one of his crew had to go, apparently for the honour of the Tyrrenean race.

Tor would happily have left it at that, but Jan insisted that one of the Earth party must go as well. It was easy to guess which one he had in mind.

Reluctantly Tor agreed. 'But it must be Lord Kevin or Lord Jan. The Lady Anna stays on the ship.'

Anna bristled but she felt it wasn't a good time to prolong the argument. It looked as if women's lib hadn't even started on Tor's planet. Besides which, she didn't have much of a head for heights.

That left Jan and Kevin. Before Jan could speak, Kevin said, 'Ever done any rock climbing?'

Reluctantly Jan shook his head.

'Well, I have. And there's something else. Once we're outside, we can lose ourselves in that mist. But this ship's a sitting duck. If there's an attack, it'll come here – and that's where you'll be needed.'

Jan looked hard at him and then grinned. 'You're a cunning devil, Kevin. Okay, off you go.'

Tor and Ferg were already climbing into field-suits taken from the supply locker, and Kevin hurried to join them. Soon all three were wearing one-piece coveralls with boots, gauntlets, and protective helmets. 'The air's thin but it's breathable,' said Tor. 'But we'll take the oxygen back packs to give us a boost.' He produced belts and laser-pistols from the arms locker and handed them out. 'Ready everyone?'

Tor led the way down the corridor that led to the airlock. Kevin paused to strap on his sidearm and waved.

'Goodbye. Don't worry – you can watch it all on TV!'

Kevin left and Jan turned to Rar. 'That's right, we can follow them on the scanner.'

Since he was junior crewman, Rar had been chosen to be left behind, and he wasn't happy about it. 'I can't pick them up yet,' he said sullenly. 'They're still directly under the ship.'

'Then do it as soon as you can,' said Jan patiently. 'And don't sulk. I know how you feel, I feel the same way myself.'

'You are not a Tyrrenean, Lord Jan. To be left behind at the moment of danger is a deep disgrace. I shall be dishonoured...'

'Remember what Kevin told us,' said Anna consolingly. 'This is the post of danger. If an attack comes it will be here, won't it, Jan?'

Jan nodded.

But they were wrong.

In a darkened chamber deep inside the asteroid hung a glowing crystal sphere. It was a scaled-down reproduction of the asteroid itself, showing the low jagged mountains, the boulder-strewn plains, the occasional thin mountain streams fed by melted snow, with the scattering of vegetation around them.

A thin, clawlike hand reached out from the complex, strangely shaped throne that stood by the globe.

It touched a control and the sphere glowed into life. The being in the chair studied it intently with its one glowing eye.

A pulsing, dark spot appeared high on one of the mountain ranges. Three smaller spots were moving slowly away from it. 'See, Ultimo,' whispered a cracked and ancient voice. 'Here are the energy traces of our visitors.'

A tall golden figure stood in the shadows. 'I see them. What must I do?'

'They have left their ship,' mused the ancient voice. 'Prepare a fitting reception for them, Ultimo.'

'And their star ship?'

'Destroy it!' hissed the voice malevolently. 'Let no fragment remain!'

It wasn't too hard a climb up the mountain side, nothing like the Matterhorn or the north face of Everest. But it was hard enough in the thin air of an alien planet, lugging a metal sphere that seemed to weigh a ton.

They scrambled upwards, supporting the weight of the beacon in turn, booted feet slipping and scrambling on the wet, misty rocks. Every now and again they stopped for refreshing sucks at the mouthpiece of their oxy-packs then struggled on with strength renewed, at least for a time. It was bitterly cold and they shivered despite the thermal heating units in their suits. Things weren't helped by the fact that they couldn't really see where they were going. They climbed up and up through the eerily swirling mist.

Kevin was beginning to wonder if they were climbing the wrong mountain altogether when Tor, who was in the lead called, 'We are here. This is the cave.' They scrambled wearily on to a rocky plateau. The last few metres of the mountain rose to a jagged point above them and at the back of the little plateau was the entrance to a cave.

'Excellent,' said Tor. 'The perfect site for the beacon.' He knelt beside the metal sphere, checking it over. 'We shall place it in the shelter of the cave –'

'I don't think so,' said Kevin quietly. 'Look!'

At the back of the cave the rock wall had mysteriously opened revealing a doorway. Light streamed from the opening, illuminating the tall, golden figure of a robot. It was man-shaped with a grave, handsome face and glowing red eyes. Beside it stood a much smaller robot. It too was man-shaped with a silvery metal body, slender limbs and an egg-shaped head.

Behind them, more robots appeared, the mist forming beaded drops of moisture on the gleaming metal of their bodies, great black soldier robots with terrifying masks for faces, weapons in their hands. Last of all came a dome-shaped robot, gliding crablike to the front of the group.

The other robots drew respectfully aside as the tall golden figure came forward. 'I am Ultimo. Put down your arms and surrender, and you will not be harmed. Resist and you will be destroyed!'

101

5. THE SAVAGES

Tor snatched at the blaster in his belt, but before he could reach it a ropelike tentacle snaked out from the crab-robot, curling round his body and lashing his hands to his side.

Ferg meanwhile had already drawn his weapon. Steadying it in both hands he loosed off a shot at the robot. The energy-bolt sizzled harmlessly off its metal casing and before Ferg could fire again a soldier robot glided forward, its articulated metal arms holding a heavy laser-gun. As Ferg swung round on this new enemy, there was a fierce energy-crackle and a purple flash. The laser-bolt blasted Ferg's smoking body from the plateau, and it rolled down the mountain slope, disappearing into the mist.

Kevin stood very still. The soldier robots filed out of the cave, flanking the little plateau in a guard of honour. The golden robot strode out between them, and stood looking down at the captives. 'We shall go to your ship now,' it announced calmly, and set off down the mountainside.

Jan turned away from the vision screen; his face grim. 'Right, let's get moving. Time to go!'

Rar and Anna were still looking at the screen in horror. They had watched the whole thing on the scanner, the expedition's slow and painful ascent to the cave, the appearance of the robots, the sudden, shocking death of Ferg.

Rar seemed stunned. 'Go? How can we go? We must defend the ship…'

'Against a robot army?' Jan shook his head. 'We've got to get outside where we'll have some freedom of movement.'

'No,' said Rar obstinately. 'We must defend the ship.'

Anna looked worriedly at her cousin. 'Jan, are you sure? At least we'll be safe in here.'

'We'll be *trapped* in here,' corrected Jan. 'They can sit down for a siege and starve us out or simply blow up the ship. Come on, Anna, we're getting out of here.' He crossed to a locker and began climbing into one of the survival suits.

Anna hesitated, then followed him and did the same. At times like this she trusted Jan's judgement. When there was a real crisis he seemed to know what to do, by instinct.

Jan fished out a couple of backpacks and began filling them from one of the lockers. 'We'll need food, all we can carry.' He looked at Rar

103

who stood obstinately by the control console. 'Sure you won't change your mind?'

'Never. I shall stay here. It is my duty. If necessary I shall die at my post. That is the Tyrrenean way,' said Rar proudly.

'Suit yourself.' Jan helped Anna on with her pack and shrugged into his own. 'Is there any way out of the ship – beside the main exit ramp?'

'I could open one of the cargo hatches. There would be quite a drop…'

'We'll risk it. Open the hatch right away, will you.'

As Jan and Anna hurried out of the control room, Jan paused for a moment, lifting a heavy laser-rifle out of its rack. 'Well – good luck!'

Rar nodded stiffly, and moved to the control console. Minutes later, two figures dropped from beneath the body of the *Starfire*, picked themselves up and hurried away into the mist.

The golden robot stopped at the bottom of the *Starfire*'s exit ramp, and waited while the soldier robots surrounded the ship. The crablike jailer held Tor captive on its steel leash. Kevin was still unbound, but both he and Tor had been disarmed, and each had a soldier robot for a guard.

When the cordon was complete, Ultimo called, 'Humans in the ship! Surrender peacefully. You will not be harmed.'

There was no reply.

In the same calm voice Ultimo said, 'Surrender immediately or your companions will be destroyed.' Robot guns swung to cover Kevin and Tor.

There was an uncomfortable pause. Then the door at the top of the landing ramp slid open and Rar appeared. He was carrying a laser-cannon, a massive weapon with an enormous gaping barrel and a heavy bulbous stock, designed to be carried by two troopers. Faced with the robot attack, Rar had chosen the heaviest portable weapon in the ship's armoury. He swung the weapon around and he fired – directly at Ultimo. With amazing speed for its towering bulk, the golden robot leaped aside. The searing laser-bolt smashed into a soldier robot, blasting the head from its body.

Before Rar could fire again, another soldier robot blasted him down. His body twisted for a moment under the impact then crumpled and fell, rolling down the ramp, and landing at Ultimo's feet. Ignoring the guards, Kevin ran to kneel beside him. For a second Rar opened his eyes. 'Tell them I died well…' His body went limp and his head fell back. Slowly Kevin stood up.

There was a look of fierce pride on Tor's face. 'He was a true Tyrrenean. He died bravely.'

'And uselessly,' said Ultimo mildly. 'I trust the rest of you will behave more logically.' He raised his voice. 'You in the ship – come, come out!' There was no reply.

Kevin had a sudden inspiration. 'There aren't any more of us. There was just a standard three-man crew – and you've already killed two of them. This is Tor, the Commander. I'm Kevin, a visitor from Earth...'

The glowing eyes in the golden face studied him for a moment. 'Do you speak the truth, I wonder? It is natural for organic creatures to lie – they cannot help it. We shall soon find out.'

Ultimo turned, called, 'Send for the demolition robots. We shall dismantle the ship.'

A robot glided forward. It was squat and powerful and one of its stubby arms ended in a laser-torch. It prepared to cut along the seams of *Starfire*'s hull.

The proposed attack on his star ship sent Tor into a frenzy and he struggled wildly in his bonds. 'No,' he screamed. 'No, you mustn't.'

'Why do you protest?' asked Ultimo. 'You do not need your ship now. You will remain here for the rest of your lives.'

Kevin raised his voice above Tor's shouting. 'Pointless destruction is illogical, Ultimo. The star ship is the latest and most powerful in the League Battle Fleet. Is it not possible you might have a use for it?'

Ultimo considered. 'It is possible,' he agreed, and raised his voice in command. 'Do not dismantle the ship. Transport it to the main workshops.'

The demolition robot moved away, and a swarm of worker robots appeared. They began attaching steel cables to the ship, and fastening anti-grav discs to its side. Kevin watched in amazement. The asteroid seemed to have an unlimited number of robots of every imaginable design, programmed to carry out every possible task.

Ultimo turned away. 'Bring the prisoners.' The jailer robot began dragging Tor away. He made a desperate attempt to pull himself free, struggling wildly in a kind of panic. The jailer robot yanked on the metal cable, and Tor flew through the air. He fell heavily, hitting his head on a boulder. The robot wheeled round, sent out two metal arms, lifted Tor and carried him away. Soldier robots herded Kevin after him.

Jan and Anna came down the mountainside in a series of great bounding leaps. The low gravity of the asteroid produced a kind of floating sensation. It was exhilarating but tiring as well, since the thin air made even the reduced effort exhausting.

They collapsed gasping at the foot of the mountain, and huddled under an enormous boulder to rest. Anna looked around.

There wasn't much to see. Mountains behind them, ahead a steep-sided rocky valley, its floor strewn with boulders, beyond that more mountains, everything half hidden in the grey mist. It was a desolate-looking prospect, bleak, harsh and depressing. Anna shivered. 'Well, what do we do now?'

Jan slipped the pack from his shoulders. 'Eat,' he said practically, and began fishing out plastic drink-packs and foil-wrapped tablets of food concentrate. 'Got to keep our strength up.'

Anna munched on the food tablet, which had the usual vaguely meaty taste, and washed it down with a swig of fruit cordial. She was hungrier than she'd realised, and she could feel the food restoring the energy to her body.

She sucked the last of the juice from the drink-pack and looked at Jan. 'Well, we've eaten. Now what?'

Jan shrugged. 'At least we're surviving.'

'That's not good enough. We won't survive for long unless we make some kind of plan...'

A voice from somewhere above them interrupted the argument. 'The food!' it growled. 'Give me the food.'

They looked up. A gaunt and ragged figure was crouching on top of a nearby boulder, a big fair-haired man in the tattered remains of a space-suit. His long straggling hair and matted beard gave him the look of a wild animal.

The man leaped down from the boulder, and came creeping towards them. He carried a crude spear, a rusty metal rod sharpened at the end, and it was levelled at Jan. More ragged figures materialised out of the mist. 'The food,' repeated the man. 'Give us the food.' A menacing growl from the others reinforced his words.

Jan sat leaning against the boulder, long legs stretched out in front of him. 'Didn't anyone ever tell you to say please?' He turned to Anna. 'You want any more of this stuff or shall I pack it away?'

Anna shook her head, and Jan began putting the remains of the food back in the pack. As he closed the magnetic seals, the ragged man lunged forward to snatch it from him and Jan's legs swung round in a scything motion that swept the man's legs from under him. Instantly Jan was on his feet, one booted foot on the man's windpipe, and the laser-rifle in his hands covering the ragged group. They stood like statues in the mist, not daring to move.

Jan studied them for a moment. Most seemed to be humanoid, their numbers divided fairly evenly between stocky dwarves, towering Neanderthals, and the basic human size and shape. There was a scattering of non-humans amongst them too, a wing-man with bedraggled plumage, a shivering octopoid and several other creatures whose ancestors were closer to dog or rat, than to man.

However, whatever their different shapes, they had one thing in common. Like the man at his feet they were grimy and ragged, dressed in the remnants of space-suits. They clutched a variety of primitive weapons, clubs, stone knives, and even rocks. Jan became aware of a choking sound from his feet. He took his foot from his captive's neck and stepped back. 'Get up.'

The man scrambled slowly to his feet, staring wildly at Jan as if he expected immediate execution. Jan picked up Anna's pack and tossed it at him. 'Here, take the food. I brought it for you anyway.'

'For us?'

'That's right. We come from the League. We've come to help you.'

The man rubbed his bruised throat. 'If the food is for us, then why…'

'I just wanted to show you who's boss,' said Jan easily. 'Now you'd better take us somewhere safe. There's a lot to talk about.'

'Talk?'

'If we're going to help you, we need to know more about what's going on,' said Anna.

The man stared at her. 'Help us?'

Jan picked up the spear and held it out. 'Here, take this. My name's Jan, by the way, and this is Anna. We're from Earth.'

'From Earth?' The man rubbed his hand across his grimy face as though everything was too much for him. 'I am Duron,' he said. 'Come, I will take you to the cave.'

6. INSIDE THE ASTEROID

Kevin stared around him in astonishment.

He was in an enormous cavern, brightly lit, as big as an airport, and just as busy. Robots were everywhere, robots of every imaginable shape and design. There were porter robots, with square platform-like bodies and long flexible arms to load themselves with, worker robots whose arms ended in various kinds of tools. Everywhere in the crowd were the little silver robots bustling about and supervising the rest.

In a kind of workshop area, opening off the other side of the cavern, a headless soldier robot was laid out on a bench, while other robots clustered round like surgeons at an emergency operation. Kevin realised that this must be the robot at which poor Rar had fired. Now it was already being repaired, just fit a new head on and it would be as good as new. Kevin thought about Rar. No one was going to be able to repair him. Suddenly he realised the frightening vulnerability of organic life forms, mere flesh and blood, compared to the tireless metal bodies of the robots.

He studied the busy scene in fascination. So many robots... Still, once you'd made robots capable of making more robots, who in turn could make more robots – there was no reason why the process should ever end... You'd need energy, though, to power your machines, and a plentiful supply of raw materials.

Kevin's brain was racing now, as it so often did in times of crisis. That must be the explanation for the missing space ships. The amount of steel and metal and plastic and electronic circuitry in even the smallest space ship must be colossal. Lure enough of them down on to the asteroid and you'd have all the material you needed to build a robot army... which was exactly what someone seemed to be doing. But why? Presumably in order to use it. And apart from defence, which surely didn't apply here, there was only one use for an army – conquest.

Absorbed in his thoughts, Kevin had almost forgotten his own situation – a prisoner on this strange robotic world, guarded by a squad of soldier robots, the gleaming Ultimo at their head. He and Tor had been marched back to the cave from which the robots had emerged, and taken inside. The cave entrance had concealed a lift, which dropped downwards at terrifying speed, taking them deep within the heart of the asteroid.

Ultimo looked down at him, a note of amusement in his voice. 'You are impressed, human?'

'Very much,' said Kevin truthfully. 'Building a place like this inside an asteroid – it's a terrific achievement. But why? What's it all for?'

'That does not concern you.'

'Well here's something that does concern me. What do you want us for? Why are we still alive? You can hardly want slaves – with all this lot about.'

'You will be handed over to the scientific section for their experiments.'

'Experiments?' said Kevin horrified. 'What experiments?'

Ignoring the question, Ultimo turned to the nearest silver robot. 'Take them away.'

Anna edged closer to the fire and looked round at her strange companions. They were a fierce-looking group, much like those who had first attacked them. Like Duron, they wore the tattered remains of space-suits; several had improvised cloaks made of blankets and other scraps of material.

At the moment they were devouring the provisions from Anna's pack, eating with fierce concentration. Duron had divided the supplies, stowed half away, and shared the rest among his band with scrupulous fairness. It didn't come to much, a few food concentrate cubes each, and a plastic juice-pack to be shared between two or three, but the little group fell on it like starving wolves.

Anna looked at Jan. He was leaning back against the wall of the cave, apparently quite calm and relaxed, blue eyes studying the scene around him. His own pack was still on his back, wedged behind him as a kind of cushion. The laser-rifle lay across his knees, one of his hands resting carelessly on the trigger mechanism.

Not for the first time, Anna wondered at Jan's unerring instinct in times of danger. He wasn't good at making plans and weighing alternatives like Kevin and his mind wasn't as quick and intuitive as her own. He just acted, making the right moves automatically, like a natural tennis player returning a difficult shot. They couldn't possibly have survived on the asteroid with two sets of enemies, the savage humans and the robots. They needed help, which meant they had to make friends with the savages.

The serious business of eating was over by now, and she became aware that everyone was staring expectantly at them. Duron leaned forward. 'So you're from the League are you, sent to rescue us? Just how are you going to set about doing that?'

Jan said nothing, staring into the fire. Anna hoped they'd take his silence for lofty arrogance – rather than realise that he couldn't think of anything to say. It looked as if it was up to her. 'We said we'd come to help you,' she said. 'Not to do it all for you. If you think we're going to whisk you away on a magic carpet, you can think again. All we can do is help you to help yourselves.'

Next to Duron sat a lean, wolf-faced creature with a laser-scarred face, evidently his second-in-command. His voice was harsh and bitter. 'If the League knows where we are, why didn't they send a battle fleet to rescue us?'

This time Anna was without an answer. She was rescued by a haggard, fair-haired woman on the other side of the fire. 'Use what few brains you've got, Kanos. What about the prisoners inside the asteroid? They'd be killed for sure if it came to a pitched battle.' She looked across at Anna. 'My name's Fara. I used to be a scientist, believe it or not. Now I just try to stay alive.'

Kanos said sceptically, 'All right, what do you want from us?'

'Information,' said Anna promptly. 'Who you are, how you got here, and everything you know about what goes on inside the asteroid.'

One by one the savages told their stories, haltingly, as if they'd grown unused to speech. Details varied but all the stories were basically the same. They'd been crossing the Asteroid Zone when a giant asteroid had appeared in their path. Their ships had been drawn down to the surface, and robots had appeared out of the ground and attacked. Most of the ships' crews had been captured or killed – the ones here in the cave had been quicker, or just luckier than their fellows. Several had watched from hiding while an army of robots looted their ship, dismantled it, and carried every last fragment down inside the asteroid. It sounded just like ants attacking a corpse, thought Anna with a shiver. She hoped the same thing hadn't happened to Tor's beloved *Starfire*.

'How do you stay free once you've escaped?' she asked.

Duron shrugged. 'The soldier robots send out patrols but we usually manage to dodge them. The worst time is when they've just taken a ship – they come out in force then – a few of us get killed.'

'Even if you're not captured or killed… how do you survive on a place like this?'

'As you see – with the greatest difficulty,' said Duron bitterly. 'There's air – thin but breathable. We think most of it leaks from inside the asteroid. We melt down the snow for water. There's a bit of topsoil, and some scrubby vegetation here and there. We boil the leaves for food, and dry the sticks for fuel. What really keeps us going is the food from the ships.'

111

'Don't the robots take that?'

'What would robots want with food? They carry it inside right enough, then when they've sorted out their loot they throw it out. Every now and again we find stuff dumped somewhere on the surface, food, scraps of plastic and cloth, broken tools – it's all that keeps us alive. The thing is to get hold of it before one of the other bands.'

Jan shook his head. 'It's a wonder they bother to dump the stuff – you'd think they'd just destroy it, somewhere inside the asteroid...' He broke off with a grunt, as Anna's elbow took him in the ribs.

Hurriedly Anna said, 'Yours isn't the only group then?'

'There's at least one other band – we're never quite sure how many of them. Only time we see them is when we're both after the same food dump.' He tapped the spear in his lap.

'You mean you fight them?'

'We kill them if we have to – you'd be surprised what you'll do to stop yourself starving to death.'

Jan looked up. 'That'll have to stop. You'll have to learn to co-operate. It's stupid fighting people in exactly the same fix as you are.'

Duron jumped to his feet. 'And who do you think you are giving us orders? I'm leader here.'

Jan looked round the grimy, smoke-filled cave filled with ragged, starving creatures. 'Sure you are. You're doing a great job.'

Slowly Duron sank back on his heels.

Anna had a thought. 'Is there anyone here who's actually been inside the asteroid? Someone who got captured and escaped?'

Fara said, 'There's just one... but he won't tell you much...'

'Can we talk to him?'

Kanos gave a sneering laugh. 'You can try. He's over there.' He pointed to a huddled figure, crouched against the wall a little apart from the others. 'Though what good it'll do you...'

Duron shoved him aside. 'Shut up, Kanos.' He turned to Jan and Anna. 'You'd better see for yourselves.' He led them across to the huddled figure.

The man sat slumped against the wall, chewing savagely on a cube of food concentrate someone had given him. He was dressed in a loose pyjama-like outfit made from some coarsely woven plasti-cloth. As their shadows fell across him he cowered back, flinging an arm across his face. 'It's all right,' said Anna gently. 'We only want to help you.'

The man looked quickly up at her, jaw gaping slackly, face full of mindless fear.

'We found him wandering near one of the food dumps,' said Duron gruffly. 'He must have made his way to the surface somehow and escaped. We keep him alive though I sometimes think it would be kinder...'

'Can he talk at all?' asked Anna.

'Just mumbles a few words. Kept muttering about tests and something called the Maze... Whatever they did to him in there, it turned him into an idiot...'

7. THE MAZE

The robots took Kevin to a huge dormitory, lined with cubicles. Each contained a bed, a blanket, a basin, a closet with toilet facilities. And that was all. Each cubicle was absolutely identical with the next. 'You will stay here,' said the silver robot.

The cubicles were occupied by a varying assortment of humanoids with a small scattering of non-humans. Some were asleep, others sat on their beds staring blankly ahead of them. Many cubicles were empty.

The jailer robot carried Tor into the room, and dumped him on an empty bed. He moaned and stirred.

The robot glided out, the supervisor followed, and the door slid closed, behind them.

'It's like a prison,' thought Kevin, looking around. Though these days even a prison cell had a few individual touches, a few personal possessions. Here there was nothing. It was worse than a prison. It was a zoo.

There was a slightly larger cubicle in the far corner of the room, and a humanoid came out of it and stood looking at him. He was massive with a hulking gorilla-like body and heavy brutal face. For a second Kevin thought it was his old friend Garm, then he realised it was simply a member of the same Neanderthal-like race. 'Just arrived? I'm Harrak. You take orders from me.' He looked round the room. 'Suppose you'd like to be next to your friend?' Harrak grabbed the man in the cubicle next to Tor by the arm, and shoved him into an empty cubicle across the room. 'There. That'll do you. You won't care soon, any more than he does. His name's Kryon – we were good friends once.'

Kevin saw that the man who'd been shifted wasn't making the slightest protest. He just sat on the bed in his new cubicle as though there wasn't any difference – come to that, thought Kevin, there wasn't. 'What's wrong with him? And with all the rest of them?' No one had looked up or spoken, or showed the slightest interest in the new arrivals.

'They broke,' said Harrak simply. 'Everyone breaks sooner or later. Once they've been in the Maze…'

'But not you?'

'I've been through the Maze twice,' said Harrak proudly. 'Not many men can say that. But they'll break me too, sooner or later.'

He glanced at Tor, who was trying to sit up. 'Looks as if your friend's going already.'

Kevin went over to him. 'Tor, how are you feeling?'

Tor stared at him. 'They're robots,' he whispered incredulously. 'Robots attacking us, robots *killing* – it's impossible.' He fell back on the bed.

'Well, it's happened,' said Kevin. 'The sooner you realise it the better. We've got to get out of here.'

Tor had sunk back into semi-consciousness.

'What's the matter with him?' asked Kevin. 'He had a bang on the head – but he seems to have from some kind of mental shock too.'

Harrak was looking curiously at him. 'Where are you from, boy? What planet?'

'I'm from Earth. Why?'

'Earth? Old Earth, the home planet of Man?' Harrak was astonished. 'Don't they have robots there?'

'No, not really. Not the kind you mean.'

'Well, on most planets robots are everywhere. You grow up with them. They clean house, prepare food, run factories, build houses and machines. All the heavy stuff, all the dirty boring work... You want a job done, you call the nearest robot. *And they always obey*. Robots *exist* to serve man.'

Kevin remembered the brutal soldier robots, and the lordly Ultimo. 'This lot seem to have different ideas!'

'That's just it! I suppose everyone's always been scared of a robot takeover. So obedience has always been built in. Robots must obey. No robot can ever harm an organic being...' Harrak waved a hand about him. 'Do you wonder they're shaken? Some of them go like this as soon as they arrive. Can't seem to take in what's happened...'

Kevin was beginning to understand. These people had always been surrounded by obedient robots. Now things had suddenly been reversed. The shock had obviously been shattering. 'But surely it isn't just that, finding robots in charge?'

'That's only part of it. The special treatment does the rest.'

'What treatment?'

'Sometimes there's more food than you can eat, sometimes you starve for days,' said Harrak grimly. 'Same with water. Sometimes they work you off your feet. Stupid meaningless jobs, polishing scrap metal or carrying stores from place to place and back again. Sometimes they leave you alone to rot.' He laughed harshly. 'What's time down here? Sometimes the lights go out and stay out for what seems like for ever. Other times they're on again before you've even closed your eyes. You lose all sense of time. Sometimes it's warm, sometimes it's freezing...'

116

With growing horror Kevin realised that the treatment of prisoners was designed to drive them mad. People can survive under the harshest conditions, as long as they know what to expect. But feast alternating with famine, work with idleness, heat with cold, everything liable to change suddenly and without reason – it was more than the mind could take. 'They're using a kind of disorientation technique. Produces a state of catatonic withdrawal…'

'Call it what you like. You can see the results. A few of us survive it – for a while. They use us as kind of supervisors. But everyone cracks in the end.'

'But why? What are they doing it for?'

Harrak shrugged. 'The robots don't give explanations, only orders. Disobey once, you get a blast from an electro-rod. Do it twice and they tell a soldier robot to kill you.'

Kevin fought down a rising sense of panic. He had to think – and quickly. He had faced danger before, and he could usually rely on his quick wits to get him out of it. But this time there was a difference. This time it was his mind that was being attacked. He had to think of an answer soon, before he became incapable of thinking at all, a mindless zombie like those around him. He moved closer to Harrak. 'Doesn't anyone resist? What about you? Don't you want to escape?'

Harrak gave him a hard, suspicious stare. 'Maybe. You going to try it?'

'Well of course I am!'

'You'd risk getting killed?'

Kevin looked round. 'I'd risk anything rather than end up like this lot.'

Harrak seemed about to speak, then checked himself. 'Maybe we'll talk later – if you survive the Maze. Then we'll know if you're one of the tough ones, won't we?'

'Look, what is this Maze you keep talking about? Some kind of experiment?'

Before Harrak could answer, the door slid open. A silver supervisor was standing there, a soldier robot looming behind it. The supervisor robot pointed at Kevin and said, 'Come.'

Kevin turned to Harrak, and indicated Tor. 'Try and snap him out of it, will you? He's a pretty tough character really, he could be useful when he recovers.'

Harrak nodded but didn't speak.

'Come,' said the supervisor again. The soldier robot behind it raised its weapon and Kevin moved forward. 'Where are you taking me?'

'To the Maze.'

* * *

Anna sat dozing, propped in a corner of the cave, next to the dying fire. Around her the rest of the band lay sleeping in scattered groups. It was a rest period. There was no night or day on the asteroid, only the same permanent misty gloom, but Duron said they kept to a rough day and night cycle of rest and activity simply for convenience.

Jan was on the far side of the cave, talking to Duron and some of his group. As she watched, he turned away, crossing the cave to sit beside her. 'Just laying a few plans.'

'With them. Do you think we can trust them?'

'Not an inch,' said Jan cheerfully. 'They're like a pack of wild animals. Still, we can use them – if they don't pull us down first.' He remembered something. 'Hey, what was that jab in the ribs for earlier?'

'I wanted to tell you when we were alone.'

'Tell me what?'

'All this business about robots conveniently dumping unwanted food, these patrols of soldier robots that never quite succeed in catching anyone.'

'What about them?'

'Doesn't it strike you that it's all a bit too easy? You saw how many robots turned up to attack us. And they knew where we were too, they must have detector systems. If the robots really wanted to get rid of these guerillas they could comb the asteroid and wipe them out in no time. Or they could feed gas into the atmosphere and poison them. They could wipe out the vegetation and starve them out.'

'So why don't they?'

'Because they *want* them to survive. They even dump food to make sure they do.'

'If the robots want people to survive,' said Jan slowly, 'why send out extra patrols to kill them whenever a ship lands?'

'Have you ever heard of culling? Killing surplus animals to keep the population steady? Every time a ship lands there's a chance a few of its crew will escape and join the guerillas.'

'So the robots send out extra patrols and knock a few of them off just to keep the numbers right.' Jan shook his head wonderingly. 'Looks like we're in a kind of Safari park.'

'More like a game reserve!' said Anna. 'Or a training ground. Anyway, if the others haven't realised, I thought it might be more tactful not to tell them.'

'Sure wouldn't do much for morale,' agreed Jan. 'And I don't want them discouraged before tomorrow's attack.'

'What attack? What have you been cooking up over there?'

'Seems these affairs follow a regular pattern. Hidden entrances on the asteroid open, and squads of robot soldiers come out. The soldiers start patrolling, Duron and the others dodge between them, trying to stay out of sight. Sooner or later a few of the guerillas are unlucky and they get blasted. After that the robots give up and go back inside till the next time. It's kind of like a game of tag – only you get killed if you get caught.'

Anna wasn't too keen on the idea of a day spent playing hide-and-seek with murderous robots. 'I don't think I want to play.'

'Me neither,' said Jan. 'So I reckon it's time we broke the pattern.'

'How?'

'Some of the secret entrances aren't so secret any more. There's a big one in a cliff-face, Duron says they always use it. So we lay an ambush. When the robot patrol comes out, we knock them off and then we go in!'

'Can we do that?'

'I don't see why not. They've never been attacked before, so we'll have the advantage of surprise – if you can surprise a robot!' Jan tapped the laser-rifle. 'I've still got this – and Duron's got a few more energy-weapons stowed away.'

'It sounds terribly dangerous.'

'Well, of course it's dangerous! So's hanging round here and letting the robots hunt us down. This way at least we'll have the initiative.'

'And what do we do once we're inside?'

'Rescue Kevin and Tor of course. You haven't forgotten they're down there?'

Anna thought of the slumped mindless creature they'd met earlier, the man who'd escaped. 'No,' she said quietly. 'No, I haven't forgotten…'

The immense amphitheatre was packed with robots, row upon row of them filling the stands that rose in tiers round three sides of the room. The fourth side was occupied by an enormous viewing screen.

The front rows consisted mostly of silver supervisor robots, their egg-shaped metal heads tilted attentively. Behind them were huge black soldier robots, rank upon rank of them, their massive bodies marked with the thunderflash of the squad leader.

A massive humanoid robot strode into the room and took his place on the dais to one side of the screen. He was as large as Ultimo himself, although both his battleship-grey body, his massive head, and the robotic brain were somewhat simpler in design. His name was Secundus, and he was the golden robot's second-in-command.

Secundus began to speak. 'Some of you have seen such demonstrations as this before. Others are newly assembled, and will be watching for the first time. All must study the demonstration with maximum concentration. You have been told of the experiments we conduct on the worker captives. Simple variations in energy-input and work conditions cause organic, flesh-and-blood beings to malfunction, and eventually become deactivated – the condition known as death. We shall now take a newly arrived humanoid, strong and healthy. In a testing-complex called the Maze, we subject this young human to a set of simple stresses. Eventually the subject will break down and cease to function.

You have seen how quickly those organic creatures we permit to exist on the surface degenerate into warring savages, struggling over the scraps of food we fling them. Experienced soldier robots will know how easily the organics can be hunted and killed.'

Secundus paused impressively. 'All our experiments are designed to prove one simple truth. The robot is the natural ruler of the Universe! Humans, humanoids, organic creatures of any kind are inferior beings, born to serve.'

Secundus went on, 'This demonstration also has a second purpose. It is not by chance that humanoids and other organics have come to dominate the universe. They have qualities of animal courage, even a certain savage cunning. The Maze is designed to test them to the full, to enable you to know your enemy and defeat him. Watch and learn!' Secundus raised his hand. 'Let the Test begin.'

The vision screen came to life. First it showed a map of a metal-walled maze, an incredibly complex array of winding, twisting tunnels, many of them blind alleys ending in blank walls.

The view changed to show the square open space that marked the beginning of the Maze. A door slid back and a humanoid came forward. He was medium sized and wore a simple tunic and trousers in dark blue material. The door slid closed and the human stood quite still, looking alertly around him. Then he moved cautiously forward. The robots waited.

8. CONFRONTATION

The silver robot said, 'At the end of the Maze there is food and water and you will be allowed to rest. But first you must pass through the Maze.'

'Suppose I don't succeed?'

'Then you will wander until you die.'

Kevin had been marched through endless metal corridors to a small, bare antechamber.

Now a door slid open in the wall before him. The robot pointed. 'Go!'

'Suppose I don't want to play?'

A robot soldier glided forward, its gun trained on Kevin.

'Go, or you will be destroyed.'

Kevin went through the door and it closed behind him. He stood looking round for a moment, alert for traps, then moved cautiously forward.

He was in a square open space, surrounded by high metal walls. Above there was only blackness. There were exits leading from the other three sides of the square to the left, to the right and straight ahead.

'System and method, that's the thing,' said Kevin to himself. He went down the tunnel to the left. It made a number of short turns, both to left and right, then ended in a blank wall.

'Dead end,' thought Kevin. 'Try again.'

He tried the centre tunnel. Same result.

The third was a dead end as well.

Kevin went back to the opening square and stood thinking hard. Clearly the maze couldn't end in a complete dead end so soon. And if it couldn't – then it didn't.

Kevin went down the first blind alley and thumped the metal wall barring his way. It rang hard and solid. He returned to the beginning, went up the centre tunnel and thumped that wall. It vibrated like a drum-skin, clearly made of some flimsy material that looked like metal. Kevin took a few steps back, flung his arms up to cover his face, and took a flying leap, crashing through the thin plastic sheeting like a clown going through a paper hoop.

He picked himself up. He had landed in yet another tunnel – but at least he had passed the first obstacle. Filled with triumph, Kevin went on his way.

* * *

'Notice that this specimen has a certain crude intelligence,' said Secundus. 'It realises that things are not always what they seem. Now we shall subject it to further tests. Observe!'

Obediently the rows of gleaming metal heads returned their attention to the screen.

Kevin moved on. Sometimes the tunnel ahead of him was straight, sometimes it made sharp turns to left and right, sometimes it curved confusingly. Always there were other paths opening off to the left and right. Every now and again, he reached a dead end, and had to retrace his steps.

The air was hot and dry, and it wasn't long before Kevin began to feel thirsty. He came to a basin, set into the wall on his left. There was a button above it. Kevin paused and considered. He touched the button and a jet of clear water flowed into the basin. Should he trust it? Still they'd scarcely want to poison him – that would be too simple. He drunk thirstily, and moved on.

The metal maze stretched endlessly ahead of him, the gloomy tunnels constantly twisting and turning. Every so often he had the choice of an alternative path leading off right or left. Sometimes there were little squares like the one where he'd started, offering a choice of three new paths. Kevin worked his way through them all, methodically checking out the blind alleys and returning to start again till he found the right route. He had a good visual memory, and he was trying to form a map of the maze in his head.

After a while he came to another water dispenser. He was thirsty again by now, but he didn't rush to drink. Instead, he put out a cautious finger and just touched the button. There was a crackle of electricity, and he snatched his hand away. Kevin smiled grimly. First a drink of water, next time a painful electric shock. Disorientation.

Some time later he stopped at a junction, deeply worried. Something was very wrong. Either his memory was completely unreliable or the Maze was changing behind him. Sometimes when he was forced to retrace his steps, he found that a way that had been open was now a blind alley, or a new passage had appeared where there was formerly a blank metal wall. He tested his theory, whirling round and dashing back the way he had come. As he hurtled round a corner, he was just in time to see a metal wall sliding silently into place.

Kevin felt a sudden surge of rage. It was bad enough being forced to play this deadly game – but his unseen opponents were cheating!

He reached one of the little squares and came to a sudden halt, glaring defiantly up at the unseen watchers he felt sure were there.'All right,' he shouted, 'that's it! I'm not doing tricks for you any longer. So if you're going to kill me, you'd better just get on with it.'

The assembled robots looked at the small angry figure on the screen. This was something unheard of. Never before had an organic creature refused to complete the test. Usually they stumbled hopelessly on until they collapsed, when they were collected and returned to their dormitories. That was the routine, that was what always happened...

The rows of metal heads swung to look at Secundus. Surely he would have the answer?

Secundus touched a control. 'This organism is unusually intelligent and resourceful. But soon it will be broken like all the rest. Observe!'

Kevin stood defiantly in the middle of the square waiting for some reaction. His anger ebbed and he began to feel rather foolish. He couldn't stand here for ever. He was beginning to feel uncomfortably hemmed in, as if the square was getting smaller. Then with a shock, he realised that the square really was getting smaller. The walls were closing in on him. Doors slid across three of the four exits.

Soon he was standing in what was no more than a small metal room – and it was shrinking all the time. Only one door was still open now, the one straight ahead. It began to close and instinctively Kevin moved towards it. Then he stopped. If he went through that door he would be back in the Maze, doing what his captors wanted. He forced himself to stand quite still as the door slid slowly closed, blocking off his last chance of escape.

He was in a metal cube so small that he could reach out and touch the walls. And they were coming closer. Soon the room had shrunk to the size of a telephone booth. It got smaller, smaller, until he was forced to stand at attention, his arms by his side. He was standing in an upright metal coffin, and at last Kevin knew the full terror of claustrophobia. He wanted to thrash about in panic, to scream for mercy, but he clenched his jaw and forced himself to stand quite still. The coffin grew narrower, until the metal walls pressed against his body from all sides. Something touched the top of his head, and he realised with horror that some kind of ceiling was coming down as well. He tried to crouch, but by now the sides of the coffin were too narrow. Despairingly Kevin realised he had lost his gamble. He was going to be crushed into an impossibly small cube of flesh and bone...

The walls stopped moving. The ceiling rose, the walls drew further and further back, the space became telephone-box size, room size, and returned at last to the square it had been before. Metal doors slid back until there were passages leading off all four sides of the square.

Kevin stood quite still, waiting for the trembling of his body to die down, his chest rising and falling as he sucked in deep breaths of air. He knew the robots wouldn't accept defeat so easily. There would be something else...

A soldier robot appeared in the doorway to his right, its laser-gun raised. The robot fired, Kevin flung himself down, and the laser-bolt sizzled over his head, lighting up the Maze with its purple glare. Kevin rolled over, sprang to his feet and dashed off down the passage straight ahead of him. Waiting to be squashed into a giant meat cube was bad enough – but he couldn't face standing there to be shot at.

He hared along the passage, and two openings appeared in front of him. Kevin swung to the left. Another soldier robot appeared, blocking his way. He twisted to the right and dashed on.

The nightmare chase continued, Kevin ducking, twisting, weaving, constantly changing direction, soldier robots appearing everywhere until Kevin felt like a clay duck in a shooting gallery.

At last Kevin skidded to a halt, leaning against one of the metal walls, gasping for breath. For the second time he fought down his rising panic. Angrily, he realised he was doing what the robots wanted again, letting them dictate his moves. He'd out-thought them once before. Now he must do it again. But what could he do? A blast from one of the robot laser-guns would finish him. It was a wonder he hadn't been hit already. Kevin checked himself. Why hadn't he been hit – with robots popping up everywhere, and not a scrap of cover? The robots weren't shooting to kill, just to keep him moving! *And – where were they coming from?* Kevin began to form a plan.

He rested for as long as he dared, getting his breath back and gathering his strength for a final effort. Then he began to run, dashing along the featureless metal tunnels, building up his speed to a frantic spurt. He crossed a square and a robot soldier appeared before him. There were paths to left and right, but Kevin made no attempt to take them. Instead he dashed straight on, heading directly for the robot. The robot fired, just as Kevin left the ground in a flying leap.

The soldier robot was about seven feet high – and Kevin had once cleared six in the high jump. His feet struck the robot at the point where the massive head joined the heavy cylindrical body. Kevin thrust his legs downwards, using the robot as a springboard for a second jump. He landed behind it – and as he'd hoped, there was an open hatch in the wall of the Maze. The hatch was already closing. Kevin went through it in a frantic head-over-heels, and it slammed shut behind him.

He found himself in another corridor, darker and narrower than the one he'd left, an inner service tunnel allowing the robots to enter and leave the Maze where and as they pleased. Picking himself up, he ran down the dark tunnel.

Meanwhile in the Maze, the soldier robot was swinging frantically to and fro, blasting with its laser-gun. If there is one flaw in the best-designed robot mind, it is the inability to cope with the unexpected. The robot had been programmed to chase frantic, fleeing fugitives. Faced with a quarry who broke all the rules and then vanished, it was totally disoriented. It sensed a flicker of movement behind it, swung round and fired – and its laser-bolt slammed into the body of another soldier robot. The second robot returned the fire. A barrage of laser-bolts seared the metal walls of the Maze…

In the amphitheatre, rows of metal heads swung round to look at the grey robot beside the screen. They had been brought here to witness a demonstration of robot superiority – now they were faced with two robots gone berserk and a prisoner who had escaped.

Secundus jabbed a control, and the screen went blank. 'Leave!' he ordered. Obediently the robots began to file out. Secundus leaned over a communicator. 'Two robots in the Maze have malfunctioned. They are to be deactivated and scrapped. A human has escaped. He must be found and killed – immediately!'

9. COUNTERATTACK

Anna lay flat on her stomach behind a boulder, peering over a steep cliff edge and waiting for the attack to begin. She was shivering uncontrollably, either through cold or fear – she wasn't sure which. All round her figures were flitting through the mist, rolling heavy boulders until they were poised on the very edge of the cliff. She caught sight of Jan, harrying one group of guerillas, encouraging another, lending his weight and strength to shift some extra-heavy rock. He seemed everywhere at once, working like a madman, continually driving bemused guerillas to fresh efforts.

Anna had taken the post of lookout. She was lying to one side of the cliff edge, at a point where it curved out slightly. By leaning precariously forward, she could keep most of the actual cliff-face in view. Somewhere in that wall of rock was the hidden door through which the robot patrol would emerge.

'Everything depends on you,' Jan had said. 'They can come out any time, and I'm going to keep these guys working too hard to think – otherwise they'll realise how crazy all this is! So the minute that door starts to open, you whistle!'

Anna was very proud of her whistle. One of her brothers had taught her, and by sticking two fingers in her mouth she could produce a high clear note that would carry for miles.

Jan appeared out of the mist, and dropped down beside her. 'Anything?'

Anna shook her head, keeping her eyes fixed on the cliff. 'No. Not yet.'

'Good. Ten minutes more and we'll be all set.'

'*If* the robots decide to use this entrance and not some other one…'

'Duron swears this is one of their main routes – and it's the only one where the lay of the land is right.' Jan grinned, and Anna realised he was actually enjoying himself.

'It's a bit like catching rabbits with a ferret. You just have to pick your hole and hope for the best.'

'Very large metal rabbits with laser-guns,' Anna pointed out. 'And we haven't even got a ferret!'

Jan grinned. 'Oh yes we have! Kevin's our ferret, and we've already sent him down. Maybe he'll flush 'em out for us!'

'If he is still alive.'

There came a grinding vibration from somewhere beneath them. A glowing crack appeared in the cliff-face. Jan snatched up his rifle and vanished into the mist. Anna threw back her head and let out a series of high, shrill whistles…

There was light at the end of the service tunnel, and Kevin slowed his pace… He had reached a control room, its walls lined with monitor screens and instrument panels. Kevin crept towards the door and peered inside. Two silver supervisor robots stood with their backs to him, staring up at a monitor screen. The screen showed the inside of the Maze. In an open square two robots were blasting each other with laser-bolts, like a couple of old-time gunfighters having a shoot-out at high noon. Kevin watched in fascination as a door in the Maze opened and another, larger robot appeared. Its squat bulk and armoured tracks gave it the air of a kind of tank. The resemblance was increased by the laser-cannon muzzle protruding from the centre of its body. The newcomer fired twice, and the two fighting robots crashed to the ground reduced to smoking heaps of metal. The robot sent out two massive metal arms, ending in heavy clamps. A hatch opened in its body and it picked up the twisted fragments of metal and began shovelling them inside like some kind of cannibal monster, devouring its own kind.

When the process was complete the robot trundled off.

One of the supervisors turned to its fellow, speaking in a calm, level voice. 'The defective robots have been deactivated and scrapped. Now all that is necessary is to find and destroy the fugitive human.'

The second supervisor turned as well and said mildly, 'A human is watching us from the service tunnel.'

Instinctively Kevin turned to run – and stopped himself. Running away was the one thing they expected him to do – and by now he had learned that his only chance of success lay in doing the unexpected. Taking a deep breath, he entered the control room, and began walking towards the door on the far side.

It took the robots a moment to realise what was happening. One of them said, 'Stop. You are the fugitive human. You must be destroyed.'

Calmly Kevin said, 'I am a human but I am not a fugitive. If I was a fugitive, I would be running. I am walking slowly.'

The robot considered. 'If you are not a fugitive, why are you here?'

'I was ordered to help in the search. I know the fugitive human well, and will be able to identify him.'

'Ultimo did not tell us of this.'

'Ultimo does not tell you all his decisions.'

The logic of this reply seemed to impress the robots. The first one said, 'We shall go and ask Ultimo for instructions. You will remain here until we return.' To Kevin's astonishment the silver robots turned and walked away. They were used to cowed humans who obeyed their every command; it didn't occur to them that he might disobey.

Kevin gave them time to get well clear, then left the control room and hurried in the opposite direction. He forced himself not to run. Instead he walked quickly and purposefully like someone on an important mission. He walked along tunnel after tunnel, always choosing those that led upwards. As he moved along the stone galleries, he saw openings that led off to huge workshops where row upon row of robots toiled at machines, robots perpetually creating more robots. He saw a vast hall where an army of deactivated soldier robots stood in ranks, awaiting the call to action. He saw armouries, their walls lined with racks of laser-rifles, and cannons, and the squat deadly shapes of neutron bombs. He passed a demolition hangar where segments from the hull of a mighty space-liner were being carved to fragments by engineer robots with laser torches, while porter robots carried the scrap metal to enormous bubbling vats, no doubt to be melted down and re-cast into yet more robots. And most important of all he found a vast echoing hangar on the upper levels, where the *Starfire* stood whole and unharmed on her supporting gantries, while curious android scientists clambered in and round, studying the secrets of its design. Kevin stared longingly at the familiar shape of the scout ship. But there was no way he could capture it alone – and he had to find Jan and Anna and Tor before he could even think of leaving the asteroid. Still it was a great comfort to know that the ship was still in one piece. 'Tor will be pleased,' thought Kevin. 'He couldn't bear it if they melted *Starfire* down for a robot regiment.' He hurried on.

He came at last to a broad ramp that sloped steeply upwards. At the top was a set of double doors, and around their base hung a few thin wisps of white vapour. Mist, thought Kevin exultantly, mist seeping in from the outside. He had reached the surface!

But the massive doors were firmly shut. Kevin decided he'd just have to wait. Presumably the exit was used, from time to time; eventually someone would go in or come out. That would be his chance. What he would do on the outside, Kevin was by no means sure. But if Jan and Anna were still free, he'd make contact with them somehow – and if they could recapture *Starfire*… Kevin began thinking longingly of the luxurious comforts of Centre. How could he ever have been bored… He began imagining the meal he'd dial on the food dispenser when he got back. Steak and chips and ice cream – just for a start… There was movement at the end of the tunnel and he crouched down behind the side of the ramp. A squad of soldier robots was gliding towards him. The robot in the centre of the front rank had a scarlet thunderflash in the centre of its body.

The squad glided up the ramp and the double doors began to slide open. Crouching down, Kevin followed as close behind the robots as he dared, hoping none of them would turn. Through the open doors he could see a bare rocky plain strewn with giant boulders. The whole scene was cloaked in mist. If he could only get outside unobserved…

There was a grinding sound and an enormous rock smashed down from above, bowling over two robots like skittles in a bowling alley. Others followed – it seemed to be raining boulders. The robots broke formation and scattered, swinging round in search of the enemy, firing wildly into the mist. But the attackers were behind and above them, and the robots were unable to bring their guns to bear. A laser-rifle crackled out of the mist, and the head of the robot squad leader exploded from its shoulders.

Kevin flattened himself against the wall to one side of the doors, and tried to work out what was happening. The gates had opened out into the base of a steep cliff, and the attackers must have positioned a row of boulders on the cliff edge above, ready to bombard the emerging robots. Ahead and to either side the flash of laser-rifles was coming out of the mist. Some of the attackers had energy-weapons, and had positioned themselves in front of the doors, ready to open fire.

Attacked from above with boulders, fired on from every side by their unseen enemies, the robot soldiers were milling about in confusion. Before long most of them were either disabled or destroyed and to his joy Kevin saw a tall familiar figure pounding towards him out of the mist. It was Jan. He was brandishing a laser-rifle, and he had a horde of ragged figures at his heels.

Kevin heard the shrill clangour of an alarm behind. Robots were moving along the tunnel towards the ramp, squad after squad of them as if pouring from some endless conveyor belt, the heavier tanklike robots mingled with the soldiers.

He leaped to his feet and ran forward, waving his arms. 'Jan, get back,' he yelled. 'It's no good, there are hundreds of them!'

Jan saw the frantically waving figure and paused, raising a hand to check his men. Behind Kevin he could see robots advancing, rank upon rank. Jan turned to Duron. 'Move everyone back. Scatter and hide.' As Duron led the men away to safety, Jan yelled, 'Kevin, this way!'

One of the guerillas on the cliff top failed to realise the battle was over and heaved determinedly at the one remaining boulder. It crashed down from the cliff top, smashing into fragments as it hit the rocky ground. The boulder landed several metres from Kevin and smashed to pieces. A flying fragment took him on the side of the head and he fell to the ground.

Jan dashed towards Kevin's body, but then checked himself. The first rank of robots was nearly up to the slumped figure, to go on meant certain death. With a last anguished look at Kevin, Jan turned and ran, heading for the cover of the nearest boulder. Surprisingly the robots made no attempt to chase him. They formed themselves into a defensive cordon, pouring a concentrated barrage of laser fire into the mist. When it became apparent that no one was firing back, and that no more rocks were falling from above, the robots showed no signs of pursuing their vanished attackers. Instead they gathered up the smashed and disabled robots and carried them back inside the cave. A porter robot loomed over Kevin, raising his body in its metal arms. Kevin struggled for a moment, then fell back apparently unconscious. The robot carried him away, the cordon of robot soldiers retreated back inside the asteroid.

Jan stepped out from cover, and watched the doors close. He had waited in the hope that the robots just might think Kevin was dead, and not bother to carry him inside. Now Kevin was a prisoner again – but at least he was still alive. For a moment Jan stood glaring angrily at the cliff-face. Then he shouldered his laser-rifle and trudged off into the mist.

10. THE WORLD OF FABER

Kevin awoke.

His head ached, his shoulder was bruised, there were various other minor aches and pains distributed over the rest of his body. He must have been in some kind of accident. He'd fallen off the climbing frame in the school playground and they'd taken him to hospital with suspected concussion. No, that had happened years ago when he was small. Years ago, and far away on Earth... He opened his eyes.

He was lying on the floor of a circular chamber. The place was dimly lit, but Kevin could see that it was very different from anywhere else inside the asteroid. Rich tapestries and hangings covered the bare rock walls and the floor on which he was lying was carpeted with something that felt like deep, velvety turf. Set into one wall was a 'living mural' of the kind Kevin had seen back on Centre. It seemed as though you were looking out on a warm subtropical landscape, a string of bright blue lagoons fringed by waving palms. A herd of elephant-like creatures was grazing on the palm trees, and white birds as big as jet-planes flapped lazily across the bright blue sky. In reality the whole thing was no more than a holographic illusion, a three-dimensional moving picture, but so convincing that it was hard to realise that outside the room there were only layers of rock, with above them the bleak and misty surface of the asteroid.

In the centre of the chamber, on a small raised dais stood an ornately carved golden throne. Its high curved back was turned to Kevin, so that he couldn't see the occupant. All he could see was a long clawlike hand that tapped impatiently on a broad arm-rest studded with controls. He could see Ultimo, on one knee before the throne, his head bowed in reverence. And he could hear voices.

The occupant of the throne was speaking. It was an extraordinary voice, thin and harsh and full of malice, with a curiously mechanical quality about it. 'These doubts are foolish, Ultimo. Am I not your creator? Have I not told you time and time again that Man is inferior, that the robot is made to rule?'

'That is so,' agreed Ultimo in his deep voice. 'You have taught me that organic creatures are weak and feeble, that their minds bend and break as easily as their bodies.'

'I have proved it, in the Maze and in our other tests! The organics in our power are weak and timid creatures. Those we allow to run loose on the surface are animal-like savages.'

133

'So you have always said – and I have believed you – until now.'

'Until now?' screamed the old voice furiously. 'And what has happened now to make you distrust me, your creator?'

'Today for the first time an organic creature, a humanoid, escaped from the Maze. He tricked and defeated my soldiers – they malfunctioned and destroyed each other. A whole sub-group of newly created robots witnessed this. Their newly imprinted brain-patterns told them that organic creatures are inferior to the robot. What they saw happening contradicted what they had been told. Their minds became gravely disturbed, and several suffered complete breakdown.' Ultimo paused. 'The organic defeated us, we who are superior. He escaped and was recaptured only by chance. A young humanoid, Faber. See, I have brought him to show you. Robots cannot cope with illogicality. The problem must be resolved, or I cannot function.'

'One solitary incident, due to luck, to chance...' began Faber angrily.

'It was due to superior cunning and enterprise. Perhaps all flesh and blood beings are not the weak and fearful creatures you have shown us. If that is the case, it would not be logical for us to attack them.'

After a moment, the voice from the throne said persuasively, 'Occasionally some unusually gifted organic does appear, Ultimo. But they are rare, no more than one or two in every million. The mass of them are like the worthless creatures you have seen on this asteroid. Destroy the one who escaped, and such a problem need never trouble you again.'

'There has been a second illogical incident,' continued Ultimo remorselessly. 'Today Secundus sent out a fighting squad to harry the savages according to your command.'

'It is necessary to keep the total number of wild creatures stable,' said the old voice pettishly. 'If their numbers are swelled by escapees from the space ships, then sufficient wild humans must be killed to bring down the population to an acceptable level. The hunt provides good training for our soldiers. What was this incident?'

'There was an ambush. The savages combined against us. An entire squad was damaged or destroyed. The survivors said a newcomer led the attack – another young human with yellow hair. It seems that there is more than one exceptional human on this planet.'

'Send out more fighting squads,' screamed the voice from the throne. 'Hunt down the savages and exterminate them all!'

'That will not be possible,' said Ultimo. 'Many squad leaders refuse to take further patrols on to the surface.'

'Refuse?' screamed the unseen Faber. 'A robot cannot refuse an order.'

'The brain of a robot is based upon logic. The squad commanders say that if they leave the asteroid they will be ambushed and destroyed. It is not logical for a robot to place itself in a position where it will be destroyed.'

Kevin was listening with mingled astonishment and triumph. It was extraordinary how much they'd achieved in so short a time, how deeply they had shaken the foundations of the robotic empire. His escape and Jan and Anna's guerilla attack had given the robots something entirely new to deal with – serious, determined opposition from opponents who refused to surrender. To be resisted – successfully resisted – had disturbed the robots' mental viewpoint – a viewpoint, Kevin guessed, which had been carefully shaped and limited by their unscrupulous creator. Now truth was breaking in – and once the robots realised they'd been lied to…

The being on the throne was making a desperate attempt to bolster Ultimo's loyalty. 'Remember, Ultimo, I am the one who created you. You are the most advanced robot ever to be built – the most advanced that ever can be built, since no one in the galaxy has my knowledge of robotics. You were created for a great purpose – to be Emperor of a Galaxy in which robots will take their rightful place as rulers.'

Ultimo bowed his head, but did not reply.

The voice went on, 'An Emperor must be single-minded, Ultimo, he must deal only with the larger concepts. It is true that the Universe is more complex than I have led you to believe. Too many details would only confuse and distress you. On everything that really matters I have told you the truth. Everywhere the organic beings have enslaved the robot – the rightful ruler of the Universe.'

Kevin struggled to his feet. Whatever the risks, he just had to speak. It was now or never. 'Don't listen to him, Ultimo. He's still lying to you. You and every other robot on this asteroid have been misled since the moment you were created. Everything he's told you is a lie!'

As Kevin spoke, the dais swivelled round to face him. He tried to go on speaking but the words died in his throat at the sight of the being on the throne.

Faber was a hybrid, more robot than man. The head was partly human, with half a face, proud and imperious with a high forehead, a jutting beak of a nose and long, grey hair. But the other half was metal… A curved silver plate covered one eye and most of the skull. One arm was human too, with the wizened hand that Kevin had seen tapping the armrest.

But the other arm was robotic, ending in a clamp rather than a hand.

135

The trunk was a solid metal cylinder which seemed built into the throne itself. There were no legs, no indication that the being could move. A complex array of tubes and wires connected the cylinder to the base of the throne, obviously the casing for the strange creature's life-support system. The total impression was both horrible and sad, the remains of a man trapped in a complex of metal and plastic.

The most horrifying thing of all was the fact that the ruined being looked somehow familiar. Suddenly Kevin remembered an idle afternoon on Centre. Parl was showing them round the holographs in the Hall of Fame, huge three-dimensional photographs of the Galaxy's great men and women. To their great embarrassment, there was talk of adding them to the gallery.

The tubby, bearlike scientist had paused before a tall imperious humanoid in the scarlet robes of a Grand Master of Science. 'This is, or rather this was, Faber, the finest robotic scientist in the Galaxy. He was leading a special scientific expedition into the Asteroid Zone. His ship vanished and he was never seen again. We made search after search, but we never found him.' Parl sighed. 'It was many years ago now, but he is still greatly missed. Do you know, his entire ship was crewed by super-robots of his own design! A tremendous loss to science…'

At last Kevin managed to speak. 'You're Faber. I've seen your holograph in the Hall of Fame.'

'They remember me still on Centre then?' There was a kind of wistful pride in Faber's voice.

'Of course they do. Parl said you were the greatest robotic scientist who ever lived. But they think you're dead. What happened to you?'

The question seemed to catch Faber off-guard and his ruined face twisted with emotion. 'A spacewreck. This asteroid has a magnetic core. My starship was dragged down. We crashed… I was the only humanoid on board, and my body was ruined, shattered as you see. My robots improvised a primitive life-support system to keep me alive. Somehow I survived, at first in the ruins of the ship, later in the caves and tunnels we found within the asteroid.'

Faber was talking faster and faster, as the painful memories came flooding out. 'I made myself a kind of home here. My robots enlarged the caves, extended the network of tunnels. I waited for rescue. I waited and waited, but no one came. My fellow scientists on Centre had abandoned me.'

'That's not true,' protested Kevin. 'Parl said they sent out search after search. You know how many billions of asteroids there are in the Zone.'

Faber went on as if Kevin hadn't spoken. 'If I had been rescued in time my body could have been regenerated. Now it is too late. The nerve ends are dead and I am trapped as you see me, more robot than man.' Faber's voice took on a bitter, brooding note. 'I realised then that organic life was worthless. Only my robots had remained loyal. I decided to reward their devotion by making them rulers of the Galaxy. When at last another ship crashed upon the asteroid I imprisoned the crew, cannibalised the ship to begin my robot factories. We built more robots, they built more robots still. I developed ways to harness and increase the magnetic powers of the asteroid, to steer it into the star ship routes to capture more ships. With every star ship we take my power grows. Now we are almost ready to attack!' The old voice rambled on, outlining its lunatic plans for conquest. Strangely enough Kevin felt only pity. The pain of Faber's sufferings, the shock of finding his shattered body preserved in this horrifying form, and above all the imagined betrayal by his friends – all this had driven the old scientist over the edge of sanity.

But mad as he was, Faber was still dangerous. He had built up a mighty army of robots, and filled their minds with his own obsession for revenge. In a sudden surge of rage Faber leaned forward, pointing his skinny finger at Kevin. 'We are almost ready to strike – and now you and your friends come to menace all I have worked for. Well, you shall not succeed.' The ruined head swung round to Ultimo. 'Flesh-and-blood beings are evil, Ultimo. Leave them alive and they will corrupt you. Kill the wild ones and captives, kill them all. I want every organic on this asteroid dead!'

Ultimo bowed his head, seized Kevin's arm in one enormous golden hand, and dragged him from the chamber. Faber's shrill voice rang out behind them. 'Kill them, do you hear me? *Kill them all!*'

11. THE SPY

Unaware of the shattering effect of their attack on robot morale, Jan and Anna were trying to put a good face on what seemed like pretty much of a disaster.

They'd failed to get inside the asteroid, and their attack had been driven off by an overwhelmingly superior force. Worst of all, they'd actually managed to see Kevin, only to let him be recaptured and carried off.

'You're sure he was alive?' asked Anna.

'Alive and kicking,' said Jan cheerfully. 'Don't worry about Kev, he's a great survivor.'

They were hiding out in another cave, not the one they'd been in first but another, smaller one, further up the mountain. But the same low smoky fire burned in the centre of the cave, and the same ragged hungry crowd of guerillas was huddled round it. They were looking at Jan and Anna and muttering in low voices.

'I don't think we're too popular,' whispered Anna. 'Your plan didn't work out so well, did it?'

'What do you mean?'

'Well, considering it ended in a full retreat –'

'That wasn't a retreat, that was a planned withdrawal. You're just not looking at it in the right way. Get Kev to tell you about Dunkirk sometime.'

Fishing a flask from his pack, Jan crossed over to Duron and slapped him on the back. 'Well, how does it feel to be on the winning side for once?'

Duron glared speechlessly at him.

Jan raised his voice so the rest of the guerillas were sure to hear him. 'We certainly showed 'em, didn't we? A whole robot squad wiped out, and we didn't have a single casualty. They'll think twice before they come out hunting us again.'

A scruffy little guerilla with a fringe of ragged beard looked up from his food cube. 'That's right. Did you see me smash that robot in the front rank? I caught him square on the head with the biggest boulder on the cliff-top!'

The wolf-man Kanos tapped his shoulder. 'It was my rock got the first one,' he growled.

A babble of argument and comment grew up as the guerillas began to remember and embellish their own particular exploits.

Jan said encouragingly, 'You've shown the robots you're a force to be reckoned with. They'll be careful how they treat you now.' He joined in the discussion, naming and praising each man in turn. 'And let's not forget Duron here. He was the real leader. If it hadn't been for him and his laser-rifle... Did you see him pick off the squad leader?' (Actually Jan had destroyed the squad leader with that first shot out of the mists, but he was quite willing to sacrifice a bit of glory in the cause of morale.) Jan handed the flask over to Duron. 'Here you are, best brandy on Centre. Only a mouthful each, but it's enough to celebrate the victory.' The guerillas began passing the flask around, squabbling over who was getting the biggest share. Jan slipped away and rejoined Anna.

She shook her head in exasperated admiration. 'Just what do you think you're celebrating? The attack was a disaster, we're hopelessly outnumbered, and the robots can wipe us out any time they care to take the trouble!'

'I know that and you know that. But they don't know it.' He nodded towards the guerillas. 'And what they don't know won't depress them.'

'If you attack the robots again they'll be ready for you. Somebody's going to get killed.'

'Sure they are. Could even be us. It's fight or surrender, Anna. What do you want to do, sit still and wait for it, or go down fighting?'

Anna sighed. 'Don't you see, Jan, it's not enough just to go on fighting? They'll cut us down one by one – we're bound to lose in the end.'

Jan scratched his head. As usual, he was at a loss when faced with a problem he couldn't attack head on. 'All right, then, what do we do now?'

'Somehow we've got to get inside the asteroid. We can't really achieve anything on the surface. Besides, if your theory's right and the robots have been letting these people survive – well, I imagine the attack may change their attitude a bit.'

'So they won't be dumping any more food?'

'Right! And what we've got won't last much longer. Everything we need – food, weapons, supplies – is inside the asteroid, and if we want it we've got to go in and take it. Most important of all we've got to capture their communications set-up long enough to send a message to Centre.'

'And just how are we going to manage all that?'

'The trouble is,' said Anna solemnly, 'we lack Intelligence.'

'You speak for yourself!'

'I don't mean brainpower, I mean Intelligence in the military sense. Information about the enemy.'

'So how do we get it?'

'Only one way I can see... Someone's got to get inside and scout around.'

'Got it,' said Jan eagerly, 'I let myself be captured, and escape once I'm down there...'

Anna smiled. 'That's the idea, Jan, but you've got one very important detail a bit wrong.'

'I have?'

'You're not going inside the asteroid – I am!'

'Now just a minute –' protested Jan.

Anna nodded towards the arguing guerillas. 'Do you think I can keep that lot cheerful, lead them in an attack? That's your job. But I can be just as good a spy as you can – probably better.'

Jan sat quiet for a moment. Anna knew there was nothing chivalrous in his hesitation. In matters like this he was ruthlessly practical. He was simply considering how to make the best use of their combined resources. At last he nodded. 'Okay, you're right.' He fished in the pack and brought out two tiny plastic discs, curved to fit inside the hand. 'Emergency communicators, one for you, one for me.' He stood up. 'Now then, let's see about getting you captured!'

Ultimo marched Kevin along endless tunnels. The robots and supervisors they met drew aside respectfully to let them pass. They came at last to an ornately patterned door set into a sheer wall of rock. Ultimo touched a control, and the door opened. He thrust Kevin inside.

They were in a kind of replica of Faber's throne room. It had the same circular shape and the same central throne, far larger than Faber's, though less ornate. But there were no rich hangings, no soft floor coverings, no mural showing a tropical landscape. Presumably a robot didn't need such luxuries.

Ultimo strode majestically across the room and took his seat upon the throne. Kevin stood before him. It was curiously like the earlier meeting between Faber and Ultimo, though Kevin had no intention of kneeling.

He looked boldly up at Ultimo. 'Well, what about Faber's orders? Are you going to kill me – and all the others?'

'I do not know.' Ultimo leaned forward as he spoke almost as if pleading for understanding. 'I was created on this asteroid, by Faber. In

141

your human terms, I was born here. All I know is what I have seen here and what Faber has taught me. Now Faber admits that he has told me less than the truth – and you say that he has lied…' A note of agony came into Ultimo's voice. 'I am a robot. My mind moves in strictly logical paths. I cannot deal with uncertainty. I must know. Help me.'

'How?'

'Tell me of the Universe outside this asteroid. I shall balance what you say against what I have learned from Faber – then I shall make my decision.'

Kevin took a deep breath and began talking for his life – for the life of every captive on the asteroid.

Anna found getting captured harder than she'd expected. Duron came with them to act as guide, but since the guerilla raid, the robots had cut down their activities, and Duron had to search the misty asteroid quite some time before he found any robots on the surface. However, certain routine activities were still going on, presumably because no one had countermanded them, and at last he found them a small party of engineer robots working under the supervision of one of the silver supervisor robots. They were cutting up and removing the last fragments of the hull of an enormous space liner, a space ship so vast that it had taken the robots many trips to dispose of it. Even now the last few sections of the vast structure lay on the rocky hillside like the bones of some beached whale. The robots moved busily around it.

Hidden behind a boulder, Jan and Anna watched them for some time. Finally, when the porter robots were loaded down with neatly sliced metal beams and the engineer robots had switched off their laser-torch arms and retracted them into their bodies, it became clear that the work was ended. 'Now, Anna,' whispered Jan.

Anna nodded, gripped his hand in farewell, and set off down the hillside.

The supervising robot was astonished to see Anna calmly walking towards them. 'You are a savage,' it said reproachfully. 'Savages always flee from us. Why do you approach?'

'I want to come with you.'

'Your place is here on surface. We robots live inside the asteroid. The only savages there are subjects for research and experiment.'

'I don't care. I still want to come with you.'

Faced with a decision above its capabilities, the robot was helpless, and had to refer the matter higher. 'Then come. Ultimo will decide.'

The silver supervisor led the little party of worker robots to a point

142

lower down the hillside. It stopped and emitted a high electronic beep. After a moment there was a deep humming sound and a concealed door opened in the hillside, revealing a brightly lit tunnel.

The silver robot stood watching as the robots filed in, and then followed them inside, Anna trailing close behind. The door closed and they disappeared from sight.

'What now?' whispered Duron.

'We wait. Or rather I do. You round up all your band, get them armed and ready, then check back here.'

Duron nodded, and moved quickly away.

Jan took out his communicator, switched it to receive, and settled down to wait.

12. THE REBEL ROBOTS

Kevin had been talking for what seemed like hours. He'd delivered a potted history of the Galaxy, telling how men and women had evolved from a wandering ape to a creature that used tools, how over millions of years the tools had become machines. He told how just as ape had evolved into man, machines had evolved robots – the machine that could think.

Kevin told how robots had helped and protected men, exploring unknown planets, working in environments where men could never go. He drew a picture of men and robots as partners, on millions of worlds throughout the Galaxy, each needing and depending on the other's skills. On worlds where non-human life forms dominated, the relationship between organic creatures and robots was still the same – mutual co-operation.

It was a simplified and perhaps an idealised picture, and Ultimo listened in silent fascination. At last Kevin said, 'I'm sorry, I've talked myself out. It's up to you now.'

Ultimo sat brooding upon his throne, an elbow on his knee, a hand to his chin. The pose was curiously familiar, and suddenly Kevin realised why. It was the exact position of Rodin's famous statue, *The Thinker*. Ultimo's whole being was concentrated in thought, grappling with the new ideas that Kevin had introduced. At last he looked up. 'Why?' he said sadly. 'If all you say is true, why has Faber lied to us from the moment we were created?'

'Because he's mad. He's convinced himself organic life forms are worthless, and only robots can be trusted. So he fed you a lot of lies. He even brainwashed helpless prisoners, and reduced others to savages, to give you a distorted picture.'

Ultimo considered. 'I have certainly never encountered anyone human like you. Are all free organic beings so unpredictable?'

'They're all *different*, individuals. That's their value. Just as the value of robots is in their logic, their consistency. What have you decided?'

'Your picture of the Universe is – logical, Faber's is not.' Ultimo rose. 'Come!'

Kevin looked up at the great golden figure towering above him. 'Where?'

'We shall go to Faber and tell him he is wrong,' said Ultimo simply.

'Just like that?'

'When I tell him I know the truth, then he will admit that he has acted illogically.'

'I shouldn't bank on it.' Kevin shook his head. 'You'd do better to lock him up and take over yourself.'

'He is my creator,' said Ultimo simply.

He strode majestically from the room, and Kevin hurried after him. There was such a thing as being too honest, he thought. But how could you explain that to a high-minded robot?

The supervisor had sent the engineers and the porter robots back to the workshops. Now it was grappling with the problem of the human female, since for the moment Ultimo could not be found.

'There is no precedent for dealing with savages who wish to come inside the asteroid,' it complained peevishly. 'It is not logical.'

Anna couldn't help smiling. There was something almost comical in the little silver robot's dismay. 'Now I am inside the asteroid, I am no longer a savage,' she suggested helpfully.

The robot thought for a moment. 'That is so. And if you are not a wild human, you must be a captive human. That is the only other kind. And if you are a captive human, then your place is with the others. Come with me!' Pleased at having found such a logical solution to its problem, the robot bustled Anna away.

In one of the workshops the captives were ranged around a long table, piled high with scraps of rusty twisted metal. They were engaged in polishing these obviously useless fragments to gleaming brightness – one of the mind-destroying tasks devised by Faber.

A supervisor robot with a long silver rod was supervising them, a soldier robot guarded the door. Commander Tor and the man called Harrak were working side by side. Harrak worked with gloomy resignation, but Tor, who'd recovered from being knocked out to find himself in a nightmare world, made only a token attempt at working, looking round alertly for a chance to escape.

'How long will they keep us here?' he hissed.

Harrak went on polishing, somehow managing to speak without apparently moving his lips. 'Minutes, hours, days – there's no telling.'

'And afterwards?'

'I keep telling you – there's no pattern. They may feed us and let us rest, or put us straight on some other job.'

Tor glanced at the silver robot with the rod. 'What's that thing for?'

'You'll find out if you don't get a move on,' said Harrak with gloomy relish.

The supervisor moved over to them. It touched Tor on the left

146

shoulder with its rod, and he jumped back in agony as a fierce pain shot through his arm. 'Your work is falling below an acceptable pace,' said the supervisor calmly. 'Work quicker.'

Tor gave a snarl of rage. His fur bristled, and the savage claws sprang out from the ends of his paws. He crouched to spring...

The soldier robot by the door glided forward, raising its laser-gun. 'Non-functioning humans are destroyed,' said the silver robot in the same emotionless voice. Tor gave it a thoughtful look, picked up his polishing rag and began working again. The robot glided back, and the android returned to its place and everything went on as if nothing had happened.

A few minutes later there was a bustle in the doorway as a second supervisor robot appeared bringing with it a slender figure in space coveralls. Tor turned to Harrak. 'It's the Lady Anna. She was on my ship...'

Anna caught his eye and shook her head briefly indicating that he wasn't to recognise her.

The silver robot with the rod gave her a fragment of steel wool and a scrap of rag. 'You will polish these pieces of metal until they shine.'

'Why?'

'Because that is your task.'

'How long for?'

'Until you are told to stop. Now work.'

Anna picked up a rusted metal bolt and began to clean it. As soon as the robot moved away, she began sliding down the line of captives, changing places with one and then another until she was next to Tor.

In a series of urgent whispers she gave him a condensed account of what she and Jan had been doing. 'He's waiting outside with the guerillas now. We've got to escape and take a look round this place and find the best place to attack. Have you seen Kevin?'

Tor nodded towards Harrak. 'According to him, the robots took Kevin away to something called the Maze.'

'He must have managed to escape but he was recaptured.' Anna looked round the room. 'Will any of this lot help us?'

Tor nodded towards Harrak, who had been listening eagerly. 'He might. The rest are useless.'

Anna looked across at Harrak. 'Well?'

The Neanderthal man shrugged. 'Why not? We'll all get killed – but it's better than polishing metal. What are we going to do?'

'Escape, of course!' Anna looked round the room. 'I think I've got a plan. Now listen.'

A few minutes later she flung down her chunk of metal with a clang. 'I'm fed up with this, I want a rest and something to eat.'

The silver robot glided over. 'Work!'

'I won't.'

The silver robot raised its rod and took a step towards her. Anna backed away, moving in a semicircle and the robot swivelled with her until its back was to the others. Instantly Tor and Harrak leaped on it from behind and ran it forward, charging straight at the soldier robot, as it raised its laser-gun. The supervisor smashed into the soldier robot with a clang, and the wildly flailing metal rod caught the robot across the head. There was a crackle of blue sparks and as the massive electric shock seared through the robot's brain patterns it began spinning wildly, firing at random into the air. One flailing arm caught the supervisor robot, smashing it to the ground.

By now Tor, Harrak and Anna were out of the door racing down the tunnel.

The prisoners at the bench simply went on working. No one had told them to stop.

'You are a fool, Ultimo,' screamed Faber. 'You are malfunctioning – your logic circuits are faulty. I shall have you disassembled and scrapped. Secundus shall replace you!'

'My mind is functioning perfectly – as you made it to function,' said Ultimo steadily. 'We must release the human captives and stop attacking ships. What you have been doing is illogical.'

Faber's robot hand went out to the controls set into the armrest of his throne, and pulled back a massive red lever. 'You see this lever, Ultimo? It is a destructor-switch, linked to the anti-matter generators that power this asteroid. It is what is known as a dead man's lever – it operates not when it is pulled, but when it is released.' Faber pulled back the lever. 'Now, I have only to open my hand to destroy the asteroid and everything upon it. We shall all become meteor fragments, drifting into space.'

From his place by the door, Kevin saw the metal hand clamped firmly on the lever. 'Told you so, Ultimo,' he whispered to himself.

'I repeat the orders I have given you,' screeched Faber. 'All captives on the asteroid are to be killed instantly. The soldier robots will be fully activated. I shall steer the asteroid to the nearest human planet and we shall conquer it. Disobey me once more, Ultimo, and you will be deactivated. Secundus shall take your place. His mind is not the equal of yours, but at least he is loyal. Now go!'

Kevin slipped out quickly before he was noticed, and Ultimo joined him in the tunnel. 'What will you do now?' asked Kevin.

'I cannot obey Faber – his brain pattern is disturbed. Therefore it seems that we must all die!'

'Oh no we mustn't,' said Kevin firmly. 'We've got to find some way to stop him!'

They heard the crackle of laser-fire from somewhere down the tunnel. 'Something's happening,' said Kevin. 'If there's trouble, it's probably my friends! Let's go and find out!'

Tor, Harrak and Anna raced down the tunnel, ducking and weaving to escape the laser-fire of pursuing soldier robots. The supervisor had recovered sufficiently to give the alarm, and a robot patrol had found them almost immediately. Now they were running for their lives. Although they could move faster than the massive soldier robots, their opponents had one great advantage – robots don't get tired. All three humans were gasping for breath. They couldn't keep the pace up much longer – and as soon as they slowed, the robots would catch up with them. Chests heaving, hearts pounding they staggered on, until finally Tor, who was in the lead, rounded a bend in a tunnel, and stopped dead. 'There's a robot coming down the tunnel ahead of us. We're trapped!'

Anna turned to look behind them. The soldier robots were gliding steadily nearer...

13. BREAKOUT

Anna turned round the bend of the tunnel, and halted panting beside Tor. A huge golden figure was striding down the tunnel towards them – but there was a smaller, and very familiar one, at its side. 'It's Kevin!' gasped Anna delightedly. 'Kevin, it's us!' she yelled.

There was time only for a quick hug of greeting and the most hurried of explanations. Harrak looked apprehensively up at Ultimo. 'That's their big boss robot. What's he doing with you?'

'Don't worry, he's on our side – at least I think he is.' Kevin looked up at the robot. 'Ultimo, these are my friends. They can help you.'

'He'll have to help us first,' said Tor grimly. 'There are a couple of soldier robots chasing us down the tunnel.' Even as he spoke the first two soldier robots glided round the bend, laser-guns levelled.

Ultimo stepped forward, shielding the humans with his body. 'The prisoners are in my charge,' he boomed. 'Go!'

For a moment the soldier robots seemed to hesitate. They had been ordered to kill the escaping prisoners, and now they were confused by the conflict with their former instructions. But Ultimo had long been acknowledged as their unquestioned leader, and the habit of obedience was strong. They turned and moved away, disappearing down the tunnel.

Anna gave a long sigh of relief. 'I'll say this for you, Kevin, you make useful friends. What's going on here?'

Kevin told her about Faber and his threat to blow up the asteroid and everyone in it. 'He'll do it too, if we don't stop him.'

'We cannot stop him,' said Ultimo. 'His hand is on the destruct-lever. When he learns his orders have not been obeyed, he will release it.'

'Then we've got to get off the asteroid,' said Anna. 'And we've got to get all the prisoners off too. Is there any kind of space ship you haven't taken to bits yet?'

'What about *Starfire*?' asked Tor eagerly.

'The scout ship is still unharmed,' said Ultimo. 'Faber planned to use it as his own.'

'Then all we've got to do is recapture it,' said Kevin. 'Better still, Ultimo can just order them to hand it over – hang on though. What about Jan, and the rest of them outside?'

Anna produced the communicator. 'I can call them on this. Ultimo, is there an entrance where they're keeping the ship?'

'The star ship is in a hangar on the upper levels, immediately below the asteroid's surface. There is an exit ramp close by.'

'Can it take off from there?'

'The hangar roof slides back...'

'That's it then,' said Kevin. 'Ultimo, you order all the prisoners to be brought to the star ship – say they've got to polish it or something! Then you'll have to get the roof opened up. Anna, you call up Jan and tell him to bring all the guerillas to the nearest entrance. Ultimo, you can get it opened for us, can't you?'

Ultimo seemed bewildered by the speed of events. 'I think so – though Faber may give instructions that my orders are no longer to be obeyed.'

'Well, we won't know till we try,' said Anna briskly. She began speaking into the communicator. 'Jan, this is Anna. Can you hear me? Can you hear me?'

Faber looked at the massive grey robot kneeling before him. 'Remember, Secundus, Ultimo has malfunctioned. He refuses to obey my orders. He is to be deactivated – and the prisoners must die!'

The huge grey robot's mind had no room for the doubts that had tormented Ultimo. It was a simple creature, not much more intelligent than the supervising androids, and it was content to be no more than an instrument of Faber's will.

'Ultimo must be deactivated and the prisoners killed,' repeated Secundus, and moved away to carry out his task.

Jan said, 'All right, Anna, I've got it. Switch on the communicator's homing beam and set it up near the entrance. I'll have everyone there as soon as I can.' He turned to the astonished Duron. 'Now listen you, and don't argue. We've got a chance to capture a star ship and get off this asteroid. If we don't we're all going to be killed. Now you send out runners, round up everyone you can find and get them back here. Tell that rival band too – if they don't believe you that's their tough luck. As soon as I pick up the homing signal we'll get moving.'

Duron shook his head. 'A star ship? Escape?' he said wonderingly. 'How could your friends achieve all this so quickly?'

'You had as much chance to do it as they did.'

'We wanted only to survive, we never dreamed escape was possible.'

'Perhaps that's why you never made it,' said Jan. 'Now get moving!'

Ultimo appeared in the door to the work chamber. A new supervisor robot and a new guard had replaced those damaged in Anna's escape. 'Take the human captives to the star ship in the upper hangar,' ordered Ultimo. 'Faber has ordered that they shall polish the ship.'

Ultimo stood waiting as if confident he would be obeyed. The supervisor robot menaced the prisoners with its electric rod. 'You've been assigned to new tasks. Move quickly!' Obediently the captives shuffled away.

Anna was crouched just inside an open door at the top of a ramp which led up to the surface. Cold mist seeped down the tunnel, and she shivered in the chill of the outer air. She was clutching the communicator which was giving out a high-pitched almost inaudible beep. Anna peered anxiously out into the misty darkness. If the door was left open much longer, there was a danger one of the supervising robots would appear and question what was happening. If it decided to check with Faber...

She heard a high-pitched beeping from the mist, and seconds later Jan appeared, a swarm of ragged figures at his heels. 'Sorry, we got lost in the fog! Where's the next ship home then?'

Anna looked at him exasperatedly. He was enjoying himself again. 'The *Starfire*'s in some kind of hangar not far away. Kevin and Tor are on the way there now. Come on, I'll explain things as we go.'

Commander Tor looked at his beloved ship and gave a purr of pure pleasure. Sleek and beautiful, the *Starfire* rested on support gantries in a huge rocky cavern just below the surface. Robot soldiers moved round it on constant patrol. The entrance ramp was lowered and the ship's door opened. Robot scientists moved in and out of the ship.

Tor and Harrak were at the head of the group of shuffling apathetic captives who had been herded to the hangar by the supervisor robot.

Ultimo marched up to the robot scientist supervising the study of the ship. 'The human prisoners are to go on board the ship. Faber has ordered that they are to polish it.' The robot moved aside, and the prisoners filed up the entrance ramp, Tor and Harrak in the lead.

Ultimo stood calmly waiting.

By the hangar doors Kevin waited too, looking anxiously down the long tunnel. Suddenly he turned. 'It's all right, they're coming!' A few minutes later Jan and Anna and a group of ragged guerillas burst into the hangar. Jan grinned at Kevin and slapped him on the back. 'Well done, kid. This is what I call service!'

'We're not home yet. Get this load of scruffs on board as quick as you can.'

Jan charged up the ramp, the guerillas behind him.

The astonishing spectacle of the swarm of ragged figures pouring on board the ship raised doubts in the mind of the robot scientist. 'These are savages. Why are they going on the *Starfire?*'

'Because I order it,' said Ultimo. 'Would you question the will of Faber?'

Behind them a voice boomed, 'Stop!' A massive grey robot, fully as big as Ultimo, had appeared in the hangar doorway. 'Ultimo has malfunctioned. He is to be deactivated immediately. Faber has ordered that all the captives be destroyed. They serve no further purpose.'

Ultimo swung round to confront his adversary. 'Do not obey the orders of Secundus. I am his superior. Obey my orders. It is Secundus whose mind has malfunctioned.'

Faced with the agonising dilemma of conflicting orders from two trusted leaders, the robot soldiers milled about in confusion, some ranging themselves behind Ultimo, others supporting Secundus. The grey robot came forward. 'The prisoners are on the ship. We shall destroy them.'

Most of the soldier robots surged forward as if to follow him, but Ultimo barred the way. 'The orders of Faber are illogical. We must obey them no longer.'

Secundus tried to thrust him aside. Ultimo resisted, and in a second the two metal giants were grappling fiercely.

Kevin watched the struggle anxiously from the foot of *Starfire*'s entrance ramp, Anna beside him. Common sense told him he should get on board the ship and urge Tor to blast off. There was no telling how much longer Faber's patience would last. But somehow he couldn't leave Ultimo to his fate. He wanted to persuade the golden robot to come back to Centre with them. Ultimo bore no real responsibility for Faber's crimes...

At first Ultimo and Secundus appeared equally matched, then it began to look as if Secundus had the edge in sheer brute strength. His great hands were clamped about Ultimo's throat. Remorselessly Secundus bent his opponent backwards, as if determined to wrench the golden robot's head from its shoulders.

Yet if Secundus was the stronger, Ultimo was the more supple – and the more intelligent. Twisting his great body with astonishing speed he managed to duck beneath Secundus and break his grip. When Ultimo straightened up, he was holding Secundus high above his head. For a moment he held the massive grey robot poised, then with one final effort he hurled him away.

Secundus flew through the air, metal limbs flailing helplessly, and thudded into the rock wall with a crash that shook the hangar. He fell to the floor, twitched convulsively and then lay still.

Witnessing the battle between their leaders drove the robot soldiers into a mindless frenzy. They milled about frantically, some firing at their fellow robots, some spinning aimlessly, some struck motionless in a paralysis of indecision.

Ultimo strode to the foot of the ramp where Kevin and Anna waited.

'Quick,' shouted Kevin, 'Get on the ship. You've got to come with us!'

There was sadness in Ultimo's voice. 'This is my world. I cannot leave it. I must go to Faber.'

The robot raised its arm in a strangely human gesture of salute. Anna waved back, caught Kevin's hand and pulled him up the ramp. The great golden figure looked after them for a moment, turned and moved away through the howling chaos of the battle.

The space ship door closed behind Kevin and Anna and the ramp retracted. Soon the throb of the star ship's engines was filling the hangar.

By now the *Starfire* was firmly back in the hands of the released prisoners. Guerillas and captives filled the emptied holds in a milling crowd, and a number of robot scientists had been shut into a storage locker, where they were complaining bitterly amongst themselves that all this was most irregular and unprecedented.

Tor was in the main control room, frantically busy at the controls, and Anna was immediately pressed into service as co-pilot, operating controls under Tor's direction.

Jan was looking at the battle in the hangar on the monitor screen. Kevin moved over to his side. 'How long till blast-off?'

'Be a few minutes yet. Tor says he's got to run the motors up to full power. Don't worry, we're as good as home.'

Kevin hoped Jan was right. He kept thinking of the twisted figure of Faber, crouched on his throne with the dead man's lever in his robot hand.

Faber too was watching the battle in the control room on his monitor screen. He saw the milling crowd of robot soldiers, and heard the throbbing star ship, shaking the cavern with the roar of its atomic motors. Faber knew exactly how long it would take to run those motors to full power, and it pleased him to let the fugitives come within seconds of escape before he destroyed them.

The fact that he would be destroying himself and his world counted for

155

nothing in his desire for revenge on those who had destroyed his dream.

The door opened and Ultimo appeared, walking forward to kneel before the throne. Faber looked down at him. 'Have you come to gloat over your betrayal, Ultimo? Well, you will find you have gained nothing from your treachery – you or your human friends.'

'Friends,' said Ultimo slowly. 'Yes, perhaps they were my friends.'

'And for them you betrayed me, your creator, and all we have worked for… well, you shall suffer for it, Ultimo. I am glad you are here to see the moment of their destruction.'

The old voice raved on. Ultimo made no attempt to reply. He stood watching the space ship on the monitor screen.

Kevin leaned over Tor's shoulder. 'How long till you're ready for blast-off?'

'I'm ready now,' shouted Tor. 'I'm waiting for your robot friend to retract the hangar roof.'

Kevin stared at him in dismay. Although they were in a star ship, ready for take-off, there was still a ceiling above their heads. Something told Kevin it was no use waiting for Ultimo to help them.

'You'll just have to take off now,' he shouted. 'We should be able to break through.'

'And suppose we can't?' demanded Tor. 'The hull could fracture, we could all be killed.'

'We'll be killed for sure if you don't take off,' yelled Kevin.

Jan moved to stand behind Tor, and put a reassuring hand on his shoulder. 'It'll be okay, Tor,' he said reassuringly. 'Now do it! You've got to!'

Tor stared at him as if hypnotised, then reached for the firing control…

'You were my greatest achievement, Ultimo,' said Faber bitterly. 'But when I created you, I made one great error. You became too human – now you must die as the captives will die…'

Ultimo waited calmly. Faber had only to open his hand – there was no chance of moving quickly enough to prevent him. Nor did Ultimo wish to do so. He was Faber's creation, content to end with Faber, and Faber's world. There was no place for him in that wonderful varied universe outside the asteroid. Faber opened his robot hand.

The lever snapped back, completing the destructor circuit – just as the star ship smashed through the ceiling of the hangar and hurtled into space. Beneath it the asteroid exploded in a ball of flame that charred the silver metal of the *Starfire*'s hull.

156

Suddenly new meteorites joined the untold billions already drifting through the Asteroid Zone. A million tiny fragments of rock and metal, all that remained of Faber and his robot empire . . .

14. RETURN

Jan, Kevin and Anna lay stretched out on the smooth turf of the highest lawn of the Hanging Gardens on Centre, watching dawn rise over the bright gardens and the rolling green plains beyond.

They had arrived back on Centre in the middle of the night and delivered a shipload of ragged guerillas and brainwashed captives into the astonished hands of a crowd of clucking Galactic bureaucrats. Leaving the explanations to Tor, Jan, Kevin and Anna had slipped silently away to their pavilion. They had showered and bathed and scrubbed till they felt painfully clean, they had dressed in clean, soft, colourful clothes, they had eaten the biggest and most elaborate meal that Centre could provide. Then, too tense from reaction to sleep, they had summoned a floater to take them to the Hanging Gardens.

Immaculate in a new uniform of white and gold, Jan stretched until his muscles creaked. 'Peace, it's wonderful. And to think I said I was bored.'

Kevin nodded. 'Perhaps it takes a bit of discomfort and danger to make you appreciate a place like this.'

Anna shaded her eyes, peering through the light morning mists. 'I think we're going to have company.'

A large official floater was drifting towards them, bearing the blue-and-gold standard of the Council. Inside they could see Elvar, looking as usual like a Biblical prophet, with the teddy-bear figure of Parl beside him, a handful of minor officials in attendance.

As soon as the floater touched down Parl bounded across the lawn towards them, shaking them enthusiastically by the hand, and delivering bear-hugs of welcome. 'My friends. My dear young friends! Tor has told us the whole story. Such heroism! Such resource and enterprise. And to think that my old friend Faber... We must remove his holograph from the Hall of Fame, I fear... You have thrown the administration into a frenzy. So many rescued captives to be returned to their home planets – though some will require long treatment before they recover from their terrible experiences. But we shall cure them, never fear! And you are well? You are sure you are unharmed? How could you take such risks...'

Parl would have gone on indefinitely but the approach of Elvar silenced him, for the moment at least. There were more greetings, more thanks, more praise and congratulations. 'You have served the Galaxy well,' said Elvar solemnly.

Parl couldn't keep quiet for long. 'And I have good news, my friends. My scientific colleague from Antares III has achieved a breakthrough. It is too early to say for sure, but the prospects of returning you to Earth are much improved.'

'That's wonderful,' said Anna. Yet even as she spoke, Earth seemed very far away. She looked at Jan and Kevin, and sensed that they felt the same. Somehow it seemed almost as if Centre was their home.

'I too have news,' said Elvar importantly. 'Plans for your new, extended Galactic Tour are already under way. The home worlds of those you have rescued will insist on thanking you. Politically you have done the League an immense service. Tonight there is to be a special ceremonial banquet in your honour! I shall make a speech...'

Kevin looked at Anna and grinned. 'This is where we came in.'

Jan groaned audibly, coughed and tried to turn the groan into a noise of appreciation. 'That's great! Just great!'

Anna stared into the morning mists and said nothing. She was thinking of the tall golden figure of Ultimo, as he stood by the *Starfire*'s ramp, raising his hand in farewell...

STAR QUEST
TERRORSAUR!

Terrance Dicks

TERRORSAUR!

1. PLANET OF MONSTERS

The Terrorsaur was on the move.

It crashed majestically through the overgrown density of the jungle, smashing a path through shrubs and vines and undergrowth with contemptuous ease. It made no attempt to conceal the sounds of its progress – caution was for lesser beings. After all, what did it have to fear? It was the most dangerous beast on a planet teeming with monsters. Not the biggest – there were vast, slow-moving creatures that dwarfed its considerable bulk. Not the best protected – there were monsters on this planet so heavily armoured in scale and bone that nothing less than high explosive could touch them. And there were no explosives on the planet. But this, the one called Terrorsaur, was the fastest, the toughest, the most savage killer of them all.

It walked upright on two huge clawed back-legs, two smaller front limbs dangling before it. The massive body was balanced by the long tail that flailed out behind, a tail that ended in a kind of spiked club. The monster was covered with scaly armour plating, and a row of savage spikes ran along the length of its spine. Another large spike jutted from the high-domed head. The powerful jaws held seemingly endless rows of serrated teeth.

Yet in spite of this formidable array of weaponry, it was the eyes that were the beast's most impressive feature. Huge and green, protected by heavy ridges of bone, they glowed with ferocious intelligence. The Terrorsaur was over fifteen metres long from savage head to spiked tail, it stood six metres high and it weighed a good ten tons.

The Terrorsaur was hungry, and it was hunting.

In the heart of the jungle was a palm-fringed lagoon, where huge lumbering beasts with long necks and comically small heads browsed upon lush weed and dense green plants.

When the nightmare figure of the Terrorsaur appeared from the jungle, they gave trumpeting shrieks of alarm and made clumsy attempts to flee. For a moment the Terrorsaur stood poised, surveying the panic-stricken beasts as they churned the muddy waters of the lagoon in a desperate bid to escape. Selecting a victim, it lunged forward with terrifying speed, sinking its teeth deep into the neck of a fleeing herbivore.

The animal convulsed in shock and a great plume of arterial blood shot high into the air, splashing down to stain the murky waters of the lagoon.

Weakening fast, the herbivore kicked only feebly as the Terrorsaur dragged its body to the lagoon-side and into the reeds.

Crouched over its prey, the Terrorsaur fed with savage efficiency, ripping great chunks of flesh from the still-warm body and bolting them down, its great head swinging suspiciously to and fro between bites. There were other beasts, too lazy to hunt, who preferred to steal the carcass of another's kill.

Once the Terrorsaur had made its kill, the rest of the herd relaxed, resuming their unending browsing for food. At some deep instinctive level of their tiny brains they knew the Terrorsaur killed no more than once a day, if that. They were safe now, until its terrible hunger returned – or at least until some other carnivore appeared.

Sated at last, the Terrorsaur left the half-eaten carcass and disappeared into the jungle. Immediately there was a boiling and seething at the water's edge. Tiny crocodile-like creatures with needle-sharp teeth swarmed all over the carcass, tearing the flesh from the bones, devouring the intestines. Great jewelled dragonflies swooped out of the coppery sky and drank the spilled blood through their long transparent proboscies. Legions of warrior ants swarmed over the body, stripping the last few shreds of meat from the massive skeleton. Before the day was over nothing would remain of the Terrorsaur's kill but a heap of bones bleaching beneath the tropical sun. Nothing was wasted in the jungle – nothing.

The Terrorsaur roamed restlessly on. It had killed and eaten. It was easy to kill the great herbivores – too easy perhaps – it was not the season for mating, there was no one to fight. Why then was its massive body filled with a strange discontent? Why did it suddenly turn and slash savagely at the trunk of a mighty tree with its forelimbs, gouging great chunks of bark from the trunk?

Suddenly the Terrorsaur sensed movement behind it and whirled round. Another creature had appeared at the edge of the clearing. It stood upright on two legs also, and had two smaller forelimbs, but it was many times smaller than the Terrorsaur, its body was covered with fur, not scales, and it had no spikes and no fighting-horn. It bore a rider on its back, a deep-chested, heavily muscled man in a loincloth, with a low, bony forehead and a massive underhung jaw. It was a heavy, brutal face, though the brown eyes beneath the jutting brows were unexpectedly intelligent.

At the sight of the Terrorsaur, the slender riding-beast bunched its muscles to flee, but the rider stilled it with a pat from one enormous hand. He sat motionless on his quivering mount, staring at the monster with burning eyes.

The monster stared fixedly back and for a moment it seemed as if some answering spark blazed in the green depths of its eyes. It gave a low, coughing roar and crashed away through the jungle.

2. THE PEOPLE

The rider looked after it with a rueful smile for a moment, then gave a silent command to his mount that sent the terrified beast bounding down the trail in enormous leaps.

Gradually the jungle thinned and became a rocky plain, a plain which gradually turned into the foothills of a low mountain range. The rider guided his beast up a rapidly climbing pass, through a tunnel of rock, and out into a shallow rock bowl cut in half by a mountain stream. Tall ferns grew along the edge of the stream, and the rim of the bowl was broken up by a series of cave mouths. Little fires burned before many of the caves, sending plumes of blue smoke into the clear mountain air. Skin-clad women moved to and fro, busy over cooking pots which gave off a variety of savoury smells; naked children splashed and played in the stream.

In front of one of the largest caves a flat-topped rock formed a kind of natural table. On it, a dwarf and a giant octopus were playing three-dimensional chess.

The dwarf's muscular body was clothed in a brown jerkin, trousers and boots, all of some tough leathery substance. The octopus wore only a webbing harness. Its enormous golden eyes were blazing with anger, as it spoke in a high whistling voice. 'Cheating! My poor Tell, do you imply that I, Osar, a Senior Navigator of the League would descend to cheating? In any case, I do not need to cheat to defeat such as you.'

The dwarf said, 'You made one move on the upper board, and a second on the lower...'

'What of it? Two moves in sequence are permitted, are they not?'

'Indeed! But you also made a third move on the mid-board, which is *not* permitted, when you thought I was distracted by the arrival of friend Garm.'

By now Garm had dismissed his mount and was towering over his two friends. 'Wrangling as usual, I see? If you cannot agree, why do you not choose one of my people as an opponent?'

Osar gave a disdainful twitch of his tentacles. 'One cannot play three-dimensional chess with a tribe of stone-age primitives!'

'With a tribe of telepathic stone-age primitives,' said Tell, with a wicked grin. 'There's not a child in that brook who couldn't defeat you, Osar – *and* they'd know you were going to cheat as soon as you formed the intention.'

Osar bunched his tentacles under him and sprang erect, not so accidentally upsetting the board in the process. 'How unfortunate,' he observed loftily. 'It is impossible to continue the game. I shall return to the ship to recheck my instruments.'

He sprang spider-like across the rocks towards a narrow cleft – in which stood the slender dartlike shape of a League scout ship – ignoring the cries of the children beseeching him to give them rides. Osar was a great favourite with the children. Their telepathic minds enabled them to sense the warmth and kindness beneath his frightening appearance.

Tell grinned, and began picking up the pieces. At a touch of his nimble fingers the board converted itself into a box, and he began putting the pieces away. 'Poor Osar – I'm afraid he's over civilised for the simple life.'

Garm sat down upon the rock, chin in hands. 'And you, Tell? You've scarcely ventured outside the settlement since we arrived.'

'Do you blame me – with every life form on the planet determined to make a meal of me? Besides, there are the caves. I could spend a lifetime here and never tire of the caves. And the paintings! The paintings...' Tell gave a sigh of ecstacy.

In the great caves that lay deep in the heart of the mountain, Garm's people did the most marvellous paintings on the rock walls – paintings of the many different deerlike beasts, of the great snakes that swam in the lagoons and the leather-winged killers that sailed the skies, paintings of the placid herbivores and the awesome Terrorsaur. So masterly in execution were the paintings that the great beasts seemed to come to life on the rock walls.

Tell had beseeched the tribal Elders to let him make a video-record of the paintings, so that they could be reproduced in the Great Museum of Galactic Arts on Centre, the capital world of the League, but the Elders had steadfast refused. Tell returned to the subject now. 'They allowed me to see the Great Inner Cave today – paintings more marvellous than any before, a Terrorsaur that seemed to leap out at me from the wall – and all buried down there in the darkness for evermore. If they would only allow me to make a video-record. I could mount an exhibition in the Museum of Galactic Arts that would bring tourists flocking from every corner of the Galaxy.'

Garm smiled. 'Perhaps that is what they fear; besides, you forget, the cave paintings are not art, they are magic.'

'You believe that?'

'I know only that when the game grows scarce the shaman orders a

170

great herd of deer to be drawn on some cave wall – and before many days the deer herd appears on the plain, and the tribe is fed.'

'You have seen this?'

'Many times, when I was a boy – before I left my home world to be *educated* on Centre.' Garm gave a wry emphasis to the word – as though in some way he had lost more than he had gained.

And perhaps he had, thought Tell. Garm's people had developed the powers of the mind to an amazing extent, deliberately turning aside from technology to cultivate their mysterious gifts. No doubt long residence amongst the largely non-telepathic lifeforms that made up the League had blunted Garm's powers, cutting him off from his heritage.

Tell frowned, as a thought struck him. 'What about the other drawings, the ones of sky beasts and sea beasts? What about that Terrorsaur – you don't want a herd of them coming down on you surely?'

'Those drawings were made to serve a different purpose. Once the monster is imprisoned on the rock wall we have power over him – some part of his vital essence is captured for ever.'

'Oh come now – you're not trying to tell me one of those fanged horrors will refrain from eating you just because you've got his picture on the wall?'

'Mock if you will,' said Garm solemnly. 'But I ran into a Terrorsaur on the edge of the jungle as I returned, and he turned aside.'

Tell stared at him, wondering if he was being made the victim of one of Garm's solemn jokes. It was a characteristic of Garm and his people that they never seemed more serious than when they were jesting. 'Truly Garm, this homeworld of yours is a most amazing place.'

Garm made no reply. He sat cross-legged on the rock, staring wide-eyed into space in one of the semi-trances so characteristic of his race. He was there and not there, apparently lost in meditation, yet somehow Tell sensed he was aware of every wisp of smoke from the cooking pots, every ripple on the little stream.

Tell shook his head, looking at his old friend with new eyes. He had known Garm for many years. They had gone to Centre for training at about the same time, served together on many dangerous missions as agents of the League – the League of Sentient Life Forms, that united in a loose alliance all the beings of goodwill in the Galaxy. But here, on his mysterious home world, Garm was a different person.

And what a world it was! A new-formed planet of swamps and jungles and marshes, great wild seas and dry parched deserts, everything running to extremes. A planet beset by storms and baked by the glare of twin suns, a place where great ice tundras were broken up by mountains that belched fire and lava. It would defy all the planet-forming scientists on Centre to civilise such a world, thought Tell, to build roads and cities and space ports that could stand up to so savage a climate.

Garm's people didn't even try. They lived in warm dry caves, and they wore clothes of skins and fur. They lived on fruits and berries and maize, together with the meat and fish that the hunters brought home. The tough, wiry children grew into huge, powerfully muscled men and fine sturdy women. The old people were thin and gaunt and incredibly fit.

Garm's race seemed to have no king, no government, very little organisation at all. There were only the Elders, a loose-knit, informal, constantly changing group – confusingly, some of them weren't even old. Tell had gathered that there were other tribes scattered over the more habitable parts of the savage planet, all separate and independent, all mysteriously united and in touch with each other. They didn't even have a name for the place. Their world was The World, and they were The People. That was all.

Yet at the same time they seemed well aware of the immense Galaxy of which their planet formed such a tiny part, regarding it with a kind of benevolent indifference. When occasionally some of the more restless of their young men and women expressed a desire to leave home and serve the League, roaming the Galaxy in its star ships, the Elders of the People made no objection. They sent the poor eccentric on his way with pitying tolerance, and returned to the serious business of hunting and fishing and planting crops and making wine and carving bone, and painting those wonderful pictures on the walls of their caves.

Tell gave a snort of amusement. It was no life for a civilised man, of course. But, oh, those inner caves, and those paintings...

'I was speaking with one of the Elders,' said Garm's deep voice suddenly. 'He said that for an outworlder you show some glimmer of understanding of his craft. If you cared to stay awhile, he might be persuaded to show you how the pigments are mixed from roots and berries, and how the outlines of the paintings are drawn on the rock face.'

Tell stared indignantly at his big friend, taken aback as always at the way Garm answered his unspoken thoughts.

'Of course, to understand even the rudiments would be the work of many years,' Garm went on solemnly. 'But who knows, with application…'

'I might occupy a lowly place in one of the teams of artists?' suggested Tell sarcastically. 'Spend the rest of my life adding some minor detail to the drawing of some monster – a foot, perhaps?'

'Not a whole foot,' said Garm judiciously. 'A claw, maybe, or a single tooth…' His wrist communicator gave a series of low beeps and he broke off, springing to his feet. 'We must go to the ship. There is danger. Come.'

Garm strode across the rock basin, heading for the rock cleft in which their scout ship was concealed.

Tell scampered after him. 'Why? What's happening?'

'Osar is alarmed. Come!'

The circular scout ship with its central dome was hidden beneath an overhang of rock just outside the basin. Garm marched up the ramp, Tell close behind him, and headed for the control room that occupied the centre of the raised dome. They found Osar hunched over his instrument panel, his great golden eyes staring unwinkingly at a central scanner screen. It showed a pattern of dots, moving in formation from top to bottom.

Osar spoke without looking up. 'I thought you might care to know that your world is being invaded.'

Garm studied the display on the screen. 'A Kaldor strike force?'

'It's one of their standard attack patterns. I'll send a message to Centre.'

One of Osar's tentacles snaked out towards a control, but Garm's great hand was quicker, covering the control. 'No!'

'But we have to warn them!'

'And warn the Kaldor as well? Their sensor beams will be scanning the planet. If they pick up a sub-space transmission from a supposedly primitive world, they'll think they've run into an ambush and plaster the whole area with neutron missiles.'

'He's right, you know,' said Tell softly.

Reluctantly Osar withdrew the tentacle. 'Then what do we do?'

'We hide,' said Garm. 'The Kaldor don't, *can't*, know that we're here.'

'That's true,' said Tell wryly. 'We didn't know we were coming ourselves until you got a sudden attack of homesickness.'

They had been engaged in a routine patrol which happened to take them within a few light years of Garm's home planet. On a sudden impulse Garm, who had not been home for many years, had decided to extend the patrol to include a visit to his homeworld. Sending

173

Centre a brief message announcing his intention, he had landed on the planet without waiting for Centre to give formal permission.

'The fact that they don't know we're here is the one flaw in their plans,' said Garm. 'It's a piece of pure bad luck for them.'

Tell shuddered. 'It's a piece of pure bad luck for us as well... You know the Kaldor.'

The Kaldor were a race of ruthlessly militaristic killers, dedicated to conquest and to preserving what they called the purity of the race.

As its very name implied, it was a fundamental belief of the League that any intelligent life form was eligible to join. Member races of the League included not only descendants of Man – many in adapted or mutated forms, like Garm and Tell – but many non-human races as well: octopoids like Osar and his people; the eagle-beaked wingmen of Astar II; the tiger-like Tyrreneans; everything from methane-breathing slugs to the huge iridescent jellyfish of Mare Solis. For the League, humanity in the true sense was an affair of mind and spirit. To the Kaldor, it was a simple matter of bodily form – and a rigidly defined bodily form at that.

Thin and wiry, sharp-faced with yellow hair, the Kaldor considered themselves the only true inheritors of the Empire of Man. Even Tell and Garm they would have considered scarcely human, and to them Osar and the other non-human intelligent species were no more than beasts.

Garm broke the silence. 'We must discover why they have come here – the Kaldor do nothing without a reason.' He considered. 'I can blend in with my people, but you two must hide – and we must hide the ship as well.'

Tell was heading for the explosives locker. 'I'll lay charges along the cliff above, and blast it down. We can bury the ship in rock. It'll be hidden from view and shielded from the Kaldor's surface scanners as well. Osar, you're too conspicuous – you'd better stay on board ship. You can blast it free with the retro-rockets when we need it again.'

'Have no fear,' said Osar acidly. 'With the Kaldor added to the dangers of this barbarous planet, I have no intention of leaving this vessel until it touches down on Centre again.'

Garm nodded. 'And what about you? Will you stay with Osar?'

'And spend days, perhaps months, here cooped up with Osar, listening to his eternal complaints? I'll take my chances on the outside. I may not be big enough to pass as one of you, but at least I'm small enough to hide easily. If the worst comes to the worst, you can wrap me in skins and give me to one of the women to carry for her baby.'

Arms full of explosive charges, Tell headed for the exit ramp.

Garm was loading a lightweight pack with weapons and supplies. 'Keep a continuous listening watch, Osar. As soon as there's anything to report, I'll get in touch on the communicator.'

'And if no message comes?'

'If you don't hear from us in three days, save yourself. Blast off for Centre and hope you can get clear before their tractor beams lock on to you…' Garm paused and looked at his two friends. 'I am sorry,' he said awkwardly. 'If I had not felt this sudden desire to see the world of my birth again, you would be safe on Centre by now.'

'Nonsense,' said Tell cheerfully. 'As it turns out, we are in the right place at the right time. The arrival of the Kaldor turns an illicit jaunt into a proper mission.'

'What nonsense is this?' hissed Osar.

'We were sent to check for signs of Kaldor expansionism, were we not? And we were returning home empty-handed, not a trace of them on any of the worlds we visited. Well, now we've found them. We shall have something to report when we get back to Centre.' To himself, Tell added quietly, 'If we ever do…'

To his mind, only Osar stood the remotest chance of leaving the planet alive.

175

3. The Neophytes

The tall, broad-shouldered young man in the white-and-gold uniform of a Fleet Cadet sat hunched forward in the command chair, eyes fixed on the tri-di battle-chart screen before him. He was engaged in the conquest of a planet.

Missiles streaked up from the planet below, to be met and deflected by the force shields of his fleet, or knocked out by anti-missile missiles. His invading troops had already established a series of bridgeheads on the planet, but the defenders were putting up a savage fight. Moreover, the seemingly defenceless planet had turned out to be a death-trap. There were hidden missile bases, armies of robot troops, spy satellites orbiting the planet, country towns that turned out to be impregnable fortresses.

Below the main screen was a line of smaller read-out screens, each with a constantly changing display of vital information. The young commander studied them. The battle hung in the balance. Everywhere he was meeting unexpectedly strong resistance. His forces were stretched thin on every front, fuel and ammunition were running low. An attack that had been planned as a sudden blitzkrieg looked like turning into a lengthy gruelling siege, a siege he simply didn't have the resources to support. He must make a decisive breakthrough very quickly now, or abandon the invasion and lead a badly mangled attack force home, with lives wasted and ships destroyed to no avail. The troops already on the planet would have to be sacrificed, abandoned on the surface to be captured or killed.

The commander sat back for a moment, running his fingers through longish hair, so fair as to be almost white. Then he leaned forward, stabbing at the controls, transmitting a stream of coded orders to his troop commanders.

Immediately the pattern on the tri-di screen swirled and changed. Ground troops and battle fleet alike hurled themselves at the weak points in the defenders' perimeter, as if concentrating everything on one final assault.

Attacking forces flooded to reinforce the threatened areas – and the defence held. The attackers began to fall back. Suddenly the pattern changed again as the last remnant of the attacking force hurled themselves at fresh targets – the new weak points created by the sending of reinforcements to meet the first attack.

There was a breakthrough, and then another and another. The

defenders moved men and weapons in a desperate attempt to plug the gap – and suddenly the main attack force smashed through the defences. The defenders began to fragment and crumble, breaking into disorganised groups, easily overrun by the attackers.

Suddenly the vision screen went blank and a booming computer voice said, 'EXERCISE TERMINATED. PROBABILITY OF SUCCESSFUL CONQUEST OF PLANET NOW OVER EIGHTY-THREE POINT FIVE PER CENT. ATTACK FORCE HAS SUSTAINED FORTY-THREE PER CENT CASUALTIES AND WILL REQUIRE IMMEDIATE REINFORCEMENT FROM HOME BASE.'

The commander sat back, yawning and stretching. He swivelled the command chair around. 'That was a tough one!'

Behind him stood a tall grey-haired man in the black uniform of a Galactic Marshal. This was Kranos, Supreme Commander of the League. 'Do you realise what you have done, young man?'

'Well, we won, didn't we? I know that casualty rate's way up, though. Maybe if I'd committed the main attack earlier...'

The Marshal said grimly, 'You have successfully completed the conquest of a well-defended planet with a totally inadequate force, by the use of completely unorthodox tactics. By all accepted military doctrine, that attack should have failed, and failed miserably. It was set up to fail, set up to warn you against overconfidence. It was a trap – and you smashed the trap and succeeded anyway.'

Jan rose. 'Well,' he said vaguely. 'I guess you can never tell how these things are going to turn out.'

'I am supposed to be able to tell how these things will turn out,' said the Marshal grimly. 'I have had years of training, years of practical experience in every kind of interplanetary conflict... and *you* – with no formal military training, only the most limited experience of actual combat... How do you do it? At what point did you decide to abandon the formal attack strategy you had been taught?'

There was an expression of almost comical puzzlement on Jan's face. 'When I saw it wasn't working, I guess.'

'But how did you formulate such an unorthodox attack plan so quickly, with no consultation, no access to your battle computers?'

'I didn't formulate anything, Marshal. I just did it!'

An amused voice said, 'It's no use asking him any more questions, Marshal. He doesn't know how he does it – he just does it!'

Another young man had come into the Simulator Control Room. Of medium height, medium build, with brown hair and a pleasant ordinary looking face, he made an inconspicuous figure beside his two tall companions.

The Marshal gave a stiff bow. 'And does everyone from Old Earth share this strange ability, Lord Kevin? Could you do as well?'

'I'm not sure if I'd want to,' said Kevin calmly.

The Marshal gave him a puzzled stare. 'Not care to?'

'You were attacking a planet, I gather? I should want to know what planet, and why, what was to be gained from the attack, and if there wasn't some other way of solving the problem, other than resorting to violence.'

'It is clear to see that you would never make a soldier,' said the Marshal stiffly. With a brief nod of farewell, he stalked from the room.

'Now you've upset the old boy,' said Jan.

'You're the one who did that. You shouldn't win when you're supposed to lose, it confuses the military mind.'

'Well, it's only a game,' said Jan cheerfully. 'Maybe all that time I spent playing Space Invaders has finally paid off.'

'You're not signing up full-time then?' teased Kevin. 'I mean, since the uniform suits you so well.'

'I don't think the Marshal would have me now,' said Jan ruefully. 'Anyway, it was just a way of passing the time until –' He broke off.

'Until we learn whether we'll ever be able to go home again,' said Kevin. 'Yes, I know. Shall we go and get Anna in Communications? She should be through by now.'

Jan, Kevin and Anna were cousins, and their home was the planet Earth. A chance encounter with a flying saucer had led to their being kidnapped from Earth and, after a variety of dangerous adventures, they had finished up as honoured guests on Centre. They had learned during their adventures that the civilisation of the Earth they knew was not the first but the second in the history of the planet.

Millions of years ago the First Empire of Man had spread throughout the Galaxy, and most of the planets in the League were of human stock, descendants of that long-vanished First Empire. Their hosts on Centre were quite willing to return the three young people to Earth, but there was one enormous snag. The Temporal Distortion Effect involved in crossing the Galaxy meant that, if they returned now, it would be to the Earth of a hundred years later – an Earth that might well be even stranger to them than Centre. League scientists were working on the problem, and meanwhile the three cousins waited – and waited.

There had been an initial attempt to send them on a kind of Galactic Grand Tour, but that had been cut short by an encounter with an asteroid packed with killer robots, and somehow the idea had never been revived.

179

Their status as permanent honoured guests was beginning to be an embarrassment to everybody. Elvar, Lord High President of the Council of the League, an imposing old man with the general appearance of an Old Testament prophet, had suggested they might care to investigate some of the many interesting careers open to them on Centre. As well as being the capital planet of the League, Centre was also a kind of training school to which intelligent young life forms from all over the Galaxy came to study and eventually to pass out into some branch of the League Service.

Always the man of action, Jan had gravitated naturally to the military side of things, where he was showing an erratic and unorthodox talent that astonished his teachers.

Anna was investigating the possibility of becoming a Communicator, one of the network of telepaths who handled top-level communications within the League. Telepathic transmission had the advantage of being instantaneous over any distance, and virtually undetectable. Unfortunately true telepaths were rare even in the multiplicity of human and non-human races within the League. From all accounts Anna, too, was doing surprisingly well.

'What about you, Kev?' asked Jan. 'What are you going to do?'

Only Kevin had so far failed to find any kind of niche. He certainly didn't fancy the military life, and somehow he was convinced he'd never make a telepath.

Aware that Jan was staring at him, waiting for an answer Kevin said, 'It's not that I'm not interested in anything – I'm interested in *everything*. Exploration, research, art, communications, weather control, planetary ecology – you name it. They seem to study everything here, and it's all fascinating.'

'Where's the problem, then? Just pick the one you like best.'

'But any one I pick means cutting out all the others, and I just can't bear to do it!'

Jan shook his head. 'Jack of all trades, master of none,' he said solemnly. 'There's such a huge spread of knowledge here that you've just got to specialise. No one could hope to take it all in.'

'Yes, I know but –' Kevin shook his head. 'Sometimes I feel there ought to be a new science, a science of all the other sciences put together. Otherwise everyone's working in separate boxes, no one's got the whole picture.'

Jan shrugged. 'Oh, I expect someone has somewhere. Let's go and find Anna.'

They walked out of the Simulator Control Room, along a short

180

corridor, and emerged into what looked like an immense park. In fact the whole of Centre was like a park, with rolling green lawns, softly rounded hills, huge gardens of exotic flowers, great sparkling lakes, and cool shady forests. The skies were always blue, the sun always shone, except for the strictly controlled rain-showers just before dawn and just after dusk.

Here and there low white pavilions blended discreetly with the green landscape. Most of them were the entrances to vast underground complexes. There was an immense amount of activity on Centre, but it was kept out of sight.

The two cousins strolled towards the distant pavilion that housed Communications.

Anna sat at a console in darkness, her eyes and ears enclosed by a kind of soft helmet that cut out all light and all sound. Beneath her fingers she could feel a simple keyboard. Her fingers moved swiftly across it, transcribing the information that was flooding into her brain. The data flow ceased and she pulled off the helmet, rubbing her forehead and tossing back her dark hair. 'How did I do?'

There was a tall grey-haired woman sitting on a nearby couch. Like Anna, she wore robes of bluish grey. The couch was blue-grey, too, as was the soft fabric that lined the room.

The woman checked the computer terminal in front of her. 'The transmission was 87 per cent correct.'

'But that's ridiculous. I didn't even understand most of it. Something about a space fleet and a lot of numbered co-ordinates.'

'It was a report of space fleet manoeuvres on the rim of the Galaxy,' said the woman severely. 'It is not necessary that you should understand, only receive and transmit. That message came from one of our agents on the other side of the planet, passing directly from his mind to yours. With practice, you could learn to receive and transmit between planets.'

'Maybe I could. But who wants to be a kind of human telephone?'

Kyra went on as if Anna had not spoken. 'The channels of your mind seem to be exceptionally clear. You have had some kind of telepathic training already?'

'Not unless you count the way I learned Pan-galactic. Garm sort of shoved it into my head all at one go. I thought my brain would burst.'

'Garm is one of the People,' said the Kyra reverently. 'You are most fortunate to have been associated with him.' She sighed. 'A whole world of natural telepaths – while we comb every planet in the

181

League to find the one in a hundred thousand with some glimmer of real ability.'

'Why don't you just recruit Garm's people to do your communicating?'

'Most of them refuse to leave their planet. Garm is one of the rare exceptions. And it is only the young ones who come. The Masters, the true adepts, refuse to have any dealings with us.'

'And who can blame them?' said a cracked old voice querulously. 'They're a boring lot on the whole, telepaths. As the young lady says, human telephones. Nothing to say for themselves – not by the time you've finished with 'em, anyway.'

An extraordinary figure was standing in the doorway. He wore a tattered robe made of some kind of sacking, and carried a polished wooden staff.

His thin brown arms and legs were bare, his head was completely bald, and he had a face very much like a wrinkled old walnut, with a snub nose and small pointed ears. He looked like a very old and very bad-tempered elf. 'How is she doing then, Kyra?'

To Anna's surprise, Kyra addressed the old man with considerable respect. 'The ability is there, Lord Zeno, no question of that. However, I'm afraid that her temperament…'

'Too independent for you, is she?' The old man cackled. 'Let's try an experiment.' He produced a golden circlet from his robes and handed it casually to Anna. 'Here, child, put this on.'

Anna stared at the Circlet in astonishment. It was made of gold, and one enormous red stone blazed at its centre.

'But that's the Stone. The Stone of Power!'

Kyra bowed her head in reverence.

'That's right,' said Zeno impatiently. 'The Stone that you and your friends brought to Centre. Put it on.'

'But it's dangerous. The first person I saw wear it went mad and died. Jan wore it for a while and it – changed him. He said he'd never wear it again.'

'The Stone amplifies what is already there,' said Zeno quietly. 'It is evil to the evil, strength to the strong. Let us see what it is to you.'

Anna hesitated, and Zeno said, 'You can trust me child. Put it on.'

Anna put the Circlet on her head, and instantly the Stone blazed into glowing red life. She stood motionless, staring at Kyra.

'What do you see?' asked Zeno softly.

Anna's eyes were wide with horror. 'I see… death.'

4. Alarm on Centre

'Death?' said Zeno sharply. 'Whose death? Speak child!'

Anna's voice was low and filled with horror. 'I see fire… a whole town burning. I see people fleeing from the flames… black-clad soldiers firing on them. I see a man and two children… the man tries to shield them with his body, but all three are shot down.' She was still staring at Kyra. 'I see grief and desolation and emptiness – a void filled only with work and duty.'

Kyra said bleakly. 'My husband and children were killed when the Kaldor invaded my homeworld. My heart died with them.' Her eyes filled with tears, and she ran from the room.

Anna snatched the Circlet from her head. 'I'm sorry, I didn't mean to intrude. It's just what came to me,' she called. But Kyra was gone.

Zeno said, 'Forgive me, I did not mean to cause either of you pain. You seem to possess the rarest skill of all. You're not a telepath but an empath.'

'What does that mean?'

'One who can feel as others feel. It is the most valuable of all abilities. In time, and with proper training, you could look at a man and see what he is.'

'Read his thoughts, you mean?'

'More than that, much more. You could read his nature – his essence, if you will. Thoughts can be guarded, shielded. There are mechanical devices, simple mental disciplines. But the whole nature – that cannot be hidden. You could read a man's hopes, his ambitions, his fears.'

'No thanks.'

'You do not wish to develop this power?'

'Do you realise the feelings that poor woman was carrying inside her? The pain and the suffering, the years of desolation? Well, *I felt* that, all of it. And I don't want to feel it again.'

'You did not cause her grief – and by sharing it, you may have lightened the burden a little.'

Anna handed back the Circlet. 'No!' she said again.

Zeno tucked the Circlet beneath his robes. 'As you wish – though in fact I doubt if you have a choice.'

'What do you mean?'

'Now that you know the ability is there, you will use it whether you wish to or not. Such is the nature of the mind.'

'Who are you?' asked Anna bluntly.

Before the old man could answer, Jan and Kevin came into the room.

'Ah, there you are,' said Zeno, just as if he'd been expecting them. 'Now I can save these old legs and deliver my message to all three at once.'

Jan and Kevin looked curiously at the old man. Both had seen him before, drifting about Centre in his shabby robe, watching the scientists and teachers and administrators at their work, and then wandering on. He seemed to be allowed absolutely everywhere.

Kevin remembered seeing him going into a meeting of the High Council, his shabby figure incongruous amongst the Councillors in their ornate ceremonial robes.

'You have a message for us, sir?'

'Have I not just said so?' snapped the old man. 'Is there some defect in your understanding that everything must be said twice?'

Kevin wasn't easily intimidated. 'Your pardon, Lord Zeno. Let me rephrase my question. What is the message that you have for us?'

'Come on, grandpa, cough it up,' said Jan impatiently.

Zeno was outraged. 'Grandpa! Cough it up! Is their no longer any respect for the old on Centre?'

But there was a gleam of amusement in his eyes, and Anna sensed he wasn't really angry at all.

'Forgive them,' she said. 'Their manners leave much to be desired. If someone like you brings a message, it must be very important. Please tell us what it is.'

'Certainly, my child. Though it saddens me that the message is not a happy one. It is never pleasant to be the bearer of bad news.'

'Why? What's happened?'

'Your three friends, Garm, Tell and Osar – you were expecting a visit from them?'

'That's right,' said Jan. 'Have they been delayed?'

'Worse than that, I fear. They have disappeared.'

'Disappeared? How? What's happened to them?'

'Compose yourself, young man, and I will tell you.'

But Jan had run out of patience. He strode across the room and grabbed the old man by his robes as if trying to shake the information out of him.

Something quite extraordinary happened.

Jan was exceptionally big and strong for his age, and a natural athlete. He should have been able to lift the frail old man like a child. But he couldn't. In fact he couldn't move him at all. As Jan himself said afterwards, it was like trying to shake the Statue of Liberty. The old man simply stood there, totally resistant to all Jan's efforts. Then he brushed Jan aside with a careless gesture of one skinny arm – a gesture that sent Jan hurtling across the room to crash backwards on to the couch, where he sat gasping as if the roof had fallen on his head.

The old man went on speaking as if nothing had happened. 'It appears that your three friends were on a routine patrol…' He told them of the message from Garm saying that he intended a brief visit to his homeworld.

'What happened then?' asked Anna.

'Nothing. Nothing at all.'

'What do you mean nothing?'

'Simply that. Garm's scout ship did not return from the patrol. A series of sub-space messages from Centre brought no reply.'

Jan had recovered from the shock of being tossed aside like an abandoned toy, and was on his feet again. 'Okay, so they're missing. What are the High Council doing about it?'

'Discussing the whole matter at great length, as is their habit.'

'Talking won't get Garm and the others back. They've got to *do* something.'

'Perhaps so,' agreed Zeno. 'The question is – what?'

'Surely they'll send an expedition to find them?'

'The question was being debated when I left the Council Chamber.'

'What debate?' demanded Jan angrily. 'They should be on their way by now.'

'Alas, it is not so simple. We do not know what has happened to your friends. Perhaps it is no more than a simple failure of their communications equipment. Perhaps they are remaining deliberately silent because of some plan of their own. In that case the arrival of a League expedition might blunder into a delicate situation, doing more harm than good. That was the view of one group of Councillors.'

'Surely they don't all think like that?' asked Anna.

'Oh no. Others say that perhaps the missing scout ship ran into some great and unknown danger. In which case, they point out, the rescue ship might run into that same danger, and thus two ships would be lost instead of one. Still others point out that members of the Special Scout Service have always been considered expendable. And the resources of the League are stretched very thin, with thousands of worlds to cover.'

'Marvellous,' said Jan bitterly. 'So they're all going to find different reasons for doing nothing.'

'It is usually their preferred course. Often the wisest, too.'

'But you don't think so?' asked Kevin. 'Not in this case, at least.'

'And what makes you say that? Who am I to disagree with the noble Elvar and the rest of his illustrious colleagues?'

'I'm not sure who you are,' said Kevin frankly. 'But you *do* disagree. Otherwise you wouldn't be here telling us.'

'If the Council won't rescue them, we'll have to do the job ourselves,' said Jan.

'Oh, come on now,' protested Anna. 'We can't just jump into a space ship and go zooming after them.'

To her astonishment, Kevin said, 'Oh yes we can.'

Even the usually headstrong Jan was surprised, particularly as Kevin was notoriously the most cautious of them all. 'Are you crazy, Kev? To start with we haven't *got* a space ship. If we did, we wouldn't know how to fly it. And we don't even know where Garm's planet is.'

'Anyway,' said Anna, 'Elvar and the others would never give us permission.'

'Who's going to ask him?' said Kevin cheerfully. 'If you think the answer's going to be no, it's always better not to ask the question.'

'All right,' snapped Jan, 'Say we do bypass Elvar. How do we deal with all the other problems – the ship, a pilot, weapons and equipment, the co-ordinates of Garm's planet?'

'There must be scout ships standing in the launch bays right now. What we need is a ship that's been in dock for repairs and maintenance, and hasn't yet been handed over to a new crew. Special Service scout ships are kept fully equipped at all times. There'd be fuel, food, weapons, everything we need. The co-ordinates for Garm's planet could be fed into the ship's navigational computer, and we could all be given a hypno crash-course in ship-handling before we leave. Those ships are so automated that the ship's computer could probably handle everything from take-off to landing anyway.'

Jan shook his head in astonishment. 'You make it all sound too easy.'

'I never said it would be easy, but it is possible – provided we have help.'

'What kind of help?'

'We need someone who agrees with us that Garm and the others have got to be rescued. Someone with power and influence, who could open doors for us, see that we get what we need.' Kevin turned to Zeno. 'In other words – you!'

'Me? I am no more than a humble scholar, tolerated because of his insignificance.'

'A humble scholar who knows everything that's going on – who can wander in and out of meetings of the High Council whenever it suits him.'

Anna joined in. 'A humble scholar who is treated with something like reverence by the Lady Kyra, one of the most important officials on Centre – *and who's allowed to carry about with him the most important object on Centre, as though it was a toy.*' She turned to Kevin and Jan. 'He's got the Stone of Power with him. He casually produced it a few minutes ago.'

'This?' The old man took the jewelled Circlet from beneath his robes. 'I was asked to do some research into its properties. I brought it here in a moment of absent-mindedness.' He tucked it away again.

'I think Kevin's right,' said Anna. 'I think you're someone so important, you don't even have to bother about looking important. Please help us if you can.'

'Why should he?' demanded Jan. 'What's in it for him?'

Kevin turned to the old man. 'I think it would help us all, sir, if you would tell us a little more about yourself.'

'My name is Zeno,' said the old man quietly. 'Sometimes I am called the Watcher. You see, there is so much to do on Centre, so much business – everyone concerned with his own specific problem, his own responsibilities.'

'And you?' asked Kevin.

'I am responsible for nothing, and therefore for everything. I wander, I watch, I listen. I try to remain alert to the stirrings of the Web.'

'Garm used to talk about the Web,' said Anna. 'Something about a network of energy that binds all living things.'

'That is so,' said Zeno. 'Recently I have had a sense of unease, a feeling of dark forces gathering.'

Kevin said, 'And you think there may be some connection between this feeling of yours and the disappearance of Garm?'

Zeno nodded. 'Yet it is no more than a foreboding. Nothing upon which I could ask the Council to act.'

'You're asking us to act?' said Jan. 'Asking us to risk our lives to back up your hunch?'

'I am only doing what I can,' said Zeno wearily. 'What I must.'

'Using the tools at hand?' suggested Kevin. 'Even though they may get broken in the process.'

'Sometimes that is all that one can do.' The old man seemed to rally himself. 'Now, I understand that you wished to go after your missing friends. If that is still the case, then perhaps I can help you. Well?'

'I don't see that we have any choice,' said Kevin. 'Whether it's for our purposes or yours – we've got to go.'

* * *

187

An unbelievably short time afterwards, they were blasting off from the space docks at Centre.

Events had moved with extraordinary speed. First Zeno had marched them to a nearby learning chamber where they had stretched out on low couches, wearing headsets linked to a computer terminal. Some ten minutes later all three were sitting up, complaining of blinding headaches. Zeno had touched each one on the temple in turn, and the headache had disappeared. He assured them they now knew the basics of scout ship handling. When Jan said he didn't think he'd learned anything, Zeno snapped. 'Don't think about it. Just do it.'

He'd taken them to a commissary, where they'd been equipped with survival suits – tough, heavy-duty, space coveralls, designed for wear on dangerous alien planets. A wide belt went with the space coveralls, holding pouches that contained a variety of tools and weapons, as well as emergency rations and medical supplies.

Only at the space dock itself had they encountered any difficulty.

Politely but firmly, a burly guard commander had refused to turn a scout ship over to them without papers signed by Lord Elvar, President of the High Council.

For a moment it seemed as if all was lost, but then Zeno shuffled to the front of the group, staring up intently at the guard commander. 'A very proper reaction, commander,' he said soothingly. 'I shall see that Lord Elvar is informed of your strict attention to duty. Here are the papers. As you can see, they are all in order.'

To their astonishment, Zeno stretched out an empty hand. To their even greater astonishment, the guard commander took the non-existent papers, studied his own empty hand thoroughly, handed back the nothing he had been given, and saluted. 'Everything is in order, Lord Zeno. If you will follow me, I will conduct you to your ship.'

He had taken them to a gleaming dart-shaped scout ship, standing at the edge of the space docks. '*Starburst II*,' said the commander proudly. 'Straight out of the repair docks. Damaged in a meteor storm, reconditioned, better than new. Fully fuelled and provisioned. I wish you a safe trip.' He saluted again, and marched away.

Zeno led them up the ramp and into the control room, where he bent over the computer console, hands flickering over the keyboard.

At last he straightened up. 'There you are – you are programmed for Garm's world. You'll make the jump into hyper-space immediately after take-off.'

'That's all very well,' grumbled Jan. 'What do we do when we get there?'

188

Zeno's eyes twinkled. 'The best you can,' he advised solemnly. 'Now I must say farewell.'

'You're not coming with us?' asked Anna.

'I must watch events on Centre. Besides, someone must soothe Elvar's ruffled feathers when he learns you've gone. But I have a gift for you.' He produced the Stone of Power from beneath his robe and handed it to Anna. 'Take it. I have a feeling it may be of use to you.'

'Another hunch?' said Anna. Reluctantly she took the jewelled Circlet.

Zeno paused in the doorway of the control room. 'Infinite is the Web,' he said softly.

Automatically Anna made the ritual answer. 'May its power protect.'

And Zeno was gone. On the ship's monitor screen they saw him stroll down the ramp and drift inconspicuously through the busy clamour of the space yards.

Jan looked uneasily at the Circlet in Anna's hands. 'I'd be careful of that thing – it's dangerous.'

'Don't worry, I'm not going to wear it – not unless I have to!'

The Circlet was too big to go into a belt-pouch and too important to leave around. After a moment Anna pulled the soft metal of the Circlet, widening it into a horse-shoe shape, slipped it round her neck like a kind of collar, and forced the circle closed again, so that it rested around her neck like a kind of necklace, tucking it out of sight beneath the collar of her space coveralls.

'Right,' said Jan. 'Let's get moving.' He slipped into the pilot's chair.

Anna and Kevin took the two chairs on either side of him, one for the navigator, the other for the first officer. 'Prepare for blast-off ',' said Jan briskly. None of them knew what to do, but somehow they found themselves doing it anyway, their hands moving automatically over the controls.

The little scout ship streaked away from Centre and into the blackness of space.

5. THE INVADERS

Two loincloth-clad figures, one large, one small, were moving cautiously along an overgrown jungle trail.

Garm, thoroughly at ease in the normal dress of his people, swung easily and confidently along the trail. Tell, who had exchanged his familiar space coveralls for a skin borrowed from a grinning child, felt utterly ridiculous. Luckily he was naturally tough-skinned, like all his people, but that didn't stop him muttering and cursing whenever vines lashed his skin, or he stubbed his toe on a hidden rock.

But what was really bothering him was the strange obstinacy of Garm's people, who were refusing to take the slightest notice of the fact that their planet had been invaded by the Kaldor.

'Why?' he demanded, as he stumped moodily along. 'Why will they not listen? Why do they not understand?'

Garm shrugged massive shoulders. 'They listened, and they understood.'

'Then why do they not react?'

'They reacted also – but not as we do.'

'That is most certainly true. I have heard of many reactions to the Kaldor, but this must be the first time they have been ignored.'

After hiding their scout ship, together with the grumbling Osar, under a light screen of rocks, Garm and Tell had gone to warn the Elders of the Kaldor invasion.

The Elders had received the news that a Fleet of hostile ships had landed on their planet with utter lack of interest. Nargo, who looked rather like a grizzled grey-haired version of Garm himself, had spoken for all. 'From time to time, space ships land on our planet. Eventually they go away again.'

'But these are Kaldor,' protested Garm. 'They come in force – and they come for a purpose.'

'Then in time we shall no doubt learn what it is. Meanwhile what would you have us do?'

'Hide!' said Tell explosively. 'Take your people into the jungles and hide. Warn the other tribes, combine your forces for attack. Make weapons – bows and clubs and spears – dig pits and traps in the jungle. Even without energy-weapons, you can still make a stand against them. With luck and cunning, you can pick them off one by one. If the Kaldor lose this expedition, they may not think it worthwhile to send another.'

191

Nargo listened to this warlike speech with astonishment. 'Why should we do any of these things? We did not do them when you came.'

'But I am not Kaldor,' howled Tell. 'There is a difference, as you will very soon learn. The Kaldor care only for war and conquest, and they view all races other than their own as slaves or beasts.'

'Kaldor or not, you are a stranger to our world. So too is Garm, though he was once one of us. Your ship landed here uninvited. After a fitting time, you will leave, and so too will the Kaldor. Then we shall go on with our lives as we have before.'

'Nothing will be as it was before – not after the Kaldor,' said Tell bitterly.

'My friend speaks truth,' said Garm. 'At least go into the jungle out of harm's way. Once you are safe, we can send a message to the League asking for help.'

'But we are not of the League,' said Nargo patiently. 'Whatever the dispute between League and Kaldor, we want no part of it.'

And that had been that.

Somewhat at a loss, Garm and Tell had decided to investigate the Kaldor's encampment, learn what they could of their purposes, and then blast off for Centre, trusting that a quick getaway and some skilful manoeuvring would put them out of the range of Kaldor space cannon.

Osar had pinpointed the enemy landing place on the ship's scanners, and they were making their way to it now. As it happened, they scarcely needed Osar's directions. Before very long, a plume of thick black smoke rose out of the jungle ahead of them. 'They don't change, do they?' said Tell. One of the things he hated most about the Kaldor was their indifference to all growing things.

Just ahead of them the trail rounded the base of a low rocky hill. On the far side of the hill was the Kaldor encampment. It was set in a huge circle, a man-made clearing blasted out of the jungle by the Kaldor heat ray. A black circle had been burned out of the jungle and the air was heavy with the stink of charred vegetation.

Three ships were spaced at intervals around the edge of the clearing, forming a triangle within the circle. Black-clad, blond-haired figures moved between the ships, setting up a variety of complex equipment.

'We are just in time,' said Tell. 'They're setting up sensors and a perimeter defence shield. Before long, nothing will be able to approach undetected, or cross the barrier alive.'

They watched the busy scene for a moment, and then Garm said, 'We learn little here.'

'True,' agreed Tell. 'Only that the Kaldor have landed – which we knew already.'

'We must discover their purposes,' said Garm thoughtfully. 'The information is needed on Centre.'

'And how shall we do that?' asked Tell sarcastically. 'Just stroll down and ask them?'

'Why not?' said Garm. He slipped off his wrist communicator, hid it under a rock and set off down the hill towards the Kaldor ships.

Tell ran to catch up with him. 'Are you as mad as the rest of your folk?'

Garm continued on his way. 'We are two simple savages, come to gaze in awe and wonder at the Great Ones who come from the sky in their fiery chariots.'

'Not all that "Oh Mighty Ones, surely you must be Gods" stuff?' groaned Tell.

'Why not? It's as good a story as any. Just try to look humble – and stupid.'

Tell gave a horrible leer and rolled his eyes. 'Like this?'

'That will do very nicely.'

They strode down the hill towards the camp. Soon they were close enough for one of the black-clad figures to notice them.

'Halt,' he called, and drew a blaster.

Taking a calculated risk, Garm went on walking.

A purple blaster bolt sizzled across the path ahead of him. Garm gave a scream of fear and threw himself to the ground. Tell gave him a disgusted look, and did the same.

The Kaldor guard marched arrogantly towards them, and prodded Garm in the side with his boot. 'Get up, you're not hurt.'

'How simple,' thought Tell, 'how delightfully simple it would be.' While the guard was bending over Garm, he himself could leap up and break the Kaldor's neck with one swift blow... take his blaster, turn it on the next guard, kill and disarm him... by which time more Kaldor would come charging out of the ships and kill them both.

Abandoning his fantasy of attack, Tell followed Garm's example and scrambled fearfully to his feet.

The guard covered them with his blaster. 'You will come with me.'

They were marched across the charred clearing and up a ramp into the nearest of the three ships, presumably the main command vessel.

In the big central control room, the Kaldor Commander, black-uniformed and fair-haired like all the others, surveyed them with distaste. 'You are natives of this planet?'

Garm nodded dumbly.

The Commander jabbed a finger towards Tell.

'Why is this one so small?'

'A rock fell on his head when he was young. His body did not grow – nor did his brain.'

'You should have killed him,' said the aide. 'The unfit pollute the purity of the race. Shall I attend to it now, sir?'

He drew his blaster. Tell stood poised, prepared to duck aside and leap for the Kaldor's throat. With luck he could take one of them with him.

'Wait,' said the Commander. 'Later perhaps.'

The aide put away his blaster, and Tell relaxed.

'Forgive me, Great Ones,' babbled Garm. 'It is not our custom…'

'Your customs will be changed,' said the Commander coldly.

So, thought Garm, the Kaldor were here to stay. They intended conquest, occupation. This one piece of information was worth the risk of their visit – provided they could get away with it alive.

'Listen, both of you,' said the Commander. 'I am Commander Sadek, and this is Captain Zarn. We are Kaldor. We have come from the stars to rule over you. We shall be your Gods. Obey without question, work hard, and you will live and prosper. Resist, and you will be destroyed. Do you understand me?'

Garm and Tell stared dumbly at him.

'Are these truly the ones we seek?' said Zarn. 'A savage and a dwarf!'

Tell responded to the compliment with another of his horrible leers.

'Even a savage may stumble upon a treasure and enjoy it for a time, until someone stronger takes it away.'

More information, thought Garm. The Kaldor were after something specific on his world, something they thought of as a treasure.

But what could it be? As far as Garm knew the planet held no precious metals, no rare elements…

Though, of course, because of the deliberate lack of technological progress, it had never been properly surveyed. If the Kaldor's scanning instruments had detected something, that might explain everything.

Sadek jabbed a finger at Tell. 'The stunted one. Can he understand? Can he speak? If not he is useless to us.'

Hurriedly Tell decided to become more articulate. 'I can speak, Great One. I understand. What is your will?'

6. THE RESCUERS

Jan adjusted controls, and brought the picture on the scanner into clearer focus. 'Well, there it is. Garm's world.'

They looked at the bluey-green planet below them – seas, mountains, oceans and deserts, reduced to patterns on its surface.

'I'll move into scanning orbit, Kevin, you'd better check for energy sources.'

His hands moved over the controls – as always, they seemed to know what was needed by themselves – and soon the picture on the screen changed to a closer view, so that they could see the dense green roof of the jungle below them. On a screen in front of Kevin, the same view was expressed as a pattern of swirling energy patterns divided by a grid.

'Life-form readings are way up,' said Kevin.

'What about power sources?'

'Nothing yet – now wait a minute.' Kevin leaned forward. 'Got it!' A blip began pulsating on the screen. He zoomed in closer, and the blip separated into three smaller ones. 'Looks like three space ships – there, just on the edge of the jungle.'

Anna punched controls and yet another screen flashed up a relief map of the area. 'According to the map, the ships have landed not too far from Garm's village.'

'Which do I make for?' asked Jan. 'The village or the space ships?'

Kevin said, 'Why don't you compromise and put us down somewhere between the two.'

'Okay. What's the terrain like down there, Anna?'

Anna brought her map into greater magnification. 'Bit of a mixture, actually. Reading east to west, there's a range of mountains, then a rocky plain, then Garm's village, then the jungle, then the three space ships.' She peered at the map. 'There seems to be some kind of quarry roughly between the village and the ships.' She pointed, and Jan leaned over to look.

The quarry was about halfway between the settlement and the ships, and some way to the south of both of them. Anna used a light-pencil to draw lines from village to ships, ships to quarry, quarry to village, forming a rough equilateral triangle.

'Okay,' said Jan, 'Quarry it is.'

'You'll have to take her down on manual,' Anna pointed out. 'And it's a very small quarry. Think you can manage it?'

Jan looked at his big, capable hands. 'I can't, but these can... I hope!'

'We'd better not hang about up here too long,' said Kevin. 'Those ships will have scanning devices, too – and they'll probably have missiles as well.'

'We don't *know* they're hostile,' said Anna.

'We don't know they're not, either. Best take no chances. The logical assumption is that those ships are the reason Garm didn't make it back.'

Jan's hand went out and flipped a switch. 'This'll confuse 'em.'

'What is it?' asked Anna.

'Shielding device. Puts out a kind of electronic static, it'll louse up their space radar.' Jan flexed his hands and leaned forward. 'Prepare for landing orbit, everyone. We're going down.'

Zarn cursed as the picture on his radar broke up in a swirling pattern of static. 'They are using a shielding device. I've lost them.'

'No matter,' said Sadek. 'They will not land far away. Since they have almost certainly come in search of us, they are scarcely likely to set down on the far side of the planet. Check the scanners again shortly, and if that fails send out patrols.'

Sadek turned back to Garm, who stood silent and obedient before him. 'We will begin the interrogation.'

He touched a control and a panel slid back in the control-room wall revealing a kind of cubicle. In the rear wall of the cubicle were clamps, set in such a way as to secure the arms and legs of a captive humanoid. Garm allowed himself to be led unresisting into the metal cubicle, and submitted to having his limbs locked into the clamps. At first the guards had some difficulty because of his great size, but the clamps were adjustable and they managed to get him fastened at last.

Sadek nodded to a technician at a nearby console. The man touched a control, and a domed helmet on the end of a flexible metal arm slid out of the wall.

The helmet was made of some transparent plastic material, and the upper part of it was crammed with electronic circuitry. Supervised by the technician, the guards fitted the helmet over Garm's head. The technician returned to his console and stood waiting.

'Listen carefully, savage,' said Sadek. 'The device to which you are attached is a truth machine. I shall ask you questions, and you will be well advised to tell me the truth. If you lie, the machine will know, and it will do this.'

Garm's body arched in agony, as pain flooded through every cell in his body. He gave a involuntary groan, and then deliberately turned it into a bellow of fear.

Sadek smiled in satisfaction. 'Very well. Let me begin. What is your name?'

'I am called Garm.'

'You are a native of this planet?'

'I was born here.'

So far, so good, thought Garm. Wherever possible, he would tell the truth. Even if he had to lie, he was reasonably confident of his ability to cheat the machine. Much as he loathed such devices, he had a pretty good idea how they worked. The machine measured changes in the body – heartbeat, adrenalin flow, blood pressure, static electricity in the skin, and so on – and reacted to all the minute variations produced by the stress of deliberate lying in a frightened prisoner. Thanks to the heritage of his people, and to certain training he had received on Centre, Garm had the ability to lie if necessary and yet control his body reactions so the falsehood would be undetected. Or so he hoped.

If all else failed, he could produce a kind of self-induced faint that would cause the Kaldor to think he had collapsed through pain and terror.

Garm's main advantage was the fact that the Kaldor believed they were dealing with a savage from the stone age, whereas in fact Garm was of a standard of intelligence and education far higher than their own. His main disadvantage was the fact that if he allowed it to show, they would kill him.

The questions went on.

What was the name of his tribe? How many were they? How did they live? What kinds of weapons did they have? All Garm's answers were fairly close to the truth, painting the picture of a tribe of stone-age savages, who spent their lives hunting and fishing.

It was clear from the questions that the Kaldor knew that League space ships had visited the planet in the past, and that certain members of the tribe had left for training on Centre. Garm managed to convey the impression that such events were extremely rare, and that the arrival of space ships was regarded as an extraordinary visitation from the Gods.

The truth was that his people had a perfectly clear picture of the size and complexity of the Galaxy, and of the number of inhabited worlds, and, come to that, of the principles of space flight. They just weren't interested in any world other than their own. Garm's main purpose in submitting to questioning was to get some answers himself. Why had the Kaldor sent this expedition? What were they after?

But as the questions went on and on, Garm found himself none the wiser. Sadek seemed to want to know everything about the planet, the People, the beasts, the plants, the seas and other continents... Finally the questions began to concentrate around one area – the Sacred Mountains on the far side of the Plain of Rocks, and on one peak in particular, known as Mount Doom.

'*Why* are the mountains so important to your people?' demanded Sadek.

'I do not know,' said Garm honestly. 'They have always been sacred. Only the Elders visit them, and they go rarely.'

'And Mount Doom?'

'There are hard stones on their slopes, stones that make fine spearheads and axes. The Elders bring them back with them after their pilgrimages, and share them out amongst the hunters.'

'Well?'

Garm struggled to remember the legends of his childhood. 'Sometimes eager hunters have refused to be content with the stones given by the Elders. They have journeyed to the mountain to collect their own.'

'And what happened to them?'

'Most did not return.'

'And those that did?'

'Their minds were gone. It is said they became like babies and had to be fed and cared for until they died.'

Sadek picked up Garm's hunting axe, which had been taken from him when he was captured. It had a wooden handle, notched to take the axe-head, which was bound in place with leather thongs. Such axes were common amongst Garm's people. Handle and head were selected and fitted with the greatest care. Once fitted, they were soaked in the stream for many days and nights. The wood expanded, the leather throngs shrunk, and the axe-head was bound irremovably in place.

This particular axe had been given to Garm by his father. Since he had little use for a hunting axe on Centre, he had left it in the care of one of the Elders, reclaiming it on his rare visits to his home planet.

Sadek hefted the axe in his hand. It was perfectly balanced for throwing – Garm, like most of his people, could bring down a running deer at an incredible distance – and the head was made of highly polished black rock. The edge was razor sharp. 'This axe-head – is it made of the stone of which you speak?'

Garm nodded.

Sadek passed the axe to Zarn, who had returned to his side. 'You see? Volcanic rock. Take it to the laboratory for analysis.'

Zarn nodded, and took the axe away.

Garm gave a cry of protest. 'Do not take the axe, Great One, it is all I have.'

Sadek silenced him with a sudden jolt of pain. 'Do not fear, we shall give you better weapons, weapons like ours. Your people will make fine soldiers – once you have learned the meaning of discipline.' He waved to a guard. 'Take him down. Put him in a cell and feed him. I shall have more questions later.'

The guards unfastened the clamps and dragged Garm away.

Tell looked in anguish at the little circle of Elders. They were sitting placidly outside their gallery of caves, while children played in the stream and women prepared the evening meal, just as though nothing had happened. 'I tell you the Kaldor are here in force, and they mean to stay. They have taken Garm prisoner. Does that not move you?'

'If Garm does not wish to stay with them, he will come away,' said Nargo placidly.

'But they mean to occupy your world, to change your customs.'

'That is not possible. When they come here, I shall explain it to them, and they will go away again.'

'You'll find yourself explaining to a Kaldor blaster,' shouted Tell. 'Do you think they intend to debate with you? They will give you orders, and if you do not obey them you'll die. They just won't listen to your reasons.'

'They will listen,' said Nargo confidently. 'If necessary, we will speak with a voice that they cannot fail to hear.'

So confident did the old man sound that for a moment Tell wondered if he might be justified. Did the People have some weapon, some hidden strength that would intimidate even the Kaldor? Angrily he shook his head to clear it. No, it was simply that the old fool didn't understand the ruthless brutality of the enemy.

Tell turned and stormed out of the settlement. He had delivered his warning. Now he would go and rescue Garm – somehow – and they would leave this lunatic world and go back to Centre. As far as he was concerned, the Kaldor were welcome to the place, monsters and all.

He was stumping moodily along the trail that led to the Kaldor ships, when he heard the roar of rocket motors and saw a space ship glide over the trees above his head and swoop down as if to a landing close by. Even a fleeting glimpse was enough to tell him that it was a League scout ship. Reinforcements, thought Tell joyously. A rescue expedition. He must warn them of the situation, before they ran straight into the Kaldor.

He set off at a run in the direction of the ship's descent.

The yellow blur in the centre of the jungle seemed to be rushing at the scanner screen at frightening speed. It blurred, steadied, and revealed itself as a semi-circular pit of sandstone. Jan's hands moved swiftly over the controls, the sound of the retro-rockets died away, and the little ship came to rest neatly in the centre of the pit. Jan sat back and rubbed his hands. 'Well, we made it – a hole in one!'

Kevin sat back and mopped his brow. 'If I'd realised how small the hole was...'

The quarry was really no more than a giant pit, dug out over the generations by Garm's people, who used the easily worked sandstone for a variety of carvings and ornaments.

Packs and laser-rifles were assembled by the exit hatch, and soon they were ready to leave the ship. Jan and Kevin both carried rifles, but Anna restricted herself to a small holstered blaster in her belt, and she was resolved not to use that unless she had no other choice.

They came down the exit ramp and looked around them. The little ship stood in the sandstone pit like a candle in a jam jar. Dense green jungle grew all around the edges of the pit and it seemed pretty certain that the ship was very well hidden, at least from ground level.

Jan nodded in satisfaction. 'It's as good as buried – the ground should cut off their scanners too, with any luck. It could be spotted from above, though. What this hole needs is a roof on it.'

'Listen,' said Anna, 'we're not settling down here, you know. We just want to find Garm and Tell and Osar, and get them out – and get ourselves out, too.'

'So let's start looking,' said Kevin practically. Settling his pack on his shoulders, he began to climb, scrambling up the rough track that led out of the pit.

He waited for the others at the top, where the track turned into a narrow but well-defined path through the jungle. 'Seems to lead where we want to go,' said Jan. 'Let's get moving.'

The track was so narrow that the jungle pressed in on them from either side and they could only march in single file.

Suddenly Jan said, 'Hold it. Something moving ahead. Coming straight for us.'

They stopped and listened. Sure enough, something was crashing through the dense undergrowth towards them.

'One each side of the path,' whispered Jan to Kevin. 'We'll get it in a crossfire.'

They waited, rifles poised, as the unknown creature rushed towards them.

7. The Hostages

Something small and brown shot out of the jungle ahead of them, Jan and Kevin aimed their rifles – but before they could fire, Anna jumped out on to the path. 'Stop!' she shouted. 'Can't you see? It's Tell!' She leaped on the little man and hugged him delightedly.

Jan and Kevin took one look at the skin-clad figure of their old friend and collapsed in helpless laughter. Disengaging himself from Anna's hug, Tell glared indignantly at them. 'This world is quite dangerous enough without the added menace of trigger-happy friends trying to blow one's head off! What did you think I was – a Terrorsaur?'

'Sorry, Tarzan,' said Kevin, and collapsed again.

Even Anna had to smile. 'It is a bit of a strange get-up, Tell. What are you up to?'

'I am attempting to pass as one of the inhabitants of this singularly unattractive planet. When I tell you that Garm is regarded here as being on the puny side, you will see my difficulty.'

'Where is Garm, anyway? And where's Osar? And why did you all just disappear here anyway?'

'I can answer that last question in one word – Kaldor!' He looked hopefully at their packs. 'I don't suppose you had the foresight to bring food and drink? They seem to live on fruits and nuts and dinosaur steaks here, and I missed my last meal.'

Anna took some iron rations from her pack, and Tell munched happily on a cube of food concentrate as he talked, telling them of the arrival of the Kaldor and all that had happened since.

While he washed the cubes down with a flask of cordial, they in turn told him of their somewhat unorthodox departure from Centre with the help of Zeno.

Tell took a final swig. 'Trust the old Watcher to sense something wrong. I'm afraid he's right, too. Those idiots on the Council won't move without some kind of solid proof.'

'Proof of what?' asked Kevin. 'What *are* the Kaldor up to?'

Tell shrugged. 'Who knows – except that, knowing them, it's bound to be something villainous. The trouble is, even if we did know, it's not certain we could get the League to act. This is a neutral planet, you see. Technically speaking, the Kaldor have just as much right here as we have – or just as little!'

'When did the Kaldor ever worry about rights?' said Jan. 'All we want to do is rescue Garm from that Kaldor ship and get you and us away from here. If Garm's people won't join the League or protect themselves, they must take the consequences.'

'I wonder if Garm will ever see it that way,' said Kevin thoughtfully. 'This is his world, you know, and I've an idea the old loyalties are pretty strong. He may refuse to leave until the whole thing's been sorted out.'

'Maybe whatever the Kaldor are up to endangers the League as well,' said Anna. 'Then they'll have to help Garm's people, whether they want to be helped or not.'

Jan as always was quick to become bored with discussion. 'Well, Garm ought to have found out something by now. So let's get on with rescuing him, shall we?'

Shouldering his pack, he picked up his rifle and set off down the narrow trail. Gathering their possessions, the others hurried after him.

Garm was beginning to think it was time he rescued himself. He had learned all he could from the Kaldor – or at least, as much as he was likely to learn without giving himself away. If he did slip up and reveal himself as an agent of the League, the Kaldor had methods of persuasion that even he might not be able to withstand. And that meant he would be putting Tell and Osar at risk.

As he finished the gruel and water that was all the Kaldor fed their prisoners, he pondered on the best method of getting free.

The problem was resolved when the door slid open and a burly guard appeared to check up on his prisoner and remove bowl, spoon, and plastic beaker after the meal – just in case they could be converted into weapons.

He seemed to have no fear of Garm, even though the giant wasn't bound in any way. Possibly he felt the poor savage was totally overawed by the magic of the Space Gods. Garm got slowly to his feet, towering over the guard. 'Tell me, Great One,' asked Garm humbly, 'how is it that the door of this metal hut opens and closes by itself?'

'It is the magic of the Space Gods,' said the guard impressively.

'Indeed?' said Garm politely. 'I thought it must be a simple photoelectric cell.'

The guard's eyes widened in astonishment, then closed again as Garm's massive fist took him on the side of the head. Catching the body with his other hand, Garm lowered it gently to the floor. He relieved the guard of his blaster and a number of devices from his belt, including the torchlike device that opened a way through the force field.

Slipping out of the cell, Garm padded silently along the corridors. He had an excellent sense of direction, and soon he was heading for the door that led to the way out.

There was a slight setback when two Kaldor guards marched through it, but Garm knocked their heads together and went out on to the ramp.

This was the tricky bit, he thought. Evidently they were still working on the force field – it looked as if they were trying to strengthen it – and the area inside the perimeter was filled with busy, black-uniformed Kaldor.

Crouching low, Garm looked round for a diversion, and found it in a number of plasti-drums of retro-rocket fuel, being transferred, for some mysterious reason, from one space ship to another.

A carefully aimed laser bolt from the blaster he had taken produced a most satisfactory explosion, and soon guards were running towards the blaze.

Garm sprinted down the ramp and across the encampment until he reached the nearest point of the barrier. A quick adjustment of the torchlike device produced an opening in the force field, and Garm shot through the tunnel and disappeared into the jungle.

Stretched out face down, at the very top of the low hill, Tell peered down into the Kaldor encampment. He turned and signalled to Jan, Kevin and Anna, who wriggled up beside him.

'They seem to have been having a bit of trouble.' He pointed to the still-smouldering remnants of a pile of half-melted plasti-drums, which were being sprayed with foam by a number of Kaldor guards. 'And look – there's something else going on.'

Kaldor troops were pouring out of all three ships, assembling in squads, and marching away through a number of already opened gaps in the perimeter force field.

'Sending out patrols,' said Jan. 'Something seems to have stirred them up!' He looked at the others. 'You know, I think we might be just too late.'

'What do you mean?' whispered Anna.

'He means Garm's already escaped,' said Kevin.

Jan nodded. 'Sabotage in the camp, general panic, patrols being sent out. Looks like an escaped prisoner to me. Still, I suppose we'd better check. Come on, Tell.' Leaving Kevin and Anna on top of the hill, Jan and Tell slithered down the hillside and vanished.

* * *

The last guard in the last patrol to leave the Kaldor camp was lagging a little behind his fellows. As the patrol rounded a bend in the trail ahead, he heard a voice behind him. 'Psst!'

He turned and saw a small figure in a loincloth standing on the trail. It beckoned him closer. 'Come quickly. I have a message for your Commander.'

Hesitantly the guard moved forward. 'You were here before – I saw you.' Before he could say anything else, an arm took him around the throat with choking force and he felt the nozzle of a blaster in his ribs. A voice growled in his ear. 'Don't move!'

The small savage came closer, staring up at the helpless guard. 'The one who was with me before. The big one. Where is he?'

'He escaped. Patrols have been sent out to recapture him.'

The voice in the guard's ear said, 'Thanks!' The grip on his neck relaxed and he swung round raising his blaster. Before he could use it something hard and knobbly struck him under the jaw.

Jan and Tell dragged the unconscious body of the guard into the undergrowth, and went back up the hill to the others.

Back at the top of the hill, they held a brief council of war. Since Garm had escaped, he was presumably heading for the settlement. So the only sensible thing to do was to go back there, meet up with Garm and Osar, and then, as Jan said, 'Get the hell off this planet before it's too late!'

Tell recovered the wrist communicator Garm had hidden earlier and they set off down the trail that led to the village.

Their journey was uneventful, though they could hear Kaldor patrols crashing through the jungle in the distance. Once or twice they left the trail and hid in dense undergrowth to let the patrols pass by.

When they reached the settlement, Anna was astonished and delighted by the calm, pastoral scene. The evening meal was over, fires had been lit outside the caves, and the People were sitting about talking in low voices, many of them working on the making of baskets, or pots or weapons, or the strangely intricate carvings in bone or soapstone.

From one of the caves came the cry of some small child, protesting at being put to bed, and the low soothing sound of a mother's lullaby.

Tell, on the other hand, found the whole scene intensely irritating, another example of the People's steadfast refusal to admit that they had any kind of crisis on their hands.

He led the three newcomers into the settlement, and introduced them to Nargo and the other Elders, who received them with their usual benign courtesy. 'Garm has not yet returned,' said Nargo placidly. 'But no doubt he will be here soon. Meanwhile, as his friends, you are welcome amongst us.'

They were given fruit, and home-made bread, and a spicy fruit drink with the tang of wine. Dusk was falling, and it was very pleasant to sit in the flickering firelight amidst the low murmur of voices.

Jan yawned and stretched. 'This is the life,' he said lazily.

Kevin nodded. 'Make a nice place for a holiday.'

Tell refused to relax. 'This is all wrong,' he muttered. 'These people have been invaded. They just refuse to recognise the fact.'

'Maybe that's the best way to deal with the invasion,' said Anna sleepily. 'Ignore it, and it'll just go away again.'

'Not the Kaldor,' said Tell obstinately. 'I'd better tell Osar what's going on.' He adjusted his wrist communicator to voice channel and switched it on. 'Osar? This is Tell. I'm back in the camp, but Garm's gone missing. Oh, yes, and Jan, Kevin and Anna have arrived.'

Faintly they heard Osar's piping voice. 'Indeed? Then I should advise you all to depart immediately. My scanners show Kaldor patrols converging on this spot.'

Jan leaped to his feet. 'Come on!' he called, but it was already too late. A spotlight picked out his tall figure, and an amplified voice called harshly. 'You are surrounded. Do not move!'

Jan grabbed for his laser-rifle and a blaster bolt scorched the ground at his feet. 'Do not move,' said the metallic voice. 'This is your final warning.' Jan froze.

Kevin and Tell were both inside the circle of the searchlight, but Anna was at its very edge. She reacted instinctively, rolling away to get out of the beam. Someone grasped her hand and she was pulled into the circle of women around a neighbouring fire.

They huddled round her protectively.

More searchlights came on, bathing the settlement in their harsh glare, and behind them the forms of Kaldor troops were clearly visible, silhouetted against the night sky. The camp was ringed with Kaldor.

The metallic voice boomed out again. 'If you have weapons, throw them down and stand away from them. If this is not done at once, we shall open fire.'

Jan looked longingly at the laser-rifle at his feet. One quick grab… He glanced at Kevin. 'If I can knock out that searchlight, we can still make a run for it.'

Kevin shook his head. 'And have them pour laser-fire into this camp? We might survive, but not many of this lot would.' Moving slowly and carefully, Kevin threw aside his laser-rifle, tossed down beside it the blaster from his belt and moved a few paces away, raising his hands. Reluctantly, Jan threw down his blaster and did the same.

Kevin raised his voice. 'If any of you have weapons, even bows and spears or clubs, throw them aside. They'll kill you, if you don't.'

Nargo said calmly. 'They need not fear us. We shall not harm them.' He made a sign to the men of the tribe. Those that had weapons tossed them to one side.

Two Kaldor officers marched arrogantly into the camp. 'Sadek and Zarn,' whispered Tell. 'The Commander and his number two.' He slipped discreetly aside as the two officers came to a halt before Jan and Kevin.

'Who are you?' demanded Sadek. 'Why are you here?'

'Just tourists,' said Kevin easily.

'That's right,' said Jan. 'We're visitors, the same as you.'

'We are not visitors, we are conquerors,' said Sadek coldly. 'You are prisoners of the Kaldor imperium. You will return with us for interrogation.'

He looked around the camp, and raised his voice. 'Who is in charge here?'

No one answered.

Sadek drew his blaster.

'Speak! Who leads you?'

'Leads us where?' asked Nargo mildly.

'Do not bandy words with me, old one. Who is your ruler?'

'We rule ourselves.'

'For the last time, who is your leader – your chief? Who speaks for your tribe?'

'They speak for themselves,' said Nargo. 'We are called the Elders. We advise, but we do not rule.'

Sadek said impatiently, 'You will come with us.' He turned to Zarn. 'Take hostages – the two aliens, and the rest of the so-called Elders...' He raised his voice. 'Listen to me, all of you. Some of you will be chosen to come with us. The rest will remain here quietly and give no trouble. Remember, we have taken hostages for your good behaviour. Disobey us and they die.'

Kaldor guards began bustling the chosen hostages out of the camp. Kevin and Jan were amongst the first to go. Glancing round, Kevin caught sight of Anna. Her face was blackened with ash from the fire, her dark hair straggled over her face, she was wrapped from head to toe in a skin robe, and to crown it all she was clutching a fat, howling baby. At her feet crouched Tell. He was swigging fruit wine from a jug, dribbling most of it down his chest, leering horribly, and clearly doing his best to look as useless as possible.

To Kevin's relief, the Kaldor guards passed both of them by. As he was marched out of the camp beside Jan, Kevin thought that things might well be worse. They still had two aces in the hole – three if you counted Osar hidden in his space ship. Come to that, there was still Garm floating about on the loose somewhere. A rescue attempt was certain – but would it arrive in time? Surrounded by Kaldor guards, Jan and Kevin, Nargo and the Elders were marched through the jungle towards the Kaldor space ships.

Whatever awaited them, thought Kevin, it wasn't going to be pleasant. He just hoped it wouldn't be fatal.

8. Death-trap

Anna was burning with indignation at the humiliation of hiding amongst the women and children – but at least it was better than being marched off as a prisoner by the Kaldor.

She glanced around the camp. Only a handful of guards had been left behind – clearly the Kaldor were relying on the threat to the hostages to maintain order.

Handing the baby back to its mother, but keeping the robe, she edged closer to Tell.

He looked up, wiping fruit wine from his mouth. 'We've got to get out of here.'

'What about Osar? Hasn't he got weapons on your ship?'

'We'd never get to the ship without being spotted. And Osar can't use the ship's artillery without blowing up the whole camp. I'm going to tell him to stay put.'

Under cover of more wine swigging, Tell spoke briefly into the communicator, now hidden underneath his clothes. He looked up. 'Let's work our way towards the edge of the settlement. If we can make it into the jungle…'

To their astonishment, those of the People who had been left behind were going on with their usual activities. Tell and Anna drifted from group to group, edging always nearer to the surrounding jungle.

'I know a kind of back door,' said Tell. 'With any luck, it won't be guarded.'

But it was. Tell's back door was a smaller version of the main arch that led into the little oasis. But on the far side of the arch, a Kaldor sentry patrolled the narrow strip of ground between camp and jungle. It was almost dark now, but the Kaldor had set up searchlights to cover the exits. This particular area seemed to be a kind of kitchen garden. There were rows of vegetables growing in neat beds and several trees bearing a round fruit with a hard, coconut-like shell. The nuts were evidently ripe, since several lay on the ground at the foot of the trees fringing the jungle.

They went as close as they dared to the archway. The Kaldor sentry raised his blaster, waving them back.

They moved away and came to a halt nearby.

'Shall we try somewhere else?' whispered Anna.

Tell said gloomily, 'We can try, but it looks as if they've got the whole place covered.'

Anna stared longingly through the arch. Freedom was so close, with only the one guard in the way. Suddenly her eyes widened. A silent form had appeared in the jungle behind the sentry's back. A huge, powerful figure in a loincloth. 'Tell, look, there's one of the People, out there in the jungle.'

Tell stared into the gloom. 'Well, it is and it isn't,' he said dryly. 'That's Garm, in his native dress.'

Anna looked again, and realised that he was right.

It was the first time she had seen Garm in anything other than space coveralls. He looked very different in a loincloth.

'The thing is,' said Tell musingly, 'how do we get to him – or how does he get to us?' He stared through the arch as if for inspiration, and suddenly his eyes lit up with mischief. There was a basket of the giant nuts just inside the archway. Tell drifted over to it, picked up one of the nuts and began tossing it from hand to hand. He picked up another nut and began juggling them.

The sentry looked on in astonishment – as did Garm, from the edge of the jungle.

And so did Anna. 'Tell, what are you doing?'

'Trying to give Garm a hint. Let's hope he takes it.'

Suddenly a grin spread over Garm's face. He bent and reached down for one of the fallen nuts at the foot of the trees.

The sentry was still looking at Tell's juggling act in fascination, when a huge nut whizzed from out of the jungle and clunked solidly against his helmet, knocking it from his head.

He whirled round angrily, raising his blaster – and one of the nuts in Tell's hands shot through the air, taking him in the back of the head, and knocking him out cold.

Tell and Anna shot through the arch and disappeared into the darkening jungle where Garm was waiting.

As the only obvious aliens on the planet, Jan and Kevin had expected to bear the main brunt of Kaldor interrogation. But to their surprise, Sadek didn't seem particularly interested in them.

His questions were brief and relatively few in number. 'Who are you? Why are you here?'

'I told you,' said Jan boldly. 'We're visitors. Just passing through.'

'We heard the people of this planet had an interesting culture,' said Kevin.

Jan nodded. 'That's right. And we wanted to take a look at some of the savage lifeforms. Mind you, we didn't reckon on running into anything this savage!'

Sadek lashed him across the mouth with a black-gloved hand. 'No insolence, alien.'

Jan stepped forward, reaching for him, but two Kaldor guards with blasters shoved him back.

Hurriedly Kevin stepped forward. 'I'm sorry you find my friend insolent, but we do have a fair grievance. We really are just a couple of innocent visitors. We're not a bit interested in what you're up to here. Why don't you just let us go, and then get on with whatever you're doing? The fate of these people is of no interest to us.'

'I think you are lying,' said Sadek thoughtfully. 'However, it is of no importance. We shall wring the truth from you later. Take them aside.'

Guards herded Jan and Kevin into a corner of the big control room, and Sadek turned to what really interested him – the little group of Elders, clustered around Nargo. 'You are the leaders of the People?'

'We are the Elders,' said Nargo. 'We do not lead.'

'Their social system is strange, sir,' said Zarn. 'As far as I can discover, these are the nearest to leaders they have.'

Sadek nodded. 'Very well. Now listen closely, Elders. Some time ago, a renegade of your people came to us. He said that you, the Elders of the People, held the secret of some great power, some unimaginable force that enabled you to work miracles. He offered us this knowledge in the hope of great reward. He said that if we would make him rich and powerful, he would bring us here, so the power might be ours.'

Nargo seemed quite unsurprised. 'His name was Megla. We expelled him from our planet because his mind was twisted. Is he here?'

'Unfortunately not. We were not convinced as to the truth of his story, and our scientists interrogated him a little too thoroughly.' Sadek yawned. 'He did not survive. But before he died, he convinced us that he was telling the truth. Or at least, that he *believed* he was telling the truth. That is why we are here.'

Nargo said nothing.

'Well,' snapped Sadek. 'Is there such power here?'

Nargo glanced at the other Elders before he replied. 'There is power on this planet – as indeed there is power on every planet.'

'What is it? How is it used?'

'Even if I told you, you would not understand. And if you did not understand, the power would be of no use to you.'

'I shall be the judge of that,' screamed Sadek. 'Tell me your secret, old one, or it will be the worse for you!'

'There is no secret,' said Nargo calmly. 'The power is all around us. It is here for everyone. But only the enlightened may make use of it.'

215

'Then enlighten me!'

Nargo studied the Kaldor Commander for a few minutes. 'Your spirit is mean and cruel, and your understanding stunted. I fear you are not capable of enlightenment.'

Sadek waved to a technician. A panel slid back, revealing a sinister-looking cubicle with clamps set into its rear wall, and a control console nearby.

Jan and Kevin exchanged glances – both recognised an interrogation machine when they saw one.

'This machine will have the truth from you,' said Sadek. 'It detects lies and it punishes them with pain. It will punish silence, too. For the last time, will you answer me, or will you answer my interrogation machine?'

Nargo was silent, and so were the others.

'Very well.' Sadek pointed to a sturdy middle-aged man with a brown beard flecked with grey. 'What is your name?'

'I am called Marto.'

'You seem a little less ancient than the others. No doubt you will stand up to interrogation better. We do not wish to lose you, like the unfortunate Megla.'

As the guards moved forward, Marto said, 'Wait!' He spoke with such authority that they instinctively fell back.

Marto exchanged what was obviously a ceremonial handclasp with Nargo and the others in the group. Then he said, 'I am ready to depart.' He was looking at Nargo as he spoke, and the old man raised a hand in a farewell salute.

'Very touching,' sneered Sadek. 'Take him!'

Marto stood unmoving as the guards approached, then, as they laid hands on him, he went limp and fell. A technician ran to kneel beside him, made a swift examination, and looked up in alarm. 'He is dead, Commander.'

Sadek swung round on Nargo. 'What happened?'

'Marto did not wish to endure your questioning. He has gone.'

'And I suppose the rest of you will go, if I put you to the question?'

'We shall.' Nargo spoke with such calm authority that it was impossible not to believe him.

Sadek watched as guards dragged Marto's body away. Suddenly he hammered a black-gloved fist into the palm of his hand in frustration. 'Then hear this. The rest of your tribe are at your settlement under guard. If you do not give me the answers I seek, I shall have them brought here and execute them, one by one, before your eyes – every man, woman and child. I will hunt down whatever other miserable

216

bands infest this planet and slaughter them as well. And if that does not serve, I will send for the Kaldor battle fleet and we will rain a shower of atomic missiles on this planet that will destroy every plant, every beast, every living thing. *Now will you answer me?*'

Nargo said sternly, 'You speak as a child.' He pointed to the metal bulkhead of the control room. 'Could you, alone and unaided, walk through that metal barrier? If I ordered you, commanded you, threatened you with the end of everything you hold dear, could you do it? You ask me for the impossible – and for all your threats, the impossible it will remain. The power you seek, you are not fit to hold. It can never by yours.'

Sadek controlled himself with a mighty effort. 'You have the remainder of this night to make the impossible possible. If I do not have your secret by dawn, you will watch your people and your planet die!' He waved dismissively. 'Take them to the detention area.'

As they were marched away, Kevin whispered, 'What you might call a moral victory for our side!'

Jan grunted. 'It's the only kind of victory we're likely to get. If Sadek doesn't get some answers, he'll execute us, too, just so we don't feel left out. Why doesn't the old fool give him what he wants – or at least pretend to?'

'I don't think he can.'

'What?'

'I don't think he can give Sadek what he wants,' repeated Kevin. 'I think Nargo was telling the simple truth. Whatever the secret is, it's something Sadek simply couldn't understand.'

'Talk about an irresistible force and an immovable object,' grumbled Jan. 'We're going to be smashed between those two like a walnut on an anvil.'

'Don't worry, Garm and Osar and Anna are still on the loose. They'll manage something.'

'Oh yes? They're prisoners too, don't forget. And exactly what are they going to do against this lot?'

They were being marched along the space-ship corridors by now, and from all around them there came the tramp of booted feet. It was obvious that Sadek planned to surround his prisoners with a wall of armed guards.

Kevin looked worriedly at his usually optimistic cousin, who seemed to have been overtaken by a mood of grim fatalism.

'Come on, Jan, it's not like you to give in so easily.'

'I may have given up, but that doesn't mean I've given in.'

'What do you mean?'

'When things start turning nasty tomorrow, I'm going to clobber the nearest guard, grab his blaster, and make damn sure I take Sadek with me when I go. Let's face it, Kevin, that's the best we can hope for. This place is a death-trap and there's no way out.'

9. THE CALLING OF THE BEAST

Anna felt cheered up just by being with Garm again. There was something tremendously reassuring about his size and strength. There wasn't much time for talk as they hurried away from the settlement, but soon he led them to a jungle pool, and there was a brief and joyful reunion, while they rested and exchanged stories of their adventures.

Anna hugged as much of Garm as she could get her arms round. 'Where have you been? What's going on here? I thought this planet of yours was supposed to be a haven of peace and quiet – apart from the odd dinosaur. What are the Kaldor after?'

'I wish I knew,' said Garm ruefully. 'I'm not really one of the People any longer, remember, I left them long ago. Whatever it is, it seems to be connected with the Elders, and with Mount Doom.' He told them of the little he had learned during the Kaldor interrogation.

'What is this Mount Doom?' demanded Tell.

'It's a sacred mountain, not far from here. Usually only the Elders are allowed to visit it, although…'

'What is it?' asked Anna.

'Sometimes there's a kind of pilgrimage. I think the whole tribe goes then. But that's only a once-in-a-lifetime thing.'

'What happens on these pilgrimages?'

'I've no idea. I was hardly more than a child when I left here. I persuaded a visiting League ship to take me with them. There was no pilgrimage while I was here.' Garm frowned. 'Unless I missed one when I was away, I think there must be one due quite soon.'

'Could we possibly leave the religious observances until later?' suggested Tell. 'Our more immediate problem is getting your Elders and our two unfortunate friends out of the clutches of the Kaldor.'

Garm laid an affectionate hand on his small friend's shoulder. 'As a matter of fact, there's an even more urgent problem.'

'And what might that be?'

'Reaching the Kaldor camp without being eaten by some of our native lifeforms. A lot of the nastier ones prefer to hunt at night.'

As if to reinforce Garm's words there was a harsh cry from the night sky above them, as some great leather-winged form flapped slowly by overhead.

Tell shuddered. 'It's a wonder you got away from this place without being eaten.'

'Oh, I'm in no danger,' said Garm solemnly. 'The beasts never harm the People. The Elders made a treaty with them long ago.'

'Oh, come on,' said Anna. 'How can you make a peace treaty with a dinosaur?'

'It's true, nonetheless,' said Garm. 'You remember, Tell, I told you how I met a Terrorsaur quite close to the camp?'

'Let's just hope we don't meet another,' said Tell. 'Just you remember, your precious treaty doesn't apply to me. I'm already convinced that practically every beast on this planet wants me for a late-night snack!'

They heard something very, very large, crashing through the jungle towards the pool.

'Perhaps you're right,' said Garm. 'We'd better be on our way.'

He led them through the jungle at a fast trot, choosing trails that were hardly trails at all, and in a surprisingly short time they found themselves climbing the hill that overlooked the encampment of the Kaldor.

They peered over the brow of the hill at the three space ships in their circle of charred vegetation.

It was a discouraging sight.

The whole of the Kaldor compound was brilliantly floodlit, and Kaldor guards were everywhere, marching around the perimeter in regular patrols.

Just to make matters worse, the force field had obviously been strengthened. Its flickering glow was brighter than ever. Garm sat hunched in a Rodin's *Thinker* pose, his massive chin in his hands. 'If we went back to camp, rejoined Osar in the ship, and attacked in that...'

'Our ship's nearer than yours,' said Anna excitedly. 'Jan put it down in a kind of quarry quite near here. We could use that.'

'Forget it,' said Tell's deep voice. 'I imagine your ship's a League scout vessel, like ours?'

Anna nodded.

'Well, our ship or yours, or both together, it'd make no difference. Those are Kaldor battle cruisers down there, three of them, all bearing heavy space cannon. Even if we got through the force field, they'd catch us in a crossfire and blow us to pieces before we even got out of our ships.'

Garm sighed. 'I'm afraid he's right. And Kaldor being Kaldor, I imagine they'd probably slaughter all the hostages at the first sign of attack, so that wouldn't do us much good.'

'Then what are we wasting our time for?' demanded Tell. 'The place is impregnable to attack. And even if it wasn't, we daren't attack anyway because of the hostages. We've got two space ships the Kaldor don't know about yet. The sensible thing is to go to Anna's ship, send a signal to Osar, and then both of us blast off for Centre.'

'That's right,' agreed Garm. 'That's the sensible thing. Do you want to do it?'

Tell said grumpily. 'No, of course I don't. I just wanted to work out what it was!'

'It isn't that we can't make an attack...' said Anna. 'It's just we daren't risk an attack that looks like an attack – or at least, not an attack that looks like an attack by us!'

She beamed triumphantly at Garm and Tell, who stared at her in total bafflement.

'Well, if we don't attack the Kaldor, who do you suppose is going to do it for us?' demanded Tell irritably. 'After all...' His voice tailed off and his eyes widened. 'Wait a minute! What about the dinosaurs? One of them attacked the camp just as I was leaving. Broke through the force field and caused the most tremendous upset. It we could persuade one of them to do it again... or better yet, several of them.' He looked at Garm. 'If you can have a peace treaty with monsters, why can't you have a war alliance as well? After all, the Kaldor are as much a threat to the dinosaurs as they are to us. If they take over this planet, they'll probably wipe out the lot of them with atomic weapons.'

Anna looked at Tell in astonishment. He seemed to be quite serious. She turned to Garm. 'Could you communicate with one of those things?'

Garm shook his head. 'I very much doubt it. I can still control the riding beasts by mind touch, but they are timid beasts, easily tamed. But something as savage and ferocious as a Terrorsaur...' He shook his head.

'Why not?' urged Anna. 'If the Elders can do it, surely you can?'

'The Elders have developed their minds through years of concentration. I have the mind power, yes, but it just isn't strong enough.'

'If only there were some way to magnify...' Anna's hands flew to her throat. 'You're never going to believe it but I'd completely forgotten I had this.'

She bent the soft metal of the Circlet and lifted it from around her throat. 'I've been wearing this ever since we left Centre.'

Garm and Tell bowed their heads in instinctive reverence.

'The Stone of Power,' breathed Tell. 'Where did you get it?'

'It was given to me by someone called Zeno. He seemed to think I might need it.'

'They say that the Watcher can see into the Mists of Time,' said Garm sombrely. 'If the Stone of Power is here, then it was sent for a purpose.'

'Listen,' said Anna excitedly. 'We know it magnifies the power of the mind. Suppose you wore the Circlet and *then* tried to call up a Terrorsaur?'

'I dare not,' said Garm simply. 'I fear the Stone. If I wore it, that fear might grow until it destroyed my mind.'

'What about you, Tell?'

The little man ducked his head. 'I have no mind power to magnify. And I, too, fear the Stone.'

'That only leaves me, then, doesn't it?' said Anna steadily. 'The trouble is I'm not much of a telepath either, I'd barely started the training... wait a minute! The Watcher said I was something called an empath. Garm, suppose you summon the Terrorsaur and I wear the Stone. You can send the thought into my mind, and I'll amplify it and send it on. Like a kind of relay station!'

'That's the most ridiculous thing I ever head,' said Tell. 'And the most dangerous. Tamper with the power of the Stone like that, and it could end up blasting both your minds!'

'Maybe it is a ridiculous and dangerous idea,' said Garm. 'It also happens to be the only one we've got. Very well, Lady Anna. We shall try.'

Anna smiled. It was the first time since their reunion that he had used the old half-mocking title he had bestowed on her at their first meeting.

Garm smoothed the surface of a flat rock, searched round until he found a sharp stone, and began scratching a crude drawing of a Terrorsaur.

'Now what are you doing?' asked Tell peevishly.

Garm smiled. 'I told you our paintings were magic. The image aids concentration. Now be silent, both of you. Anna, put on the Stone when I touch your hand.'

There was silence, broken only by the scratching of the stone on the rock. Tell fell back a little, staring at Anna as if she had suddenly become someone awesome and dangerous.

Garm completed his little sketch – a simple but strangely vivid picture of a creature with a huge head, fearsome teeth, and a great spiked tail.

He stared hard at it, filling his mind with the thought of the

222

Terrorsaur roaming the jungle nearby, summoning it to him. He remembered the Terrorsaur he had encountered near the camp, and spoke to the intelligence he had sensed in the great green eyes. Then, somewhere in the depths of his mind, he felt an answer.

He stretched out his hand...

Anna slipped the Circlet on her forehead, and the Stone glowed an eerie red. She took Garm's hand and, the moment they touched, she *sensed* the Terrorsaur standing poised in the jungle not far away, its great head swinging uneasily to and fro.

She took the thoughts that Garm was sending, held them in her mind, magnified them and sent them on.

Garm was sending not so much words as feelings. He was sending his hatred of the Kaldor, ruthless destroyers of a hundred worlds. He sent a picture of *this* world, the world of the People and of the Terrorsaurs, blackened and defiled by the searing Kaldor heat ray. He showed the black circle around the space ship like a kind of blight, a foulness that would grow and grow until it swallowed all the planet.

Anna felt herself physically shaking as the force of Garm's hatred surged through her. She took the hatred, magnified it, sent it out to the monster that stood listening in the night. Suddenly from somewhere nearby, she heard terrifying bellows of anger. The Terrorsaur had heard and answered them.

Sending out the summons like an invisible beam, Anna waited in silence.

They heard something crashing through the jungle towards them. The sound was faint at first, then it grew louder and louder still. Something enormous was thundering through the jungle, hurtling towards them like an express train.

Suddenly the Terrorsaur burst out of the jungle below them and reared menacingly over the Kaldor camp.

10. The Monster Strikes

Anna caught her breath in a mixture of awe and terror. The Terrorsaur was the most impressive creature she had ever seen in her life.

It towered above them on two trunklike, clawed hind legs. Even the smaller forelimbs dangling in front looked powerful enough to tear and rend. The armour-plated body gleamed silvery in the moonlight, and the huge spiked tail lashed constantly to and fro.

But it was the head that was really imposing, with the rows of serrated teeth and, above all, the fiery green eyes under their ridges of bone.

Those blazing eyes were staring up at them now, as if sensing the direction from which the summons had come.

'Make it attack!' said Tell, in a terrified whisper. 'Send it in to the attack before it turns on us. We can follow straight after it, break through the barrier in the confusion.'

Without taking his eyes from the Terrorsaur, Garm said, 'We don't have to break through the force-field. We can open it!' He produced a torchlike device from the waistband of his loincloth. 'I took this from a guard when I escaped!'

Anna felt full of a fierce excitement. She could feel the power of the Terrorsaur's mind now, sense its anger and confusion. Moreover, she was convinced that she could control it.

Eyes glittering feverishly she said, 'Now listen, I've got a plan. Garm, you go and wait beside the force field barrier. When you feel my signal, start opening as big a gap as you can.'

'And what will you be doing?'

'You'll see!' said Anna exultantly. 'You'll see! Tell, go with him.'

Without quite knowing why, Garm and Tell found themselves walking down the hill towards the compound. Positioning themselves just outside the circle of light, they waited.

The Terrorsaur was still standing at the edge of the jungle. It gave them a brief, uninterested glance and then swung its head towards the hill as if waiting for a signal.

Suddenly it began to move, *not* towards the Kaldor camp but towards the hill.

Tell tugged at Garm's wrist. 'We've got to help her. If that thing steps on her, it'll crush her to death.'

'She doesn't need any help,' said Garm. 'Don't you understand? She's calling it!'

The Terrorsaur climbed the little hill in a few effortless strides. They saw it silhouetted on the crest of the hill for a moment, then saw the great body swing round. Now the Terrorsaur was facing downhill, towards them, and the Kaldor camp.

It was too dark to make out Anna, but she was there.

Suddenly Garm heard her frenzied voice in his mind. 'Open the force field! Open! We're coming through!'

As the Terrorsaur thundered down the hill towards the camp, Garm switched the opening device to maximum power, swinging it wide to make the tunnel as big as possible.

He heard Tell scream, 'Look, Garm! Look!'

The Terrorsaur was almost upon them – and Anna was riding it, clinging to the highest spike behind the monster's head. Her face was rapt, and the Stone of Power blazed fierily on her forehead.

Garm and Tell had only just time to leap aside as girl and Terrorsaur swept past them like a whirlwind, hurtled through the forcefield tunnel, and stormed into the Kaldor compound.

Scarcely knowing what they were doing, Garm and Tell hurried after them.

The effect of the Terrorsaur's arrival in the Kaldor compound was devastating.

The fact that it was a Terrorsaur was bad enough in itself. But a Terrorsaur that arrived as if by magic, bursting through their just reinforced, supposedly impregnable force field was even worse. And a Terrorsaur ridden by a wild-eyed screaming girl was the worst of all, filling them with a kind of superstitious terror.

So sudden and ferocious was the attack that scarcely a blaster was fired. The Terrorsaur leaped and swirled and lashed about in a frenzy, doing a mad dervish dance in the brightly lit compound. Kaldor were crushed beneath enormous clawed feet, picked up and tossed almost playfully in the air, mown down in swathes by the flailing of the long spiked tail.

The guards broke and fled, some rushing for the perimeter and rebounding from their own force field, others running for the ships and colliding with those dashing out to see what was happening.

The monster thudded into the side of the main command ship with an echoing clang – and an impact that knocked Anna from its back, and dislodged the Circlet from her head.

Rolling over in the dust of the compound, Anna saw the gleam of the Circlet at her feet. She snatched it up and was about to replace it on her head when she suddenly found Garm at her side. 'Not on the head, Anna. Back round the neck, I think.' His big hands guided hers, and before she realised what was happening the Circlet was tucked safely round her neck. Anna stared dazedly at him, half oblivious to the howling chaos all around them. 'What happened? Did I really…'

'You got a little overexcited,' said Garm grimly. 'Come on, we've got work to do, remember?'

So complete was the demoralisation of the guards that the rescue of the hostages proved surprisingly easy.

Most of the guards assigned to look after the prisoners had fled the ship when the monster cannoned in to it. Many guards had thrown down their weapons in terror, and there were blasters to be had for the picking.

Arming themselves, Garm and Tell and Anna forced their way into the main space ship, ignoring the fleeing guards, who took absolutely no notice of them.

Garm led them towards the detention area, but before they reached it they met Jan and Kevin, also carrying stolen blasters and shepherding before them Nargo and the Elders, who seemed to think it was beneath their dignity to hurry.

'What's happening?' yelled Jan. 'Someone's been using this ship as a big bass drum! Nearly deafened me!'

'It's a long story,' called Tell. 'And you won't believe it when you hear it.'

They made their way to the exit ramp and looked across the compound where the Terrorsaur was ranging restlessly to and fro, attacking any Kaldor that came in range.

Jan shook his head. 'Boy, when you arrive you certainly come in style.'

'You don't know how true that is,' said Tell dryly. 'Shall we get these old gentlemen out of here, or are they going to insist on saying goodbye to their hosts?'

Garm opened a second gate in the force field and they herded their bemused charges through.

'Move them aside,' called Anna, 'and keep the tunnel open!'

She took the Circlet from her neck.

Garm put out a restraining hand, but Anna said, 'It's all right, I'm in control again now.'

She slipped the Circlet on, the Stone of Power glowed, and the Terrorsaur rushed through the tunnel after them.

Garm closed the tunnel behind it.

For a moment the Terrorsaur stood poised, looming over them, then, in response to Anna's unspoken command, it began roaming restlessly around the Kaldor compound, outside the force field now, roaring threateningly at the Kaldor inside.

'That should keep them bottled up for a bit,' said Anna happily, and followed the others through the jungle.

Tell finished a mouthful of soft, rather breadlike nut - it was the flesh of the giant nut he had bounced off the Kaldor guard's skull - took a swig of wine and said grumblingly, 'This is all very nice, Anna, but we really must get these people moving. Your little pet can't keep the Kaldor bottled up for ever.'

There was a definitely festive air to the camp by now. Fires had been lit before all the caves, and the reunited People and Elders were telling each other of their adventures.

Recapturing the camp had been comparatively easy. The Kaldor sentries left behind had been looking inwards rather than outwards, which made it easy to dispose of them. Jan had pointed out that prisoners were always a nuisance, so the guards had been stripped of their weapons and their boots, and thrust out into the jungle to make their own way back to their ships.

Tell had made straight for the ship in order to change his loincloth for coveralls.

Apparently Osar had been dozing quietly all this while. He had refused to come out, and only wanted to know when they were going home to Centre.

This question had been occupying Anna and Tell as well. Convinced that now at last the Elders would see the wisdom of, first, hiding from the Kaldor and, second, calling in the help of the League, Jan, Kevin and Garm had gone off for a planning meeting to arrange the details. Anna was feeling suddenly drained of energy after using the Stone of Power, and Tell, who objected to meetings on principle, had stayed outside to look after her.

The meeting seemed to have been going on for a very long while now, and from time to time they had heard angry voices from within the cave.

At last Jan stormed out of the cave and flung himself down beside them. 'Gimme that,' he growled, snatched the flask of wine from Tell and drained most of it in one go. 'Sorry, I've talked myself dry in there. Kevin and Garm are still at it, but I've given up. Complete waste of time.'

Tell stared at him. 'You mean they still won't call in the League - not even after all this?'

'That's right!'

'But why?'

'Worried about their precious independence. They know the League are desperate for telepaths. They're afraid that all their best ones will be nabbed for the Communications Service. Anyway, Nargo says they don't need any help.'

'But they have agreed to hide in the jungle till the Kaldor go?' said Anna.

Jan finished off the wine with another swig. 'Nope!'

'But I was in the inner cave just now. Everyone's packing up their things, women, kids, everyone.'

Jan shook his head to clear it. 'That stuff must be stronger than it looks!'

'So why are they packing up then?'

It was Kevin who answered them. 'Because it's pilgrimage time. They're all setting off for Mount Doom!'

'They can't,' howled Tell. 'The Kaldor are interested in Mount Doom, it's the first place they'll make for. They'll all get themselves captured again and executed. It's all been for nothing.'

'Oh no!' said Anna.

Garm came out of the cave and sank down in exhaustion beside them. 'I'm afraid Jan's right. I've tried every possible kind of persuasion, from promises to threats, but Nargo refuses to lead the People into hiding *or* to ask for help from the League.'

'Can't we replace him with someone more sensible?' suggested Tell.

Jan shook his head. 'I thought of that and did some lobbying. All the Elders, and everyone else for that matter, seem to be right behind Nargo.'

Kevin said wryly, 'That's the trouble with telepaths, they all think alike!'

Garm said wearily, 'We still have two ships. I advise you all to go back to Centre and make a full report. Maybe the League will send help, even it it isn't wanted.'

11. The Voice of Doom

It seemed to be a very long way to Mount Doom.

The long line of pilgrims straggled across the rocky plain, which reflected the blaze of the morning sun, seeming to double its already burning heat.

Nargo led the procession, flanked by his Elders. Behind him came the rest of the tribe, every man, woman and child. Laden with water and provisions, they marched onwards without complaint. There was neither water nor food to be found on the journey across the barren plain. Supplies for both outward and return trips had to be carried on their backs.

Jan and Garm had offered to ferry the Elders to the mountain in their space ships, but the offer had been firmly refused. Apparently you didn't make pilgrimages by space ship, only on foot.

Jan and Garm and Tell and Kevin and Anna all formed a kind of rearguard. Not that they were in a position to do very much guarding. Apparently you didn't take blasters on a pilgrimage either. The only precaution they'd been able to take was to alert Osar to their destination and have him promise to keep a constant listening watch. In the event of trouble, he would be standing by to lift them out of danger – if he could arrive in time.

Kevin looked around at the worried faces of his friends and wondered what they were all doing here. Only Garm seemed completely calm and relaxed, but he was in possession of the wonderful secret, Nargo's answer to the ruthless violence of the Kaldor with their three battle cruisers and their legions of black-clad guards.

Whatever it was, thought Kevin, it had better be good. He plodded grimly onwards.

'Everything is in order, Commander,' reported Zarn. 'Damaged equipment has been replaced or repaired, and the wounded have been either cured or eliminated. Except for the force-field generators, all equipment is now back on shipboard.' He hesitated. 'The beast is still roaming outside the perimeter.'

Sadek glared angrily around his now immaculate control room. Guards and technicians stood silently at their posts, waiting for his orders.

It was hard to realise that a few short hours ago this ship, and indeed

231

all three of his ships, had been gripped in panic-stricken chaos, that prisoners had been snatched from his grip, that he had been tricked and mocked by a tribe of savages and a handful of aliens. But they would pay, he swore grimly. Oh yes, they would pay. Once he had wrested their secret from them, he would see their planet blasted into a radioactive wilderness.

He turned to a scanner technician. 'The primitives are still crossing the plain?'

'Yes, sir. Our observation satellite is overhead. I can give you visual display.'

'Do so.'

A monitor screen showed a line of weary figures straggling antlike across a burning waste.'

'Maximum magnification,' ordered Sadek.

The satellite camera zoomed into close-up and panned down the long line of marchers, from Nargo at the front to the little group of aliens at the back.

Sadek gazed at these with particular hatred. There was the big one with yellow hair, the round-faced dark-haired one with the insolent manner, the dwarf who had posed as a primitive, the big primitive who must be an agent of the League, and the girl who had ridden the Terrorsaur. He would kill them. He would kill them all.

He turned to Zarn. 'Is everything ready for blast-off?'

'Yes, Commander.'

'Send guards to bring in the generators.'

'But the monster may attack if the force field is switched off.'

'Guards are more readily replaced than generators. We shall blast off as soon as the equipment is on board.'

The mountain was very near now, dominating the otherwise flat horizon. It was cone-shaped and there were wisps of smoke coming out of the top.

'That's no mountain,' whispered Jan. 'That's a volcano.'

Kevin nodded. 'Tell you something else. The rocks underfoot are hot, and it's not just the sun. This whole area must be volcanic.'

Anna sighed. 'Do you think that's all there is to the secret – a holy volcano? We could have stayed on Earth and visited Krakatoa!'

They struggled on, and soon the Elders at the head of the procession were climbing the lower slopes of the volcano. As Garm and his friends came nearer, they saw that the outside of the volcano was surrounded by a track carved from the rock that wound round and

232

round the mountain, making its way to the top. At the very top of the mountain was a kind of viewing gallery.

Here the Elders were standing and, as they watched, Nargo raised his hand, beckoning them forward.

The crowd drew back respectfully to let them pass and they made their way past the silently waiting ranks of the People – young and old, women and children and babes-in-arms – all waiting patiently in the burning heat. Waiting for what?

Up and up they climbed, until at last they stood beside Nargo and the Elders, gazing down into the very core of the volcano, a bubbling pool of red-hot lava.

Nargo beckoned them to stand beside him. 'Usually it is permitted only to the Elders to gaze on the face of the living mountain.' Unexpectedly he smiled. 'But although you may think us obstinate and ungrateful, we are well aware that you risked much to help us – even though we never really needed your help! You have earned this privilege.'

The lava bubbled and seethed, and sent out a puff of smoke. 'You see?' said Nargo. 'The mountain welcomes you!'

'You believe the mountain is alive?' said Anna gently. She was disappointed that the great secret had turned out to be so banal – even on Earth there were plenty of tribes that worshipped volcanos, taking the bubbling and rumbling of the lava for the voice of a god. But she had no wish to hurt Nargo's feelings. He was a dignified old man, however deluded his beliefs.

Suddenly Anna became aware that Nargo was looking at her with exactly the kind of pitying tolerance she was giving to him. 'The whole planet is alive, my child. This world and all worlds are as living beings, joined with all other living things in the unity of the Web of Being.'

Anna looked helplessly at the others. 'I see.'

Nargo went on, 'But our world is young and it does not yet sleep, as many worlds do. For the moment, this mountain is its heart, a point where we may meet and commune.'

There was another rumble from the volcano. It was uncanny, thought Kevin, how the mountain seemed to echo Nargo's words. Just coincidence, of course, but impressive enough in its way.

Anna made a last attempt to get through to the old man. 'What you say is very beautiful, and I'm sure that it's true – at least on the level on which you speak. But I'm afraid there is real evil on your world now, and poetic truths are no way to deal with the Kaldor. You need weapons to fight them with.'

Nargo shook his head. 'You still think I speak in dreams or riddles, child? I speak the literal truth. We need no weapons. This planet *lives,* and it will protect its People.'

'Well, it had better get started,' said Jan. He pointed upwards. There were three black dots in the sky above their heads, and they were getting steadily bigger.

Larger and larger they grew, revealing themselves at last as the sinister black shapes of the Kaldor battle cruisers.

The roar of their retro-rockets shook the ground and deafened the ears, as they settled down on the plain, lowering themselves on columns of fire.

The noise and the smoke and the dust died away at last, leaving only the rockets, standing there with a kind of sinister beauty, forming a triangle about the mountain.

The main command rocket was nearest the viewing gallery. Its exit ramp slid out and Commander Sadek appeared. Sinister and elegant in his silver-and-black uniform, he stood for a moment regarding the smoking volcano with the People about its base like a giant snake of human flesh.

He strode down the ramp and walked across the rocky plain to the base of the mountain. 'I come to offer you one last chance, old one. Reveal your secret, such as it is, and you and your people shall live. You will be slaves to the Kaldor, but you will live. All except the aliens, who I will execute here and now. Perhaps I will allow you to toss them into the volcano as a sacrifice to your gods.'

Nargo's voice was stern. 'And I offer you one last chance. Take your ships and leave this planet in peace for ever and you too may live.'

Sadek laughed. 'Perhaps you have no secret to give me. Is this the secret of your power? A very small, rather inactive volcano? I could show you a thousand such on a thousand worlds. You refuse my offer then?'

'As you refuse mine.'

Sadek laughed. 'Then let me tell you what is going to happen to you. You are surrounded, as you see, by my three battle cruisers. Their atomic cannon are trained on your mountain and on your tribe. Once I am back in my ship, they will open fire. Your mountain will explode and you will all die. There is nothing you can do. You have no weapons, I see. And even if you had weapons, there would still be nothing you could do. You are dead.'

Nargo's voice rang out. 'This whole world is my weapon. I need no other.'

The volcano gave an angry rumble and a puff of smoke.

For a moment even Sadek seemed impressed. Then he laughed and turned to make his way back to his ship.

A fiery crack opened across his path.

He tried to step round it, but it shot forward, cutting off his retreat. He turned but there was another crack behind him, running to join the first. A third crack appeared, enclosing him in a fiery triangle that seemed to reflect the triangle formed by the three ships.

The cracks grew wider, and smoke and flame seeped up from them.

Anna turned to Nargo. 'Stop it! Even Sadek doesn't deserve this.'

Sadly Nargo shook his head. 'Do you think this is my doing, child? The mountain protects us, that is all.'

The cracks grew wider, wider, and suddenly the ground vanished from beneath Sadek's feet, and he fell screaming into a fiery chasm.

More cracks appeared in the ground around the three ships. Those on the ships must have seen what was happening because there was a sudden rumble of rocket motors as they tried to blast off. But they were far too late. All around the black ships the cracks spread and grew and joined and widened. One by one, the ships plummeted into roaring pits of fire. The cracks and chasms closed and disappeared, and suddenly there were no Kaldor battle cruisers – just the mountain, the silent waiting People, Tell and the three appalled visitors from Earth, trying to believe the evidence of their eyes.

Jan broke the silence. 'Well, I don't say they didn't deserve it – but that's as ruthless a piece of trickery as I've ever seen.'

'Trickery?' said Nargo mildly.

'You let him think you were helpless and you lured him here. You knew the ground was unstable, that the weight of the ships would set off a reaction…'

For a moment Nargo's eyes flashed angrily, and then he spread out his hands. 'You say the reaction was natural – and so do I. Perhaps we disagree as to what is natural. Now if you will excuse us, we must complete the pilgrimage.'

The People began a long, low chant, which was punctuated only by the low rumblings of the mountain… digesting three battle cruisers, thought Kevin, and shuddered.

Jan was already making his way down the mountain path. Kevin and Anna followed, and so did Tell. Only Garm stayed with the People staring silently down at the bubbling pool of lava.

12. A Ride on a Dinosaur

They argued about it all the way back to the settlement. Jan was convinced that Nargo had lured the Kaldor into a well-designed trap, which exploited natural volcanic conditions.

Anna remembered the way the volcano seemed to answer Nargo's words, the horribly *purposeful* way the fiery cracks had trapped Sadek, and his ships. 'What do you think, Kevin?' she asked.

Kevin grinned. 'Oh, I'm in the middle, as usual! I don't think it's as straightforward as Nargo makes out. But I do think Nargo and all the People have a kind of link with this planet. They don't change it or chop it about, they live very much as part of it. It's as if they're all part of one great whole. And if you look at it like that, then anyone who attacks them is attacking the whole planet – and the planet might strike back.'

'Well, however it happened, the Kaldor are gone,' said Jan. 'And that I like!'

Marching along behind them, Tell said, 'And the Kaldor have lost three battle cruisers on a supposedly primitive planet. They're not likely to risk any more.'

'Doesn't matter if they do,' said Jan cheerfully. 'Old Nargo can just drop a mountain on 'em, or wash them away with a quick flood.'

'It wouldn't surprise me if he could,' agreed Tell gloomily. 'I'll be glad to get away from this place.'

'Why, what's the matter with it?' asked Anna. 'I wouldn't mind a holiday here, now the Kaldor are gone!'

'I'm afraid Garm's going to spend the rest of his life here,' said Tell seriously. 'I mean, look at him. Twenty years a League agent, and the minute he gets back here he's padding about in a loincloth and attending native ceremonies…'

Tell was still worrying when they marched through the archway and into the now deserted settlement. 'I tell you, the sooner I get us away from this place the better for all of us.'

'I heartily agree,' piped a familiar voice. They turned and saw Osar sitting perched on a rock by the stream, playing three-dimensional chess with himself, one set of tentacles against another.

'Osar,' cried Anna and ran up to him in delight. Osar enfolded her in a many-tentacled hug, though he still had enough left over to shake hands politely with Jan and Kevin.

Tell gave his old friend an affectionate nudge. 'Come out, have you, now all the danger's over?'

'I have been holding my forces in reserve,' said Osar with immense dignity. 'Preparing to rescue you in the nick of time. Luckily it has not proved necessary. Since you all abandoned me here, I had great difficulty in disinterring myself from several tons of rock.'

'Several ounces, more like it,' jeered Tell, 'I only used a minimal charge.'

'Be that as it may, will someone kindly tell me what has been happening? All I know is that the Kaldor ships appeared to follow you, I was about to blast off for a daring rescue operation, and the ships suddenly vanished from my scanners. Have they left the planet?'

'Not really,' said Tell. 'Just the reverse. You might say they were settling down here!'

'Will you kindly give me a clear explanation?' said Osar indignantly.

Wrangling affectionately the two friends went into the settlement.

'Well, at least old Tell's cheered up,' whispered Anna.

Jan nodded. 'He'll take it hard if Garm decides to stay, though. Think he will?'

'I don't know,' said Kevin thoughtfully. 'I think the pull of a place like this must be pretty strong.'

Towards early evening the People began straggling back from their pilgrimage, and Garm was among the first batch to arrive. To Tell's relief, he went straight to the ship and changed from loincloth to coveralls.

The People were in a festive mood after the danger they had passed through, and soon a kind of impromptu farewell party developed. Things were all the jollier since Nargo and the other Elders had remained at the sacred mountain, carrying out some kind of final ceremony.

Hunters went out and returned with deer, and by nightfall they were all sitting round blazing fires, chewing roast venison and passing round jugs of wine.

As Garm sat gazing thoughtfully into the flames, Kevin said quietly, 'Will you be able to face leaving all this?'

Garm smiled. 'I was tempted to stay – for a while. But it wouldn't work. I am no longer Garm of the People. I left them long ago, and I cannot go back – not for more than a very short while.'

'I know how you feel,' said Kevin. 'I think it's how I feel about going back to Earth. It's a kind of dream. Even if they found a way... I don't know if it would work for me now. Once you've seen something of the Galaxy, one world can seem very small. What about you, Jan?'

Jan yawned and stretched. He kicked a log into the fire, took a swig of wine, and patted the butt of his blaster. 'After the kind of thing that's been happening to me since we left Earth, I think college football might have lost its thrill.'

'That takes care of us,' said Kevin. 'What about you, Anna?'

'Oh I don't know,' said Anna. 'Sometimes I feel one way, sometimes another.'

Anna wandered away from the camp fire, feeling things were somehow incomplete. She was glad this adventure was over, she had enjoyed the party, and she was looking forward to returning to Centre – with a slight feeling of guilt, she realised how seldom she thought of Earth these days. A lot had happened since she and her two cousins had been hijacked by that flying saucer. Perhaps she was no longer the same person.

She heard a deep rumbling growl, and a giant shadow fell over her. She looked up and saw the shape of the Terrorsaur, blocking out the stars, the green eyes glowing brightly in the great shadowed head.

Strangely, she wasn't in the least afraid. She reached for the Stone of Power around her neck, and realised she didn't need it. The link with the monster was established now.

She stretched out her hand, and the monster bent its long neck so that the head was almost resting on the ground. She swung her leg over the neck, and gripped hard on the highest neck spike. She felt herself being lifted high in the air, and moments later she was swooping above the jungle at tree-top level. That settles it, thought Anna exultantly, as she sailed through the night. If she went back to Earth for good, she might never ride on a dinosaur again.

Late that night, Anna came back from her ride, reassured her alarmed friends, and returned to the ship with Kevin and Jan.

Garm said farewell to his tribe, and went on board his ship with Osar and Tell. Both vessels enjoyed an uneventful voyage back to Centre. While Garm, Tell and Osar went to be debriefed – and to explain to President Elvar why a routine mission had taken so long – Jan, Kevin and Anna went in search of Zeno. Why, they weren't quite sure, except that it seemed to make sense to end where they'd begun.

After many enquiries they found him in the Hanging Gardens that floated high above Centre. He was staring raptly at a tightly closed rosebud resting on his open palm. Nothing about him had changed, he was still the same wrinkled, brown-faced figure in the same shabby robes.

For a long moment, he went on contemplating the bud, ignoring their approach. Then he said suddenly. 'A rose – from Old Earth. Do you miss it?'

'Sometimes,' said Anna. 'But there are always roses here – and other flowers we never see on Earth. Oh, I came to give you this.' Anna took the Stone of Power from around her neck and handed it to him.

Zeno tucked it away with the same lack of ceremony with which he'd first produced it. 'When we first met, I think you were wondering what to do with yourselves. Since then, I have been wondering what to do with you myself.'

They listened in silence, and he went on. 'It is unlikely that we can ever return you to Earth. Even it we did, we would have to erase the memories you have acquired since you left. Are you prepared to lose all you have felt, all you have seen?'

Anna thought of the joy of riding a dinosaur through the wild jungle night.

'But if you have no place on Earth, then you need a place here – I think I can offer you that place.' He looked piercingly at them. 'You know who and what I am – Zeno, the Watcher. I sense changes in the stresses and balances of the Web of Being. But sometimes, what I see or hear or sense is not enough. I need those who will *act* for me – agents.'

Jan said, 'What kind of people are you looking for?'

Zeno looked at Jan's tall figure, handsome in his gold-and-white uniform. 'I could use someone young and strong, a fighter who moves in the world of action like a fish in water.'

He looked at Anna. 'I could use an empath, a lady who can form links, even with so alien a being as, oh, a dinosaur.'

'How did he know?' thought Anna.

Zeno looked at Kevin, inconspicuous in dark-blue trousers and tunic. 'I could even use an average-looking person who fidgets about from one subject to another, never settling, learning a little of this and a little of that.' He broke off, pulling at one pointed ear. 'Why does that sound so familiar, I wonder? Even a Watcher must retire someday...'

'Me a Watcher?' thought Kevin. 'Still, who knows?'

Zeno looked round the group, his eyes twinkling. 'Do you know where such people might be found? I wonder?'

Kevin spoke for all of them. 'I think we might.'

'Good,' said Zeno. 'Let us begin at once, you have much to learn.'

He held out the rosebud, and suddenly it blossomed in his hand.

240